William Sanders

WARNER BOOKS

A Time Warner Company

WARNER BOOKS EDITION

Questar® is a registered trademark of Warner Books, Inc.

Cover illustration by GNEMO
Cover design by Don Puckey

Warner Books, Inc.
666 Fifth Avenue
New York, NY 10103

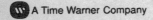 A Time Warner Company

Printed in the United States of America

First Printing: July 1991

10 9 8 7 6 5 4 3 2 1

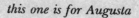

this one is for Augusta

. . . when our country struggled for its life, one hand reached across the sea, one great power stood behind and then beside us in our battle for independence. . . . Now Britain is herself hard pressed by cruel and powerful enemies. Even were we not linked by sacred treaties, would our Southern honor permit us now to turn our backs on our oldest ally, without whose support our own nation might never have come to be?

I therefore ask that this Congress declare that a state of war now exists between the Confederate States of America and the Empires of Germany and Austria-Hungary. . . .

—President Leontine Butler to the
Confederate Congress, August 15, 1914

I see the Confederate Americans have now joined the general rush toward Armageddon. My God! They must be as mad as the Irish!

—George Bernard Shaw, in a letter
to H. G. Wells, August 18, 1914

August, 1916
Northern Europe

1
_____

AMOS NINEKILLER was six thousand feet above northeastern France when he hit the enormous bird. Or the bird hit him; it could have been argued either way.

Later he decided it must have been a stork, if only because there was nothing else that big flying over Europe at this time of year—nothing with feathers, anyway—but at the time all he saw was a sudden huge whitish-gray thing that rose up out of nowhere and slammed into the propeller. There was a tremendous bang, the little biplane lurched and shuddered and for a sickening moment seemed about to go out of control, and then the rotary engine in the nose went completely crazy as the wooden propeller shattered into a lot of very expensive toothpicks. By the time he got the engine shut down the bird was nowhere to be seen.

The pilots of the other two gray-painted biplanes in the group missed the whole thing. Deafened by their own blatting engines, locked into the tunnel vision of the very inexperienced, they flew doggedly and somewhat unsteadily on eastward, leaving Amos Ninekiller alone in a large and empty sky with a powerless aircraft.

Amos said, "Hell," and, "Shit," and, "Son of a *bitch*,"

1

and after that he began to use bad language. Normally, when alone, he did not think or soliloquize in English, but Cherokee lacked any real profanity. His grandfather had often said that cursing was one of the few really useful contributions of the white man to civilized living, along with the horse and the repeating rifle and frilly underwear for women.

Having expressed himself enough to cool down, however, Amos decided that the situation wasn't as bad as it might be. The Nieuport 17 was a lightweight aircraft, with a good glide angle and decent power-off handling qualities—in fact it seemed somewhat more stable without the torque of that spinning rotary engine—and the countryside below was flat and open, and for once the weather was fine over Picardy.

Settling back into the uncomfortable little seat, he steadied the Nieuport and began looking unhurriedly for a place to land. The wind whined in the wires and he sang softly to himself in harmony:

"*U-ne-hla-nuh-hi u-we-tsi*
I-ga-gu-yuh-he-yi. . . ."

The ground floated slowly up toward him. He glided over the tops of a row of trees—closer than he had intended, a nasty moment there when his wheels brushed twigs and leaves—brought the nose up just a hair as he cleared a hedgerow, and dropped the Nieuport neatly at the end of a big green oblong of weed-grown field. The wheels bounced and rumbled a little as they rolled along the bumpy ground, but the surface was solid and there were no holes or ditches in his path. He had, he reflected, made worse landings at permanent airfields with undamaged aircraft.

The Nieuport stopped moving, settling its weight onto wheels and tail skid like a middle-aged woman sitting down to wait for a late train. Amos reached automatically to switch everything off, realized he had already done so, and began to unbuckle the chin strap of his leather helmet.

Climbing down from the cockpit, he walked around the Nieuport, looking for damage. The propeller was a complete write-off, of course; you wouldn't, he thought, have expected a mere bird to do that much damage, but there were tremendous and poorly understood stresses on a whirling propeller, and sometimes it didn't take much to set up destructive vibrations. And that had been such a *hell* of a big bird. . . .

Other than the prop, though, the little biplane seemed unharmed. The tail skid looked a bit banged up and might need attention; otherwise everything seemed intact. Bolt on a new prop and you could probably fly her out of here.

Since he didn't have a spare propeller on him, it appeared that the Fourth Virginia Pursuit Squadron, Confederate States of America Expeditionary Force, would have to struggle along a bit longer without his services or the aircraft's. He imagined they'd manage somehow without him, but they had probably needed this new plane pretty badly.

He sighed and walked back to get his valise out of the plane. Down near the end of the field a lot of khaki-clad men were coming in his direction. The morning sun glinted on rifles and bayonets. Amos hoped none of them were the impulsive type.

The dispatch rider pulled his big Norton motorcycle over to the side of the narrow road and said, "Here y'are, Lieutenant. Fourth Virginia Pursuit, right over yonder. Hope you don't mind walking a little," he added apologetically as Amos Ninekiller got out of the sidecar. "I ain't really supposed to pick up passengers, even officers. Might be some brass over at the field, give me hell."

He helped Amos unstrap his bag from the luggage rack. "Think nothing of it, Lieutenant," he said when Amos tried to thank him. "Us Southerners got to stick together over here, right? Shoot down a couple of them Kraut bastards for me. They kilt my brother last year—he was up at Loos with the Eleventh Arkansas Infantry." He kicked the Norton's starter pedal without immediate result. "God-damned piece of Limey shit," he said feelingly. "I wisht Richmond would break down and buy us some of them Harley-Davidsons. Hell of a lot better motor, I don't care if the damn Yankees do make it."

Amos lifted his bag and began walking toward the scatter of buildings and tents and canvas-covered hangars that lined the far border of the grassy field. He saw no aircraft; it was late afternoon now, and he guessed they would all be inside the hangars except for those still out on patrol. Above the largest building a big Stars-and-Bars Confederate battle flag snapped and curled in the wind.

Behind him the Norton finally coughed into life. Amos half-turned and waved, but the dispatch rider was already vanishing down the road in a huge cloud of yellow dust.

Amos walked on across the field: a medium-sized young man, maybe even a bit shorter than average, though his erect carriage tended to make him look taller. Lean and wiry of build, he could almost have been called slight, but for a pair of extraordinarily muscular shoulders and a deep barrel chest. He was not very dark for a full-blood—the legacy of a Delaware great-grandmother—but he had the classic Cherokee features, including a really impressive nose. On the ship coming over, and on his way across France, he had at various times been addressed in Greek, Italian, Yiddish, Arabic, and what he thought might be Armenian; and once a really strange police inspector, with an even larger nose of his own and a silly mustache besides, had been certain Amos was an Algerian deserter.

It was quite a long walk across the field, and the sun was hot. He began sweating heavily under his heavy flying suit. His boots and trousers were muddy from the ditches he had had to cross to get to the road from the pasture where he had landed. All in all, this promised to be a less than impressive arrival at his new operational squadron, looking like a farm hand, smelling like a horse, and oh yes, missing the small item of one Nieuport 17 pursuit aircraft, CSA property . . . fine representative of the Cherokee Nation he was turning out to be. He was glad Chief Watie couldn't see him just now.

As he neared the end of the field, he could see a group of men in butternut gray standing in front of the biggest building. They appeared to be waiting for something; there was an air of expectancy in the way they stood, and most of them were gazing toward the western sky, even though the light from the late sun was blinding.

Amos realized suddenly what was going on, and he hurried

to get off the field. Now he could hear it, very faint but growing steadily in strength: the buzzing drone of distant engines.

No one paid any notice as Amos came up to the group of officers; no one even looked at him. A tall, thin, rather sad-faced man, wearing the shoulder insignia of a Major, seemed to be the ranking man present, and Amos started to speak and salute, wondering if he should have gotten his orders out for presentation. But a stocky, fierce-looking Captain, without turning around, said, "God damn it, man, not *now*," and Amos stopped with his hand halfway to shoulder level, stood for an irresolute instant, and then moved around to the rear of the group, where he tried hard to be invisible and to breathe as little as possible.

Squinting into the sun's glare, Amos could see the approaching planes now: five tiny flyspecks against the yellow sky, spread out in no particular formation, already beginning to lose altitude as they headed for the field. The locust rattle of their engines was now quite loud.

The angry-faced Captain was studying the flight through a pair of heavy black binoculars. "They look all right, sir," he said.

"Ah." The cadaverous Major nodded solemnly. "Let's hope so, Captain Clay."

The five biplanes had arranged themselves into a rough line-ahead formation and now they began to drop rapidly, like migratory birds about to alight on an autumn field. As the lead plane floated down toward the field Amos found himself momentarily transfixed with a throat-thickening rush of indescribable emotion, something near to awe and not altogether unlike love. It had been the same, years ago, when he had first watched a clumsy, flimsy Wright pusher, not much more than a box kite with a crude engine, coming in for a cow-pasture landing; it had been so ever since.

The lead plane touched down gently and rolled down the field: a small, snub-nosed, comma-tailed airplane, its gray paint streaked with oil and smoke. Captain Clay, still looking through his binoculars, said, "That's Moore. Looks like he's picked up a few holes, but he seems to be all right."

The next two planes came in, one after another, to uneventful landings. Captain Clay said, "Rogers and Hatfield. Hatfield's got a really ugly hole in his lower port wing. Got to be ground fire . . . wonder if that silly son of a bitch has been chasing balloons again."

The fourth plane came in crookedly and too low, its engine sounding rough. There was a soft intake of breath from all the watchers. Someone said, "Oh, sweet Jesus."

The pilot tried at the last minute to get the Nieuport up, but he had run out of room. The wheels slapped at a treetop; the plane sailed down and slammed heavily onto the field. The right wingtip dropped and the Nieuport went into a vicious ground loop. The sounds of breaking and tearing were incredibly loud.

Captain Clay said tightly, "Shoemaker. Can't see whether—"

A man appeared from the middle of the tangled wreck, lurching across the grass in a drunken zigzag. A couple of men in ground-crew coveralls dashed up and began to half-carry him away. There was a sudden yellow flare from the twisted fuselage and the Nieuport began to burn. There was no explosion, just a great whoosh and then a bonfire on the runway.

The last plane cleared the blazing wreckage and dropped in for an almost casually flawless landing. The Captain said, "And Eubanks, as usual, hasn't even got his hair mussed." He sighed. "I'll take their reports, sir."

"Do that." The Major turned, a slow dreamy movement, as if he were moving underwater. Vague, slightly watery eyes considered Amos. "Ah, Captain Clay . . . this man . . . ?"

"Well, God damn it," Clay said to Amos, "aren't you going to report to the Squadron Commander?"

Amos jerked hastily to attention and saluted. "Sir, Lieutenant Amos Ninekiller reporting under orders."

The Major continued to stare, as if seeing a talking alligator. Captain Clay said, "The Indian, sir. The Cherokee officer they told us about. Attached to us for observation or some damn thing."

"Oh, yes." The Major nodded. "Ninekiller? Nine what?"

"I don't know," Amos said. "Family name. Sir."

Clay said, "Say, weren't you supposed to be with that flight that came in today? The ones bringing in the new machines?"

"Yes, sir. I'm afraid I had some trouble, had to make a forced landing. The plane's not badly damaged, though," Amos said quickly, seeing Clay's eyebrows starting to fuse. "I left it near some British infantry in bivouac. Tried to reach you on their telephone, but I couldn't get through—their CO promised they'd try again for me—"

The Major brightened suddenly. "That's right, they did," he said, and looked at Amos with interest. "I remember. You're the one who ran into a duck."

"A stork, sir," Amos said diffidently. "Or possibly some kind of large heron—"

"No, no." The Major shook his head decisively. "I was there when the call came in. No question about it. Definitely a duck. How did you manage to hit a duck with your airplane, Lieutenant?"

Amos wondered how he was supposed to answer that, but the Major wasn't listening for a reply. "You'll have to be more careful in the future, Lieutenant," he said seriously. "We need all the aircraft we can get. Can't go damaging them running into ducks and suchlike, you know. Looks terrible on our unit's efficiency report."

He waved both hands in a vague way. "Take charge, Captain Clay. Carry on." He turned and began walking away, ignoring the flurry of salutes. A large black man in a white jacket appeared from nowhere and fell in at his heels.

Captain Clay stared after him for a moment. "And that," he said, apparently to Amos, "is Major Culpepper. . . ."

He looked at Amos. "Welcome to the Fourth Virginia Pursuit Squadron," he said flatly. Neither his voice nor his face held the slightest trace of enthusiasm. He raised one hand and for a second Amos thought he was about to offer a handshake, but instead he merely rubbed his face. "God *damn*," he said. "I wish I knew what fool got the idea of using replacement pilots to bring up new aircraft. I'd kick his ass, I don't care if he's the Commanding General of the CEF."

Amos said, "The other two pilots I was with—did they make it here all right?"

"Oh, yes," Clay snorted. "Of course one of them managed to flare too high, coming in, and banged up his plane enough to keep it out of action a couple of days, and the other one got lost and came in on his last drop of gas, but they're here."

He gave Amos a sourly amused look. "You know neither of them even noticed you'd dropped out of the flight? Let alone that you'd rammed a duck."

"Stork," Amos said hopelessly.

"Damn fine replacements they're sending us these days," Clay went on, ignoring him. "If that duck had been a Fokker you'd all have been dead, you realize that?"

He glared at Amos for a moment and then turned to look at the burning wreck on the runway. A great many people were running around wielding various implements or simply waving their arms and shouting. It all seemed rather futile, since the airplane was obviously a total loss and anything that could burn was doing so, but perhaps regulations required some sort of exhibition of general dismay.

The Adjutant said, "And now I've got to figure out what to do with you." He looked at Amos again, this time with something strange, almost a defensiveness, in his expression. "Look," he said, "I don't have time to bother with the paperwork and the bullshit just now. I've got about a million things to do and they're all more urgent than booking a new pilot in. Here." He took out a pencil and a pad of yellow paper and scribbled something on the top sheet, which he tore off and folded and handed to Amos. "Go to the Orderly Room, find Sergeant Hawkins, and give him this. He'll show you to your quarters and issue your bedding and so on. You can come in tomorrow morning and we'll get the rest of it straightened out."

Amos said hesitantly, "Uh, Captain? If you're sending out a detail to recover that Nieuport, do you want me to go along . . . ?"

"Jesus Christ, no. Haven't you done enough to the poor thing already? Next time you might decide to run over a cow.

Go on,'' Clay said fiercely. ''Go kill a buffalo or put up a teepee or something. I've got *work* to do.''

The Squadron Headquarters was housed in a big stone building that looked as if it had been a farmhouse. Ranked alongside were several long, low, crudely-built structures, their walls covered with weathered tar paper, their interiors divided by flimsy partitions into cell-like two-man cubicles. The lighting was bad and the ventilation worse. Amos wondered if he *could* get permission to put up a teepee. Claim it was a religious requirement of his tribe or something, these people would never know. . . . True, he had no idea how to put up a teepee—in fact he had never seen one, outside of pictures in books—but he thought he could figure something out. Reluctantly he shelved the idea as probably impractical, and followed Sergeant Hawkins down the narrow corridor.

The cubicle to which Hawkins showed him appeared to be much like all the others: two narrow wooden beds, a couple of rickety chairs, and an assortment of lockers and boxes, crammed into an entirely inadequate space. One of the bunks was occupied by a small, thin-faced young man who put down the book he was reading and got to his feet as Amos entered.

''Hello,'' he said, and stuck out his hand. ''My name's Bill Faulkner.''

''Amos Ninekiller.'' Amos shook the young man's hand, realizing suddenly that it was the first handshake anyone had offered around here.

Faulkner's face broke open in a grin. ''Oh, sure, the Indian fighter pilot. They told us about you . . . and Clay put you in with me, of course. I should have expected it.''

Amos set his bag down on the floor and sat on the unoccupied bed. ''Is there something I'm missing here?''

Faulkner sat down opposite him. Amos saw now that Faulkner was trying to grow a mustache. Either that or he had missed a spot shaving; things were at the stage where it was hard to tell.

''Look,'' Faulkner said, ''don't be offended, but, well, hell, you're an *Indian*, right? Most of the men in this squadron won't give a damn about that one way or another—as long as you can fly and shoot, most of them wouldn't care if you were a Negro.'' He sighed and looked away. ''That's speaking of serving and flying with you. Sharing living quarters —there's no telling how some of them would react. I'm sorry, but that's the way it is.''

Amos nodded. He had been through this a few times before; it hadn't ceased to bother him, but it didn't bother him as much nowadays. He said, ''But what's that got to do with Clay putting me in with you?''

Faulkner laughed. ''Oh, I'm the squadron radical—Eubanks calls me 'the nigger-lover,' in his charming manner. I've been known to make remarks to the effect that the colored people aren't much better off now than they were before slavery was abolished, and that this isn't really a good state of affairs . . . and I'm afraid I've said a few other things that weren't too well received by the more reactionary Southern gentlemen in this outfit. Anyway, I read books, which makes me a suspicious intellectual. So Clay decided, I suppose, that I was the logical person to share quarters with you.''

Amos began taking off his heavy flying boots. ''Son of a bitch,'' he said, and couldn't think of anything else to add. He glanced around the little cubicle. A set of raw-lumber shelves held rows of books. ''Looks like you're not kidding,'' he said, since the subject seemed to need changing. ''About reading books, I mean.''

Faulkner nodded. ''I do some writing myself. That's what I want to do after the war—write novels.''

''About the war, flying, that sort of thing?''

Faulkner shrugged. ''That's really all I know about—except, of course, life in a small Mississippi town, and who'd want to read about that?'' He leaned back on his elbows. ''Didn't know the Cherokees had an army, let alone an air corps.''

Amos stood up and began undoing his long leather flight jacket. ''We don't, really. Just a small mounted force, more police than army, and some border guards. *Phoo.*'' He made a face as he pulled off the sweaty flying trousers. ''Anyway, we're trying to modernize, so I'm supposed to be learning all about air warfare from our clever white allies.''

He opened the leather valise and began taking out a fresh if somewhat wrinkled gray uniform. "So," he said over his shoulder to Faulkner, "what's it like? You might as well be first to tell me."

"What's it like? What a question . . . we try to shoot them down and they try to shoot us down. That's about all these things are good for, you know, shooting each other down. When you get right down to it," Faulkner said, "all the romance and poetry of flight hasn't got a damned thing to do with it. A Nieuport, or a Fokker, is just a complicated mechanism for carrying a man and a machine gun into position for shooting another man in the back."

"You sound pretty cynical about it."

"Just being realistic. We're certainly not going to win the war killing Germans one at a time—shoot down thirty or so of them and you'll be the hero of the year, but any machine gunner in the trenches will kill more than that in a few minutes of an unimportant action. True, the observation planes accomplish a hell of a lot more—spotting for the artillery, watching for enemy movements, and so on—and we do sometimes give them a bit of protection, if we don't get excited and run off chasing the first Germans we see. But that doesn't matter either, because our peerless leaders inevitably manage to throw away any advantage the observation might give them."

He stretched out on the bunk and looked at the ceiling. "Right now," he said, "they've got this big push going on. It started back in June and it was supposed to break right through the German lines and end the war within weeks. It's been going on all summer and they've lost God knows how many men, charging across open ground against dug-in machine guns, and I think in a few places they've actually managed to advance as much as six or seven miles. We've had a fine view of the whole thing . . . what was it the Bard said? It is a tale told by an idiot, full of sound and fury, signifying nothing."

Faulkner stopped, looked thoughtful, and suddenly produced a small pocket notebook and a pen and began scribbling.

Amos said, "Is it really that bad?"

Faulkner put up his notebook and looked at Amos. "My friend," he said cheerfully, "it's not just that bad, it's so much worse that I couldn't begin to describe it for you. You'll see for yourself soon enough—and incidentally," he added, "our brilliant Confederate brass, the heirs of Lee and Jackson, can't seem to think of anything better than slavishly following the lunatic schemes of British and French High Command. And, of course, our heroic lads in gray are always ready to rise up and answer the bugle and show the world that Southerners know how to die."

He didn't, Amos thought, sound particularly bitter; he was just describing a set of facts, as if he'd been telling Amos what the weather was like around here.

Faulkner sat up suddenly and laughed. "Now I've raised your morale and cheered your spirits," he said, "get dressed and we'll go over to the mess. May as well meet the rest of your stablemates."

The officers' mess was housed in a long narrow stone building, apparently another structure from the original farm. "Probably used to keep the goats in it," Faulkner remarked as they entered. "You could argue that the caliber of the clientele has gone downhill."

There were a number of large tables, all covered with immaculate white cloths. Around the room men sat on chairs and benches, playing cards, writing letters, talking, or simply staring into space. A piano hulked in the shadows at the far end. Pictures—mostly French landscapes, with a few portraits of Confederate generals—hung here and there on the whitewashed walls.

All the men present wore some variant of the basic butternut-gray Confederate officer's uniform, but Amos saw that there was considerable individual interpretation; indeed the only standard item seemed to be the regulation gray trousers with the light-blue stripe of the Flying Corps. Of course, non-uniform uniforms were an old Confederate tradition; it had always been an army of anarchic individualists. . . .

A loud drawling voice said clearly, "I be damn. I always thought this was a white man's outfit."

The hum of conversation in the mess dropped to almost nothing. There was a scrape of chairs on the floor as men got up or changed positions, either for a better view or a safer place.

The voice had come from near the window, next to a table where several pilots were playing cards. As Amos looked, the voice went on:

"I mean, it's a hell of a note when they expect white men to sit down and eat with God-damned Indians. Next thing you know they'll be bringing in niggers."

The speaker was a tall, rangy, fair-skinned man with curly blond hair and a lot of flashy white teeth. Amos noticed he was wearing Western-style riding boots with pointed toes and high heels. He was looking straight at Amos, and he was smiling. It wasn't a friendly smile; it was just a smile that said the smiler was enjoying himself.

"How about that, Chief?" he said. "You even know how to sit at a table and eat like white folks?"

Amos looked at him for a moment. The blond said, "Oh, you don't talkum English, Chief?" He waved his hands in what was evidently supposed to be sign language, almost upsetting the drink on the bench beside him. His face was flushed. "Look, me talkum with hands like redskin. Hey, somebody go get that stray dog that's been hanging around the enlisted men's mess. If Indians can eat here I guess dogs ought to get in too."

Amos sighed. He was supposed to stay out of trouble—Chief Watie had been explicit—and he had had plenty of practice ignoring obnoxious drunks of various races. On the other hand, it had been a very long day.

He walked slowly over to the seated blond. "It's not too late to let it go," he offered. "If you'd like to back off now."

The blond grinned up at him. "Going to do something about it, Chief?" he said, and stood up. He was a head taller than Amos and quite a bit heavier.

One of the card players said, "Come on, Eubanks, leave it alone."

Eubanks said without looking around, "God damn it, I'm not backing down from any lousy stinking redskin son of a—"

Amos sighed again and hit him in the stomach with the fastest right anyone there had ever seen.

There was a muffled chorus of surprised exclamations, one or two sounding almost like cheers. Eubanks said, "*Uh*," and began to double up, a look of intense surprise in his blue eyes. Amos hit him again in the midsection, with a left this time, and then drove a right cross to his jawline as he started down.

Amos stepped back as Eubanks crashed to the floor, waiting for him to get up. He would not have done that back home, but then back home this would not have been a matter to be settled with hands. Better not make too bad an impression on these people.

Eubanks was still lying there, shaking his head and feeling his jaw, when the door opened and Major Culpepper came in. "What's this?" he said cheerfully, while everyone came to attention, even Eubanks. "High spirits and horseplay in the mess? Little early, isn't it?" He beamed vaguely at Amos. "Glad to see the boys are making you welcome. Gentlemen," he said, "I do believe it's just about supper time, don't you?"

2

DINNER WAS an informal affair, lacking the elaborate ritual of the British mess. Everyone stood at attention while a scratchy gramophone played "Dixie," after which Major Culpepper delivered a rambling and wholly incomprehensible prayer; that was all the ceremony. The food was surprisingly good, served by a hustling phalanx of white-coated black orderlies. Amos noticed the same large Negro stood behind the Major's chair and waited on him personally, occasionally glaring at one of the other orderlies who made a bit too much noise or moved clumsily.

Amos sat in an inconspicuous corner, along with Faulkner and the two other new pilots, and took no part in the table conversation. Eubanks, to his relief, sat at the far end of the room and did not even look his way. The only bad moment during dinner came when Amos distinctly heard Major Culpepper saying to the people at the head of the table: "—hit a *duck*, if you can believe it, and had to come down in a cow pasture. Can't imagine why he did that."

Dinner finished, there was a short awkward pause, while conversation lagged and everyone looked slightly uncomfortable. But then Major Culpepper got up and left the mess, followed by the mysterious Negro, and there was a sound of mass exhalation. The noise level rose sharply as officers ordered drinks, scooted chairs across the stone floor, and asked each other for lights. Collars were loosened and smoke rose from cigars and cigarettes and pipes; a poker game began, and showed signs of becoming serious. Someone began banging on the piano; half a dozen pilots immediately gathered around and started singing, in somewhat non-Euclidean harmony. A voice called, "Do y'all know 'That's The Wrong Way to Tickle Mary'?"

Amos bowed his head and closed his eyes and pinched the bridge of his nose between his forefingers. Faulkner said, "I know, I know. When they start to rollick, it can be pretty hard to take. Let's have a drink." He flagged down a waiter. "Bourbon all right with you? That's about all anyone drinks here, except for a couple of brandy-sniffing snobs."

While they waited for their drinks, Amos glanced about the room for Eubanks, spotting him at last at the poker game. "Forget him," Faulkner said, seeing where Amos was looking. "He won't give you any more trouble. Anyone stands up to him, that's the end of it. Texan," Faulkner added, as if that explained everything. "Seems to think that gives him the right to act like an obnoxious jackass."

"What's he doing in a Virginia squadron?"

"Oh, these state titles are mere tradition nowadays. Maybe in the infantry they still mean something, but not in the Flying Corps. I'm from Mississippi myself, Captain Clay's from North Carolina, the fellow with the ten thumbs," Faulkner gestured toward the piano, "is from Louisiana—name's Lahaie, and if he were any more French he couldn't talk at all. Ah." The drinks had arrived. "I'll sign for those . . . now our dear Major is indeed a son of Old Virginny, bless his addled head. Which he would probably misplace if Tyrone didn't keep track of it for him."

"Tyrone?"

"The Major's large saturnine black shadow, surely you noticed? Some sort of old family tradition—body servants to the Culpepper men since Colonial times, I understand. Unwritten rule there," Faulkner said, lifting his drink. "Field-grade officers get to bring personal servants to the wars. We junior types have to make arrangements with whatever hewers of wood and drawers of water we can hire—mess stewards, or the odd enlisted man in need of extra cash. Tyrone,'' Faulkner added, ''according to credible rumor, is the one who actually runs this squadron. I don't believe it, though. He'd probably do a better job.''

Amos nodded. ''Major Culpepper reminds me of a professor we had at school. Taught political science . . . Wilson was his name,'' Amos remembered. ''Dr. Woodrow Wilson. Nice man, but hopelessly muddled. Come to think of it, he was a Virginian too.''

The group at the piano had begun singing a really obscene version of ''When You Wore A Tulip.'' Amos listened with interest. They had had a different set of verses at the flight training base in Texas; he decided he liked these better.

''About Eubanks,'' Faulkner said, ''don't be misled by his tinhorn posturing. Much as I hate to admit it, the son of a bitch is a brilliant pilot—much better with a Nieuport than with his fists.''

He looked curiously at Amos. ''Where'd you learn to box like that, anyway? Is that Indian-style fighting?''

Amos grinned. ''Boxed welterweight at the University of Virginia.''

''I'll be damned. That's right, you were saying something about school and professors . . . what were you doing at the . . . ?''

''Some other time.'' Amos shook his head and reached for his drink. ''It's a long story.''

The pianist was now hammering his way through ''Hello My Baby, Hello My Honey, Hello My Ragtime Gal.'' The effect would not have been measurably worse if all his fingers had been webbed. Someone dropped a glass. At the poker table Eubanks's Texas bray rose suddenly through the general mutter: ''Aces and cowboys, God damn it, beat that if you can!'' There were groans and oaths. At a nearby table someone said, ''So there I was upside-down at eight thousand with three Fokkers for company and the God-damned gun jammed—''

Amos drained his drink very quickly and signaled for another. "Better get used to it," Faulkner grinned. "This is a quiet night."

"Shared a field with a Brit squadron in Sopwiths," another voice said somewhere behind Amos. "CO had this white beagle, used to take it flying with him, sitting on his lap. From some angles it looked like the dog was flying the plane. . . ."

Later, settling in for sleep, Faulkner said, "Did you really hit a duck?"

Amos sighed. "A stork. And he hit me."

"Oh. How did you manage—"

"It's a long story," Amos said crossly.

"That's your standard answer, isn't it?" Faulkner mused. "I get the feeling your whole story's a long one."

"You've got no idea," Amos said into his pillow. "And it just keeps getting longer."

Closing his eyes, making a darkness against the darkness, Amos reflected sleepily that life *had* been a bit long lately. Ever since last summer . . . God, had it only been a year?

The honorable Albert Watie, Principal Chief of the Cherokee Nation, rested his elbows on his desk and looked at Amos over the tops of rimless glasses. "Son," he said in English, "you see before you the elected leader of a nation with its tit in the wringer of history."

Amos shifted his feet slightly on the worn carpet and said in the same language, "Yes, sir." One good thing about English, there was an endless supply of little phrases that sounded good and filled in the holes in conversation and didn't really mean anything. In Cherokee it was almost impossible to talk at all unless you were actually saying something.

Chief Watie levered himself up out of his chair: a burly, paunchy, white-haired man in a slightly rumpled brown suit. He walked around the desk and stood looking at the big map on his wall, the map of what had once been called Indian

Territory and was now divided among the more or less sovereign Five Nations.

"Little over half a century now," Chief Watie said, facing the map, "we've managed to survive—fifty-some-odd years during which it hasn't been very good for Indians, anywhere. The Yankees finally got all the Plains tribes whittled down and the survivors penned up on some dirt-poor reservations in Montana. The God-damned Texans just about wiped out the Comanches and Kiowas, all but a few raggedy-ass bands that made it across Red River and settled down to make the Chickasaws nervous. And, of course, down in Mexico, and way up north in Russian America, there's been things to make the Trail of Tears look like a stomp dance . . . and in all that time, by God, we survived. *We*," the Chief added with a gesture at the map, "meaning the Five allegedly Civilized Tribes—although I'll never know who decided those crazy Seminole bastards counted as so all-fired civilized—and, of course, several thousand Shawnees and Delawares and Senecas and all those other Eastern tribes that Washington managed to shoehorn in here with us back before the War."

He turned and faced Amos. "*How* we survived wasn't always very noble—coming in on the Southern side just before they started to win the war, and then year in, year out, playing the Yankees and the Confederates off against each other, like a girl keeping a couple of young bucks competing to buy her presents while she never puts out for either of them. And we've survived as half-assed little rump states, under the 'protection' of the Confederacy, and we've had to put up with a lot of shit from Richmond, and so on."

Amos wondered why Chief Watie was going on like this. Everybody knew all those things; you learned them in school, like Sequoyah's alphabet. But then he reflected that it was a matter of style. Albert Watie might wear a suit and live in a big white house and own a telephone and a Ford automobile, but he was still Indian enough to want to talk all around the world before getting to the point.

"I know," Watie said, "lot of people, some of the old conservative full-bloods—like your grandpa and his brothers in the Keetoowah Society—say we've gone too far down the white man's road. And maybe they're right, maybe we had to learn to play the white man's game by his rules, but by God, *we survived*."

Watie snorted. "Of course, we survived mostly because we didn't have anything anybody wanted all that bad. No gold or silver here, just a lot of red dirt and a lot of rocks and not enough water."

He pushed his glasses up on his nose. "The Confederacy, by a fifty-year-old treaty, guarantees to protect the independence and territorial integrity of the Five Tribes. The Union never has recognized our independence at all, and would be severely pissed off at any Confederate invasion of what Washington still insists on calling 'Indian Territory.' But," Watie said, "the question is, does any of that crap really mean anything? Would anybody on either side of the Mason-Dixon Line be willing to start the War Between the States up again over a bunch of Indians?"

He spread his hands. "Nobody knows. There just never was anything here worth creating an international crisis. As the man said when he screwed the pig, it's not something you take pride in, but sometimes you take what you can get."

Chief Watie sat down again at his desk and leaned back in his creaking old chair, lacing his fingers over his paunch. "You're a bright young man, Amos," he said. "You always did take an interest in the outside world, even before those missionaries fixed it up for you to go to that fancy university back East. So you know what's been going on in the world."

"You mean in Europe?"

"Right. Last summer some crazy son of a bitch shoots one of those inbred dukes, down in the Balkans, and the whole damn world goes up in flames. Down in Richmond old Butler makes a big flapdoodle speech about how much the Confederacy owes to England—which is true enough; the Yankees would have kicked their ass from Paducah to Tampa Bay if the British hadn't dealt themselves in—and asks Congress to declare war. Which they do with great enthusiasm, partly because they're just as crazy as their grandpas were back in the last century, but also because the Confederacy has been in bad economic shape and this promises to be good for business. Up in Washington, William Jennings Bryan announces the United States wants no part of this war, proving that even a damn fool can be right now and then. Of course,'' Watie grimaced, ''everybody on both sides of the water expected the war to be over in a few months, tops.''

He gave Amos a crafty look that was almost a leer. ''And what, I hear you asking yourself internally, has all this got to do with the price of pokeweed in Goingsnake District?''

Amos cleared his throat. ''Something like that did occur to me.''

''Aha.'' Watie pulled open the top drawer of his desk and pulled out a large cardboard folder, tied with ribbon, and held it up. ''This, young man, is the final report of a secret mineral survey, done for the Five Nations—at considerable expense, but well worth it. Turns out,'' Watie grinned, ''all this piss-poor land the whites figured was good enough for Indians, well, it's just floating on top of the God-damnedest puddle of oil you ever saw.''

''Oil?'' Amos wasn't bored now; he was stunned. There had been rumors and speculation along those lines for a long time, but he had never really taken the oil talk seriously. ''There's oil under our land?''

Watie chuckled. ''Damn near unbearably ironic, isn't it? The whole white world's at war, and the one thing they have to have to fight their war turns out to be the one thing we've got in abundance.''

He tossed the envelope on his desk. ''So,'' he said, ''all of a sudden we've got a hell of a lot to think about. If we play this particular card just right, it could be the best break we've had in a long time—it could finally buy us the right to stand up on our hind legs and face the whites as equals. And then again, if we put one foot wrong, it's going to be the worst catastrophe since Columbus got the idea he knew a short cut.''

Amos whistled softly. ''I see what you mean.''

''You probably do. The leaders of the Five Nations have a lot of tricky decisions to make, and the stakes are God-awful high.''

Chief Watie got up again and walked to the window. Outside, the early-summer sun shone hot and bright on the main street of the Cherokee capital, where farmers' wagons rattled and clattered and long-skirted women picked their way through the piles of horse turds. A few automobiles were parked along the street; Tahlequah was certainly getting modern lately.

"One way or another," he said, "it all keeps coming back to that God-damned war in Europe. Long as that business goes on, the Confederacy will need all the oil it can get—hell, just a couple of destroyers, patrolling for U-boats off Charleston or Pass Christian, will drink the stuff by the trainload. We'll be Richmond's little pals—they'll have to kiss our ass for a change, instead of the other way around."

"If," Amos said skeptically, "they don't just take it by force."

"True, true," Watie nodded. "But they'd have to divert troops and equipment from the front in France, and even though they'd whip us eventually, we'd sure as hell keep them from pumping any oil for a long time. Then, too, the Union may not give a damn about us Indians, but you bet your natural red ass they'd react very strongly to the Confederacy grabbing an oil field in territory they still claim. Long as we don't get too unreasonable, it's cheaper for Richmond to play it straight—more or less."

He turned and faced Amos. "But all that assumes the war's going to go on awhile longer. The oil's still in the ground—takes some time to drill for it and pump it out and get it to where they want it. If the Germans are about to collapse any day, like the Allied newspapers claim, then it's a whole different hand. My feeling," he said, "the war's going to drag on for years, but what the hell do *I* know?"

His face went grim. "And if the Germans were to *win*, run. The reaction will bring down the Confederate government, and the Texans might well take that opportunity to secede, like they've been threatening to do for years. An independent Texas next door, with nobody to keep them in line—Amos, that's so scary I don't even want to think about it. They've been eyeing this country like a rattlesnake watching a rabbit since they got shut of the Mexicans.''

Chief Watie stopped, closed his eyes for a moment, and took a deep breath. ''So you see the problem,'' he said at last. ''We need to know what's going on over there—how long the war's liable to last, who's winning and why—and I mean *know*, not just read the papers and guess.''

He began pacing back and forth next to the window. ''Now as you know, there are already quite a few Indians from the Nations serving with the Confederate forces in Europe. Mostly just young bucks out for adventure, of course—they'd have run off and joined up on their own, only old Chief McIntosh from the Creek Nation had the bright idea we should make an official show of support for the Confederate war effort, score a few free points with Richmond.

''Trouble is,'' he said, ''they all wind up as rifle-carrying mud soldiers, private troops in the trenches. Don't see much beyond their own little corner of the war—and anyway,'' he added with a wry glance at Amos, ''they're mostly country boys, you know, damn fine soldiers but not much good at analyzing the big picture.''

He beamed suddenly at Amos. ''And that, son, is where you come in.''

Aloud Amos said, ''Yes, sir?''

To himself he said: oh, shit.

''I've heard tell,'' Chief Watie said, ''you've told a number of people around here that you'd like to visit Europe some day. See Paris, all those intellectual places . . . also,'' he went on, in the warm confidential tones of a man announcing he just happens to have a deck on him, ''I'm told you took a few lessons, while you were back East at school, driving a flying machine.''

A terrible knowledge began to form in Amos's mind. ''Only a few hours,'' he said weakly. ''Only made one solo flight, and that was a short one.''

Chief Watie came across the room and put his hand on Amos's shoulder. ''Well, there you go, then,'' he said. ''This is your chance to continue your studies in aviating.''

Amos said, "Sir, I'm not quite following you." Or rather, he thought, I hope I'm not following you.

Watie patted his shoulder in a fatherly way. "Well, you see, son, you're about to make history. Indian history, anyway. After months of tricky negotiations," he said, "the Confederate government has agreed to allow the Cherokee Nation to send one of our officers to be trained in military aviation. Said officer," he went on, smiling predatorily at Amos, "on completion of flight training, to be sent to France and attached to a fighting squadron on active duty, so that he may study, by observation *and* experience, the science of modern aerial warfare; said officer further to be entitled to the rank and uniform of an officer in the Confederate forces, and all courtesies and privileges thereto appertaining."

Amos said helplessly, "Sir, I'm not even in the militia, let alone—"

"Now, now. Don't interrupt your Chief, my boy." Chief Watie went over to his desk and reached into the same drawer from which he had pulled the mineral report. "Here you are. Your commission. An officer and a gentleman, by act of Council."

The document was certainly official-looking, with seals and ribbons and elaborate print in both English and Cherokee. It announced to whom it might concern that Amos Ross Ninekiller was hereby commissioned a Lieutenant in the Army of the Cherokee Nation; it was, Amos saw, backdated over a year.

"Congratulations," Chief Watie said, shaking Amos's hand. "You are now a member of—no, come to think of it, you *are* the Cherokee Flying Corps. Just think, Amos. A moment ago you were a private citizen with no particular prospects. Now, you're not just an officer, you're an entire branch of the service, all by yourself. Why, Napoleon himself never moved that fast."

"Thank you," Amos said bleakly. "Sir."

Chief Watie grinned, an honest grin this time. "Hell, Amos, it's not a lot we want of you. Just keep your eyes open while you're over there, try to get an idea how the fighting's going—flying over the front, you ought to have a fine view of the proceedings. See if you can pick up any other useful information, too, such as the state of morale among the Confederate troops, how well they get along with the British and French, that sort of thing.''

Amos said, "Sir, wouldn't it have been better to attach someone to the Allied General Staff? Or at least a Confederate headquarters? I'd think he'd learn more there than a single pilot—''

"Oh, hell, Amos, nobody at headquarters ever knows what's going on—just a bunch of Generals and Field Marshals talking a lot of bullshit and an army of ass-kissers telling them how wonderful they are. Of course," he added, looking sly, "you don't want to assume we aren't working on that, too.''

He chuckled. "Don't get the idea you're the only one we'll have over there, Amos. You're a smart boy and all that, but we're not ready to pin our whole intelligence effort on one man—especially one who's going to be flying around in the sky trading shots with Germans.''

Amos digested the implications of the last remark. He wished Chief Watie had left that part out.

"Before you leave," the Chief said, "we'll give you the address of your contacts in Paris. Whenever you get a chance—don't go so often you make anybody suspicious—drop by and give them a written report. Now all the real spies," he went on, "they've got codes and secret inks and so on, but we've got a little something of our own. Just write your notes and your report in Cherokee—I guarantee they'll be safe.''

He reached up and patted Amos's shoulder again. "You'll be all right," he said in Cherokee. "The worst part will be the part that comes first—you've got to go to Texas for a few months. Flight training," he added in English. "Try to behave yourself, Amos. Texans can be awfully hard to take sometimes, but try.''

Amos wondered if he was supposed to salute. Though it didn't matter, since he didn't really know how. You did something silly with the right hand to the forehead, didn't you, or—

"Hell, son," Chief Watie said, "let's have a drink."

He dug a pint bottle out of his desk drawer—that was certainly an interesting drawer, Amos thought; it seemed to contain the damnedest things—and, after some rummaging, a couple of small glasses. "Don't worry," he said, pouring. "I know your daddy's a Baptist deacon, but he won't mind this time."

The whisky was powerful but excellent. Amos said, "When do I leave?"

"Soon as we can arrange transportation. Not long, not long." Chief Watie gazed at Amos over his glass. "Amos, I'm so full of bullshit sometimes . . . don't go trying to be a hero, son. That's one of the reasons I picked you for the job. You're a tough lad, sure—hell, you're a Cherokee, it goes without saying you're no sissy—but you've always had this sneaky streak. I remember when you were little. Big kid pick on you, you'd smile at him sweet as a possum eating shit and then when his back was turned you'd bust his head with a rock. Just the kind of man we need," Watie said, nodding approvingly. "Get yourself killed, you'll be no use to us."

Well, Amos thought, at last he's said something that makes sense.

The Chief laughed suddenly. "What's really going to be hell," he said, "if the Yankees decide to get into the war. Have to find some way to slip a few observers in with their bunch, then, and the U.S. Army isn't going to be near as hospitable toward Indians—civilized or not—as our old Johnny Reb neighbors."

"You think the Union will come into the war?" Amos asked.

"Probably. Their election's next year, you know. Bryan's sure to run for a second term—he's already got people running around beating the drum, 'He Kept Us Out Of War' and all that crap. Looks now like Teddy Roosevelt's got the Republican nomination in his pocket, barring something really strange. And Teddy, of course, never saw a war he didn't like. In fact, that's sure to be the main issue in the campaign."

Amos nodded thoughtfully. After a sip of whisky he said, "So who's going to win?"

"The Yankee election?" Watie snorted. "Don't make an old man laugh. Teddy Roosevelt isn't all that popular in some quarters, but William Jennings Bryan has as much chance of getting another term in the White House as he has of growing another ear."

He backed up to the desk and draped his rump over a corner. "Look, Amos. William Jennings Bryan has been President of the United States for two and a half years now, going on three. In that time he's managed to completely wreck the economy of the nation, create a major recession, and throw thousands of people out of work, with his God-damned loony economic theories. His administration has had one scandal after another—practically everybody he's appointed has turned out to be a crook, and a couple just may be going to jail. He makes good speeches, but when you analyze the words you find out he never really says anything. And every day, just about, he says or does something that makes it clearer than ever that he hasn't got a clue what he's doing and in fact doesn't know shit about much of *anything*, and doesn't really *want* to know.

"Now you think about it," Chief Watie said. "There's just no way the people of the United States would ever re-elect a man like that to a second term as President. No way in hell."

3

THE FLYING strength of the Fourth Virginia Pursuit Squadron was divided into three flights, unimaginatively named A, B, and C Flights. Each consisted, theoretically, of five aircraft. All the planes were French-designed Nieuport 17 fighters, built under license in Alabama and fitted with French-made engines after arrival in Europe; despite various attempts, the Confederacy had not yet produced a single airplane of its own design.

C Flight was commanded by a squat, flat-faced, pale-eyed Captain named Jack Yancey. Amos found him in the armorers' shack, an open box of cartridges between his feet, loading ammunition drums by hand.

He held up a single round and, with a look of disgust, handed it to Amos. "Look at that." His voice was surprisingly high and slightly hoarse, with the nasal tones of eastern Tennessee. "See the kind of shit they expect us to fight a war with?"

Amos examined the dull brass cartridge, unsure what he was supposed to see. It appeared to be just another regulation .303 round, the standard British rifle and machine-gun cartridge, used throughout the Confederate forces for over a decade. Yancey said, "If you can't see it, run your finger across the hind end."

Amos felt the base of the cartridge, then looked more carefully. The primer had not been seated all the way into the brass case.

"A God-damned jam waiting to happen." Yancey took the round back from Amos and tossed it into a bucket with several others. "You want to think about that. Nothing says you *have* to fool with your gun or your ammunition or your engine or anything else—the ground crew will do it all, you can just hop in the plane and trust everything to work like it's supposed to. But just remember, a Nieuport's only got one gun and it only takes one bad round to stop it, and then you're fucked. Those nice people at Griswold Small Arms of Macon, Georgia, won't be there in the middle of a dogfight to say, 'Oh, sorry, our mistake, let us fix your gun for you.' They won't even know they've killed you."

He pushed the last round into the drum on his lap. "And the Krauts," he said grimly, "are mounting *two* guns on the latest Fokkers, and their Spandau is the best machine gun in the world. While we got—this."

Both men stared for a moment at the oily gray machine gun lying on the workbench beside Yancey. The Travis machine gun represented one of the Confederacy's few contributions to the technology of the current war. Designed by a professor at Virginia Military Institute, manufactured at a former cotton-gin works near Birmingham, the Travis gun was an air-cooled, gas-operated weapon, fed by a hundred-round drum, its action basically a copy of the French Hotchkiss gun. In the virtually universal view of everyone who had to use it or work on it, it was a piece of shit.

"Something else to think about," Yancey went on. "Considering how much these things like to jam, you don't want to go spraying lead all over the sky. Get in close, close enough to see whether the asshole's wearing an Iron Cross First Class or Second Class, and aim and nail him with the first few rounds, because you never know how many you're going to get to fire before the fucking Travis gun goes constipated on you."

He seemed to realize something. "Say, you're the new man. The Indian. Something you want?"

Amos said, "Captain Clay said I was to report to you. I'm assigned to C Flight."

"Oh?" Yancey stood up, laying the filled drum carefully on the workbench, and picked up a rag and wiped his hands. "You're the one who knocked Eubanks on his ass, by God. I remember now." He stuck out his hand. "Anybody does that has to be all right. They ought to give you a medal or something."

He moved toward the open doorway, motioning Amos to follow. "As it happens I've got some time free right now. Might as well get you checked out . . . how many hours you got in?" he asked as they stepped out onto the sunlit field. "Hope you know more than the last few replacements they gave me."

"Sixty-seven hours altogether," Amos said. "Most of that back in Texas, of course, and some of it was on pretty crude aircraft—old Wright and Curtiss pushers they got before the Yankees slapped that embargo on military equipment for the Confederacy. But I did get in a little over twenty hours on Nieuports at the advanced training base at Tours."

Yancey looked impressed. "Christ, that's a hell of a lot more than usual. Generally they send pilots up here, maybe forty hours if they're lucky. Back last year, when the Fokkers were eating us for lunch every day, we were getting these poor bastards with under twenty hours. Some of them barely knew how to take off and land."

Amos shrugged. "I spent a lot of time waiting around while they decided what to do with me. Flying was about the only thing to do."

"Yeah, well, let's do a little of it right now." Yancey waved his arm toward the line of canvas-covered hangars. "Let's go let you have a look at the war."

After completing his walk-around inspection of the Nieuport, Amos climbed into the cockpit. Yancey leaned against the side of the fuselage and said, "Look, Ninekiller . . . nine what?"

"I don't know," Amos said, buckling his seat straps. "Family name."

"That right? Well, anyway, Ninekiller, all we're going to do is just fly over the front lines and come back—give you a look at the area, the general layout."

He didn't say, "And let me see if you actually know how to fly this thing." It wasn't necessary.

"I mean," he said, "we won't be sticking our noses into serious enemy territory, probably won't even see any Kraut planes. If we do, we don't get in any fights, right? We get our asses out of there. If we get jumped, we only do what we have to do to get loose and then we run like hell—a Nieuport will outrun a Fokker in level flight, luckily. This is *not* a combat patrol."

He pointed at the Travis gun mounted on top of the Nieuport's upper wing. "In case it gets out of hand, I assume you've at least fired one of these things?" Amos nodded. "Good," Yancey said. "Better and better."

He frowned. "I don't suppose they bothered to tell you what happens if you dive a Nieuport too hard."

"The fabric tears off the upper wing. Maybe the whole wing comes off. We lost a man that way at Tours," Amos said. "I saw the whole thing."

Yancey looked relieved. "Christ, is it possible I've actually got somebody here who knows his ass from a hot rock? Okay, let's go do it."

Amos buckled the leather helmet in place, wondering as always what good the silly thing was supposed to be. He wiggled the stick and kicked the rudder pedals, watching the control surfaces, making sure everything moved freely. Seeing Yancey climbing into his own Nieuport, Amos signaled to the mechanic who stood waiting in front of Amos's plane. "Switch off," he called.

The mechanic stepped forward and grasped the horizontal blade of the wooden propeller. "Suck in, sir," he shouted.

Amos turned on the fuel, opened the throttle and closed the air flap. "Suck in."

The mechanic yanked the propeller through two grunting revolutions. The engine made hissing and farting sounds as it ingested the rich mixture. The mechanic yelled, "Contact."

Amos opened the air value, closed the throttle, and flipped the switch. "Contact."

Amos heard the sudden coughing roar as Yancey's engine fired nearby.

The mechanic took a deep breath and yanked hard on the propeller blade. The engine popped, snorted, hesitated, and then burst into a deafening bellow. The propeller blurred to invisibility and the airplane surged forward against the chocks that held the wheels. Amos ran the power up to full throttle briefly, while the ground crew hung on to the wingtips. Nothing exploded or fell off. He saw Yancey's machine beginning its takeoff roll. He pulled down his goggles, made a small adjustment to the mixture controls, and waved to the ground crew.

The chocks came free and the Nieuport charged down the field into the wind. Amos held the stick forward, keeping the plane on the ground, letting speed build and using the rudder to counter the torque-induced tendency to swing to the right. The tail came up off the ground and Amos began to ease the stick back. There was a sudden tightening of bracing wires as the wings took the weight of the aircraft. The Nieuport ceased to roll and flew. Amos exhaled and began to climb after Yancey.

The two biplanes climbed steadily into the bright midday sky, heading east and a little north. The ground below turned into a patchwork of oddly-shaped green and brown segments, like a Seminole quilt. There were a few patches of cloud off to the north but otherwise the sky was clear.

And it was so enormous . . . that was one thing Amos had never gotten over, this hugeness of the sky, the tremendous expanse of air that seemed to go on to infinity, grays and off-whites down at the horizon, shading up into deep near-violet blues at the zenith. People who had never flown often said they would be frightened to look down and see the ground so far below; but in fact it was in the other directions that the real awe lay. Compared to the great endless depths that stretched all around and above him, the ground seemed close and friendly, a minor drop hardly to be taken seriously.

Not that the sky was empty by any means. Apart from the wisps of cloud in the distance, there were specks that were other aircraft, moving singly or in groups on whatever missions, too far away to identify. There was Yancey's Nieuport a little ahead and to the right, still in its shallow climb, wings rocking minutely in the currents of air, the sun catching the bright-painted insignia—the blue St. Andrew's cross and white stars of the Confederate battle flag, superimposed on a red circle—on the light-gray wings.

And there was the air itself, which seemed to have a visible texture, like perfectly clear water. To Amos the sky had never seemed a void, but rather a great ocean of air with tangible currents and waves . . . an ocean, he thought, in which he sat in his little island of noise and vibration and stench and tried to stay afloat.

That was the other thing that always struck him when he flew. From the ground, an airplane in flight looked graceful, even serene, soaring and banking and diving elegantly among the clouds, inspiring all sorts of poetic and even spiritual thoughts. More than one person had remarked to Amos that it must be so peaceful up there. . . .

The reality was something else entirely. The central fact of life in a small single-propeller airplane was the engine, a heavy, ugly, foul-smelling lump of metal that thrashed and rattled and shook constantly—it had *better* do it constantly, else the pilot was in serious trouble—only a few feet away from the pilot's face. The harmless, almost comic buzz people heard on the ground was in fact an incredible giant drone that went clear beyond the merely deafening to numb all the senses and deaden the mind. The vibrations took on complex harmonics that set a man's teeth on edge.

The Le Rhône rotary engine used in the Nieuport 17 was, like all rotary engines, particularly nasty to live with. The whole concept of the rotary engine was inherently grotesque, and its tremendous popularity with aircraft builders of the period stood as a monument to the strange attractions of really bad engineering: the entire engine rotated around a fixed crankshaft (rather than the reverse, as God clearly intended), which kept a good flow of cooling air over the cylinders and had absolutely no other discernible advantage. The torque made the aircraft tricky to handle; worse, the spinning engine spat out incredible quantities of oil, which coated the wings and the control surfaces and the pilot (not to forget the pilot, he of the oil-soaked leather clothing and the oil-smeared goggles and the permanently oily face) with a steady spray of waste lubricant. And there was an extra misery: for complex reasons, the rotaries were lubricated with pure castor oil, so that the pilot steadily inhaled fumes and droplets of powerful natural laxative throughout the flight. As if, Amos often thought, flying an airplane didn't already present enough strain on the sphincter muscles. . . .

People talked of aviators as "birdmen" and gave aircraft names of birds; but the truth was that any bird that roared, vibrated, and stank like this would have been ostracized for life by everything else with feathers. The only people who experienced the peaceful flight of birds were glider pilots, or perhaps free balloonists.

And if he raised his eyes a bit, Amos could see a new addition to the picture: the slender wicked shape of the machine gun, perched on its clumsy mount atop the upper wing. Sooner or later he would be making even more noise, and other people would be making noises at him, trying to cause fires and explosions and if at all possible distinctly non-tranquil impacts of aircraft against the earth. That part of it, he had to admit, was not yet quite real to him; but he was sure that would be taken care of quite soon.

It took the two Nieuports about half an hour to climb to eight thousand feet, flying steadily eastward all the while. Now Yancey rocked his wings to get Amos's attention, turned in his open cockpit, and pointed vigorously downward with his left hand.

Amos looked, and was transfixed. His mouth opened involuntarily; he said, "*E-e-e!*"—the rising-pitch three-tone exclamation which in Cherokee expressed shock, amazement, dismay, or all of these at once. It was something he had deliberately stopped doing, having found that it made white people laugh; but the sight below was enough to burn away the thin mental tissues of the last few years, and send his mind recoiling into disused channels of the past, seeking the comprehensible.

He had heard, as had everyone, about "the front lines" or "the trenches," and he had seen a few pictures and read newspaper and magazine accounts and studied the maps; he had thought he had at least some general idea what it must be like. He had envisioned, in a hazy way, a couple of lines of narrow ditches, neatly dug and running straight—something like irrigation ditches, only drier—in which men stood and fired at each other; he had even wondered if it would be possible to see such minor earthworks from high altitude.

Nothing at all had prepared him for the reality.

The face of the world had been ripped by titanic claws. Great dark gashes ran parallel across the earth below, on and on in either direction, vanishing out of sight to the north and south without a break. Shorter trenches connected the main ones in a complicated network without symmetry or pattern; behind the front-line trenches lay the black scars of earlier positions, abandoned in attack or retreat. Rutted, churned-up roads, pocked by shellfire, ran here and there, though Amos could see nothing moving along them, could not in fact see how such a road could be used at all, even by the new armored "tanks" the newspapers had been chattering about.

Down the center, between the two sets of trenches, ran a broad stretch of bare, gnarled earth, so cratered by shells and bombs and God knew what else as to resemble the surface of the Moon. Amos guessed this must be what was called No Man's Land. Suddenly the expression no longer seemed overstated or melodramatic; it was surely impossible for anything to live down there, let alone fight, let alone advance on foot across that dreadful naked ground.

The devastation stretched for miles on either side of the front. In all that area nothing green was growing, no square foot of earth had not been violated. And, Amos realized, it would be much the same all the way from the border of Switzerland to the shore of the English Channel. An immense strip had been plowed and ditched and turned under, halfway across a continent; but it had been planted only with barbed wire and rusting fragments of metal and the blood and bones of men.

A terrible vision began to form in the dark backstage of Amos's mind. I am looking on the face of Hell, he thought; and something answered: No. It is worse than that. You are looking on the face of the future.

Aloud, his voice lost in the din of the engine, he said, "And they call us savages."

As he watched, a section of the German line suddenly disappeared under clouds of smoke and dust. It took some time for the muffled booming to come up to him, but when it did the Nieuport's wings rocked in the shock waves even at eight thousand feet. Artillery fire, of course; British or Confederate or even French, he had no idea. The bombardment seemed wholly arbitrary, even whimsical; there was, as far as Amos could see, nothing going on in that area, nothing to distinguish it from any other part of the line at that moment. He remembered Faulkner's words from the night before: sound and fury, signifying nothing.

He realized suddenly that Yancey was waggling his wings again and gesturing with great urgency. While Amos had been mooning and philosophizing over the horrors below, they had, of course, been flying straight into enemy territory at almost a hundred miles an hour. Now Amos became aware that the air in their general vicinity had inexplicably blossomed with a number of dirty-looking, irregularly-spaced puffs of blackish smoke.

Someone down there, he thought with real shock, is shooting at us. With *cannons*. What an *insane* thing to do. True, none of the shell bursts seemed to be coming very close, but still—

He blinked rapidly, shook his head hard, and followed close on Yancey's tail as the lead Nieuport dropped its right wings and swung sharply about in a tight bank. For a few minutes Yancey twisted and turned and bounced about the sky, evading ground fire and, Amos suspected, testing his new man at the same time. At length Yancey broke off the game and led the way back toward home. The high early-afternoon sun glinted off the whirling arcs of their propellers.

Back at the field, Yancey began to question Amos about what he had seen over the lines; but almost immediately one of the orderly-room clerks appeared to tell Yancey that the Adjutant wanted to see him about something. Amos watched him leave with some relief. He liked Yancey, but it had already become embarrassingly clear that there had been quite a few aircraft in their vicinity—including German aircraft, a truly worrisome thought—that Amos had not seen at all. Better start looking around up there, he told himself; all very well to bend a horrified gaze on the landscape of modern warfare, but not if it caused you to become part of the landscape yourself.

Faulkner was not in the cubicle when Amos went to change out of his flying suit. After an irresolute pause Amos decided to wander over to the mess and see who might be around.

But as he came up to the open door of the officers' mess he heard from within the querulous tones of Major Culpepper's voice, raised in what sounded like reproof. Amos stood still, one foot almost to the doorsill, unsure whether or not to go on in.

"This just won't do," Culpepper was saying. "You'll have to do better than this, boy."

The response was too low and indistinct for Amos to pick up.

"Look here, boy," Culpepper went on, less angrily. "You've got a real opportunity to better yourself here. Most of your race, if they're accepted for military service at all, wind up serving in labor battalions, digging trenches and graves and the like. Here you're getting to wait on white officers, pilots at that. If you apply yourself, you might get a very good position after the war, on the staff of some hotel or restaurant. I'd be glad to write a letter of reference for any colored boy who served conscientiously under my command."

The other voice again made its muffled response. It sounded like, "Yassuh."

"All right." Culpepper sounded mollified now. "See to it, then. I don't want to have to speak to you again. You know," Culpepper went on, "you people aren't slaves any more. After we'd fought a war for our independence, we went ahead and freed you Nigras on our own volition, just as we'd have done if the Yankees had let us alone. That was before you were born, you know."

"Yassuh."

"So you've got no master to tell you everything to do now. We expect you to take some responsibility and show we didn't make a mistake."

Footsteps came toward the door. Major Culpepper said, "Tyrone, I'm counting on you to shape these boys up. Some of them seem to be fresh out of the cotton patch. I know you'll handle it."

Tyrone's deep bass rumble said, "Yes, suh, Major."

"Outstanding. Carry on, then."

Amos stepped quietly back and to one side as the Major came out the door and strode off down the boardwalk toward the headquarters building. He did not seem to see Amos at all.

Amos started once more to enter the mess building, only to stop once again as he heard Tyrone say distinctly, "Yes, sir, yassuh, yowzah, Mars Culpepper *suh*. You ambulatory advertisement of the horrors of premature senility."

Another voice, sounding choked with rage, said, "I'll kill him. Next time that fucker calls me 'boy' I swear I'm gone kill him."

"Be at peace, brother." Tyrone's voice had the low carrying tones of the bottom pipes of a church organ. "Be at peace, for now. You will not kill anyone. Even that purulent pustule on the scrotum of humanity known as Eubanks."

"Shit. I ain't taking any more—"

There was the sound of a light but solid slap. Tyrone said, "You will take whatever you have to take, brother. You will kill no one. Until the day comes when we kill them all."

It did not really seem to be a good time to walk in.

Tyrone appeared in the doorway, large and looking very black in his white uniform. "Getting an earful, red brother?"

he said without apparent surprise. "I don't suppose you'd be inclined to report anything you might have overheard."

Amos shrugged. "Not my affair."

"Indeed. Not that you would be believed anyway. The Major is as convinced of the love and devotion of his faithful darky as he is that God closely resembles Robert E. Lee." Tyrone gave Amos a cool appraising stare. "Of course you people have had your own difficulties with the Caucasian breed. I have read about you Cherokees. Lived in big houses, rode carriages and fine horses, dressed like whites. Had schools and newspapers in your own language, raised cotton and tobacco, yes, owned slaves too, some of you."

Amos inclined his head in assent. "I'm afraid so."

Tyrone chuckled without humor. "And much good it did you. When my more timid brothers and sisters argue that we must learn to be like the whites, earn their respect and acceptance, so that they will graciously grant us our at present nonexistent rights—I point to the example of your people as proof that it does not work."

Amos said, "Then why take part in the white man's war?"

"For much the same reason, I suspect, that you are doing so—to learn things that will one day help us stand up to them and even the score." Tyrone smiled suddenly. "Ninekiller. Tell me, Lieutenant. Between the two of us, were the nine white men?"

Amos nodded. "Yes." Actually they had been Catawbas, according to his grandfather, but it seemed to mean so much to Tyrone.

"Delightful. Go inside," Tyrone said, "and tell Desmond I said he is to fix you a very large drink, of your choice, from the Major's private stock. Good day, Lieutenant."

In the days that followed, Amos gradually became part of the unwieldy machine that was the Fourth Virginia Pursuit Squadron.

The routine was simple, and altered only by bad weather or the occasional special lunacy dreamed up by higher command. Each morning, and again in the afternoon, a flight of Nieuports would take noisily to the air and head for the front lines. Now and then they might have orders to escort bombers or observation machines, but usually their mission was simply to cross into German territory and look for trouble. The flights were rotated on a strict schedule: one flight on morning patrol, one on afternoon, and the third occupied with non-flying duties or simply resting.

Amos's first few patrols were uneventful. The Germans were not all that eager to fight, these days; the old Fokker monoplane, which had swept the sky of Allied aircraft only last year, was becoming obsolete, and only the best or most foolish German pilots would willingly take on a flight of Nieuports.

"It won't last," Yancey said positively. "The Krauts are damned good engineers. Any day now they'll throw something at us to make these Nieuports look like Wright pushers."

On his sixth patrol Amos finally met the official enemy.

C Flight had the afternoon patrol that day: Yancey, Lahaie, Faulkner, Amos, and a skinny kid from Georgia named Shelby. They were at nine thousand feet, a little south of Bapaume and well inside German airspace, when the German planes appeared from under a low patch of cloud.

There were three of them, lumbering slowly along in a rough V formation: LVGs, obsolete two-seater observation planes, their westward course taking them almost square across the Nieuports' path at seven or eight thousand feet. A quick check established that the area was free of German fighters at the moment. Yancey waved his left hand and C Flight went down to attack.

It was a messy business. Teamwork and disciplined group tactics were rare in 1916 and unknown among the individualistic Confederate pilots. C Flight broke up into five independent entities, each pilot picking his own target and his own approach; except for a perfunctory effort to avoid actual collisions, there was no attempt at coordination.

Bringing up the rear, Amos had time to study the targets as the distance shortened. The LVGs were painted in a mottled pattern that made them difficult to pick out against the patchwork background of the fields below, but the effect was rather spoiled by the huge black-and-white Iron Cross insignia on wings and tail and fuselage. Their long old-fashioned wings tilted clumsily as their pilots tried to haul them out of the paths of the fast Nieuports. Slow, flapping old airplanes, almost comic, no business at all in combat. . . .

Suddenly Amos realized that there was a man standing in the rear cockpit of the nearest LVG, a man in leather helmet and jacket who was pointing a machine gun straight at Amos. There was a flicker of yellow-red flame and bullets popped as they passed close to the Nieuport; Amos could hear them even over the blare of the engine. A number of small holes appeared in the fabric of his lower wing.

Amos reacted wholly by instinct, his body solving the equation without clearing the solution with his brain. The observer made a dark blot in the center of the ring-and-post gunsight. Amos fired.

He was moving fast and there was time for only a short burst before he had to yank the Nieuport's nose up to avoid ramming the LVG. There was time, however, to see the observer slump tiredly over his gun and then slide down into the rear cockpit, one arm hanging grotesquely out into the slipstream.

It was Amos's only contribution to the fight. Yancey came around again, attacked from astern, and shot the now defenseless LVG out of the sky. Faulkner and Shelby chased another machine until it vanished into a cloud; they might or might not have damaged it. Lahaie, after a careful stalk, came up beneath the third LVG, tilted his Travis gun back on its mount, and riddled the two-seater's belly until it burst into flames. The entire affair lasted only a few minutes.

On the way home, Amos decided that the whole thing had been rather like the night Melissa Bearpaw had finally let him do it. After all the anticipation and the buildup, it was over before you had a chance to think about how it felt; and afterward the excitement was quickly replaced by depression and a vague embarrassment. And yet you knew you had passed through a door that only swung one way.

* * *

That evening the five of them celebrated in the mess. It was the first time in weeks that anyone in the squadron had downed an enemy plane, let alone two. Lahaie even managed to leave the piano alone for the occasion.

"Dis Indian, he's good luck, him," Lahaie declared theatrically, draping an affectionate arm over Amos's shoulders. "Don' care if he do ron into docks."

Faulkner said quietly, "Do you *have* to do that? That bogus Cajun or Creole or whatever kind of accent that's supposed to be?"

Lahaie shrugged and reached for his drink. "Somebody has to do it."

Yancey grinned at Amos. "Good luck for me, that's for sure. That Kraut was easy meat after you took out the observer. You really ought to get credit for half of that kill."

Amos shook his head violently. "Christ, no." The idea of keeping score, like some gunman notching his gun, seemed worse than childish. "Anyway, it was just luck. He was shooting at me so I shot back, without even thinking."

"Yeah," Yancey said drily. "I checked with the armorers. You fired exactly *eight* fucking bullets, Ninekiller. To hit, not just a plane, but a man, in a full-throttle beam attack. Either that Kraut gunner was the unluckiest human on the Kaiser's payroll, or you're one hell of a dead-eye shot."

Faulkner said to Amos, "If it makes you feel any better, Amos, in a German two-seater it's the observer who's in command. The pilot is just an enlisted man, treated as a mere chauffeur. Anyway," he added, "if you hadn't shot him he'd just have burned to death when Yancey shot the plane down."

Amos shrugged. He understood what Faulkner was trying to do, but it wasn't necessary. The Mississippian could not imagine how wild things were, even now, in the Nations. Amos did not want to talk about it, but the truth was that this was not the first time he had killed a man.

He said, "I'm all right."

Faulkner looked sharply at him. "Yes," he said slowly, "you are, aren't you?" He seemed about to say more, but then he shook his head and reached for his drink. "Lucky you," he muttered.

Shelby said, "I just wish we'd got the other one."

"Not to worry," Lahaie reassured him. "Maybe tomorrow, hien?"

But nobody did any flying at all next day. A great gray wall of rain and clouds moved in during the night, grounding everyone along the front. The field became soaked and bare patches turned to mud. The pilots sat around the mess or in their quarters and tried not to think what it must be like in the trenches now.

Amos was sitting on his bunk after lunch, finishing a written report on his observations so far, when Faulkner came bustling in. "Never mind writing letters now, you can do that some other time. Get up," Faulkner said happily, "pack your spare eagle feather or whatever. Let's go."

Amos folded his notebook. "What's happening?"

"The war gods smile on the heroes of C Flight." Faulkner was throwing various articles into a small kit bag. "Or the Major does, anyway. We're to be rewarded for saving Democracy from the menace of overage observation aircraft, and incidentally for giving our noble commander some sort of victory to report after a long embarrassing dry spell. Since the weather forecast says it'll be like this all week, Clay didn't talk him out of it this time. We're free as cats till Thursday morning."

He threw a small French dictionary at Amos. "Paris, my old! We're going to Paris!"

4

BY THE second decade of the Twentieth Century, Paris had become securely and indisputably established as one of the world's great centers—perhaps even *the* center—of what might be called entrepreneurial erotica. However bizarre the fantasy, however Gothic the taste, it could be satisfied for a price somewhere in Paris. From the streetwalkers of Pigalle to the domination specialists who collected fortunes for whipping Field Marshals and humiliating Cabinet Ministers, there was someone to cater to the most esoteric desires.

It might have been thought, then, and indeed had been said, that Paris had seen it all. But that was before the coming of Dixie Land. Nothing like Dixie Land had ever been seen or even imagined in all the convoluted history of Paris; or (it seemed reasonable to assume) ever would be again.

And yet it was as with all truly great ideas: once the thing was done, it was seen to have been not merely obvious but inevitable.

On the day that President Leontine Butler announced that the Confederate States of America would send an Expeditionary Force to France, an enterprising and public-spirited lady of Atlanta, Georgia, made an instant and acute analysis of the implications. There would soon be large numbers of Confederate officers—Southern gentlemen from the best families of the thirteen states—serving their country in a distant land. Torn by duty from their wives and sweethearts, they would have need for solace and feminine companionship and, well, other things.

And it was not right that they should be driven to the company of foreign women (*French* women at that; everyone knew what *they* were like) and perhaps fall into unspeakable vices and sully their Southern honor. Clearly, there ought to be some place in France where they could find a little bit of Southern culture and hospitality, an island of graciousness and gentility amid the horrors of war. It would help them remember what they were fighting for.

"Girls," Miss Rhetticia announced to her employees, "we're going to France."

Subsequently, on the outskirts of Paris, astonishing things began to happen. A large house, somewhat run-down but once stately and elegant, was stripped and rebuilt completely, its front remodeled to incorporate a long verandah with tall white columns. Wagons unloaded chandeliers, mirrors, gleaming brass beds, and other things supposedly unobtainable in wartime Paris. There were even several magnolia trees, carefully planted about the grounds, though these unfortunately died in the harsh French winter. A number of strikingly beautiful young women were seen to move in, as were several black persons of both sexes.

And soon there began a steady stream of gentlemen visitors in the butternut-gray uniforms of Confederate officers. Lights twinkled all night, every night, in the tall windows, save only when Zeppelin bombing raids mandated the closing of shutters; and even then, the sounds from within continued unabated, however near the explosions might come. People in the neighborhood listened and told each other that someone in the big house did truly miraculous things to a piano.

Such were the origins of Dixie Land; such was the contribution of Miss Rhetticia O'Hara of Atlanta to the preservation of truth, justice, and the Confederate way.

* * *

Faulkner said, "I'm telling you, Amos, this isn't just a whorehouse. This is an *institution*. You owe it to yourself to see Dixie Land before you die."

He had said that more than once during the taxi ride from the railroad station. The truth was that Lieutenant William Faulkner had had a fair amount to drink, having nursed a bottle through most of the long uncomfortable train ride. He wasn't really drunk yet, just starting to get repetitious.

Yancey said, "Christ, Bill, shut up about people dying. You can be the *morbidest* son of a bitch sometimes."

The taxi screeched around a corner, heeling over violently on its worn-out springs. Amos tried to brace himself against the door. The stories about Paris cab drivers seemed to be true, at least in this case; he had been in crash landings that were less terrifying than this ride. Outside the cab windows the lights of Paris swam and ran in the pouring rain.

"An institution," Faulkner said yet again, and nodded vigorous agreement with himself. "They should put up a statue of Miss Rhetticia in Atlanta. Hell, Richmond. The Yankees have Barbara Frietchie, we have Miss Rhetticia. Put her picture on a stamp or something."

The taxi slowed suddenly, bald tires sliding on the rain-wet street, and turned through a large ornate gateway lit on either side by gas lamps. Several automobiles were already lined up along the white gravel drive, but the driver pulled up opposite the brightly lit entrance and sounded his horn. Seconds later, a group of black men in livery had materialized around the taxi, holding umbrellas, and were bustling the pilots toward the big house.

As they handed their caps and raincoats to the Negro maids in the front hallway, a small dark-haired woman in a full-length white evening dress came hurrying to meet them. "My goodness!" she cried. "It's Captain Yancey!"

Actually what she said was more like, "Mah *goo*-wud-niss, iyit's Cayaptyn *Yay*incih!" Her accent was the thickest Amos had ever heard; it had never before occurred to him that English, like Cherokee, had several mutually unintelligible dialects.

"And the boys from the Fourth Virginia! Well, aren't we the lucky ladies here tonight." She tapped Faulkner on the arm with the folded fan she carried. "You must tell me the news from home, Lieutenant Faulkner. I'm dying to know more about that nice Sartoris family. Such fine people. The Colonel often visited us in Atlanta."

She was, Amos saw, somewhere in her middle years; the dark hair was streaked with gray and the glittering ropes of jewelry about her neck did not entirely hide the lines and folds of age. Her body, however, was still worth looking at, particularly in the low-cut dress that fit her like a coat of paint. A bright, chattering, pretty little woman, and, Amos decided immediately, an extremely dangerous one.

Yancey said, "Miss Rhetticia, the newest officer in our squadron. Lieutenant, ah, Amos."

Miss Rhetticia extended her hand. Amos took it and bowed slightly, wondering if he was supposed to kiss it. She said, "How nice . . . Captain Yancey, just a teeny little word with you?"

She pulled Yancey aside and spoke urgently behind her fan. Her voice was low but not as low as she seemed to think; Amos clearly heard, ". . . awfully, well, *dark*, you know, I don't mean to—"

"Quite all right," Yancey assured her, straight-faced. "The Lieutenant is, um, partly of Italian extraction."

"Oh. Oh, well, that's *fine*, then. *Love* Italian men, so romantic." She fluttered her eyelashes over her shoulder at Amos. "Sorry, Captain Yancey," she added behind her fan, "but we have to be so careful. You remember that awful business last month when those Navy officers tried to bring that *Mexican* in here."

She waved her fan at all of them. "Gentlemen," she cried, "welcome to Dixie Land!"

And ushered them down the hall and into a spacious, high-ceilinged parlor, where bright lights twinkled from crystal chandeliers and flashed off tall gilt-framed mirrors, and in-credibly beautiful women in white crinoline sat on plush couches and love seats talking with men in butternut gray. The air was full of tobacco smoke and perfume; through the tinkle of glass and crystal and the hum and twitter of conversation came the rolling chords of a piano being played by an authentic genius.

Amos wandered, a little dazedly, through the room, trying not to stare too openly. It was difficult; for one thing he had never seen so many square feet of female breasts in one place in his life. The women all wore long, full-skirted dresses, coming clear down to the floor and flared by numerous petticoats, so that what lay underneath from the waist down was a matter of conjecture; but farther up, necklines plunged to awesome levels to reveal expanses of soft bosom and even, here and there, the rosy borders of nipples.

And the girls were all so beautiful, Amos thought with something not far from reverence. Blonds, brunettes, a couple of redheads, and there were several colored girls, he saw, most in servants' uniforms, but some dressed as elegantly as any of the white women. All were attended by enthusiastic-looking men in gray.

Amos wandered over toward the long shining bar that occupied the entire end of the parlor. Nearby, he saw, Miss Rhetticia and several of the girls sat talking with the rest of C Flight. He heard Lahaie saying, "So last week zis Fokker nearly got me—"

"Now, now," Miss Rhetticia said reprovingly. "No need for that kind of talk here."

The girls all giggled. Faulkner said, "It's all right, ma'am. The 'Fokker' is a type of German aircraft."

"Zat's right," Lahaie agreed. "Only zis focker was flyin' a Halberstadt."

A stocky black bartender, his hairless scalp gleaming softly in the light from overhead, took Amos's order and brought him a bourbon and water. The bartender had a dazzling smile and a deep chuckle and a genial manner; Amos remembered Tyrone and suspended judgment.

Miss Rhetticia's voice floated back to him: "Lieutenant Faulkner, I do believe you're growing a mustache! Oh, I always say a mustache is so becoming. My daddy wore one, you know. Of course," she sighed, "I only remember him from the pictures Mama had around the place, but I do remember how handsome he looked with his mustache. Mama told me once she never really liked it, but whenever she told him she wished he'd shave it off, he always just said, 'Frankly, my dear, I don't give a—' ''

At Amos's elbow another female voice, this one low and slightly husky, said, ''Enjoying yourself, Lieutenant?''

Amos turned and saw a tall, black-haired woman, about his own age, looking at a him with an expression of quiet amusement. He said rather stupidly, ''Hello.''

''My name's Julia,'' she said, still in that throaty low voice that was already beginning to set up disturbing harmonics along his spine. ''The others,'' she said with a toss of her head that included the entire room, ''all have names like Lucy Faye and Debbie Sue and Tammy June, because Miss Rhetticia feels it's expected of them. But I told her, look, I'll chirp and flutter with the best of them, but I draw the line at calling myself Becky Lou.''

Amos said, ''My name's Amos.''

''Amos?'' She tilted her head and considered him. ''You're an Indian, aren't you?'' she said unexpectedly. ''I just realized it. My God, how did the old bitch ever let you in? Come to that, when did the lily-white Confederate officer corps start admitting Indians?''

Amos glanced a bit nervously around, but no one seemed to be listening. ''Cherokee Flying Corps,'' he said. ''Attached as an observer—''

She laughed, not the high-pitched giggle that seemed to be standard here but a strong deep laugh from somewhere down inside. ''For God's sake, now I've heard everything. Cherokee Flying Corps . . . come on,'' she said. ''Let's sit somewhere. Miss Rhetticia doesn't like her girls to stand at the bar and talk with the customers; it doesn't look refined. Makes the place look like a whorehouse or something.''

She paused and laid a hand on his arm. Something changed in her eyes. ''Or,'' she said, looking straight at him, ''we could just dispense with the preliminary rituals and go on upstairs right now. It's entirely up to you.''

Amos nodded. ''Let's do that.''

* * *

Upstairs, she stripped with unhurried graceful movements, hanging the white dress carefully in a carved wardrobe, stepping out of her crinoline petticoats and folding them neatly. "All this old-fashioned stuff we have to wear," she said, undoing her camisole, "like we're going to a plantation ball, wonder the old cow doesn't have us in bustles and hoop skirts. . . ."

She shucked her step-ins and stood naked except for sheer black silk stockings held up by bright red garters. "Want me to leave these on? I thought so." She walked long-legged and white across the room, her big breasts swaying and bouncing, while Amos struggled with the remaining bits of his uniform. The buttons seemed to have become unaccountably hard to manage. "Come here," she said. "Any special . . . preferences?"

"However you want," Amos said with some difficulty.

She nodded. "All right."

She sat on the edge of the bed and grasped him, dipping her head to address his now rampant erection with her rosebud mouth. When things began to reach the point of explosion she released him and lay back on the red satin sheets. "Contact," she murmured as he mounted her. Her long black-stockinged legs were raised past the vertical, resting against his shoulders. "Don't hurry so, we've got all night. . . ."

Later, she told him she was from Charleston and that she had been with Miss Rhetticia since just before the war. She said she was twenty-five: three years older than Amos, older than he would have guessed.

"If you're working up to asking the standard question," she said, "I've got three or four pretty good tales I could tell you. I'm rather partial to the one about my mother being betrayed by a British sea captain, myself, but you might prefer one of the others. Or," she said with a toss of her black curls, "you might even want to hear the truth."

"Try that," Amos said a little sleepily. His left hand stroked her smooth bottom in a gesture that right now was more companionable than erotic. "The truth, I mean."

She made that deep gurgling laugh. "The truth, Lieutenant, is that I started doing it early, I found out right away that I liked it a lot, and later on I found out I could get paid for it. All right?"

Amos shrugged. "Speaking of, uh—"

"Don't worry about the bill, Lieutenant. It won't be more than you can handle. Miss Rhetticia has a very reasonable price schedule for junior officers. It's only the high-ranking brass who get cleaned."

"They come here too?"

"By reservation, special appointment, and a very discreet private entrance. Generals seem to have very strange tastes." She rose up and crouched over him. "Speaking of taste—"

"Uh, I don't think I'm ready for that yet."

"Oh, yes, you are," she said firmly. "You just don't know it yet."

As it turned out, she was right.

Early in the morning, Amos rose and dressed in silence, leaving her still asleep in the big bed. On the bedside table was a small silver tray, bearing a slip of scented pink paper on which was written, in a fine copperplate hand, the bill for the night's entertainment. As Julia had said, the total was surprisingly reasonable.

Amos laid a small stack of Confederate bills in the tray, adding a little something on impulse, and walked quietly from the room, his boots sinking into the thick soft carpet. Downstairs, he collected his things from the sleepy-eyed maid in the cloakroom and asked the liveried hall butler to call a taxi. He saw no one else about; he seemed to be the only one up.

The rain had stopped, though the sky was still heavily overcast and threatening. The streets of Paris were still wet. He breakfasted on croissants, which he liked very much, and French coffee, which he didn't, and later he walked the streets a bit, watching Paris come awake. He had never been here before, even though he had been in France for quite some time. The ship from Charleston had docked in Bordeaux, and a train had taken him to the big Confederate Flying Corps base at Tours, where he had several times intended to go to

Paris on pass but somehow never quite made it. On his way north with the other replacements to the field where they had picked up the Nieuports, he had gotten a distant glimpse, through a dirty train window, of the Eiffel Tower on the horizon; that had been all, till now. . . .

It seemed to be an interesting city, but the people did not strike him as all that exotic. At least they were no stranger, as far as he could see, than most other white people; they did seem to gesture a lot when they talked, like Kiowas. The local style of driving was every bit as bad as he had heard, but the women he saw on the streets were far below advance billing.

He ate an early lunch at a sidewalk café—excellent food, served by easily the most insolent waiter Amos had ever encountered; Amos considered slicing off an earlobe just to improve his manners, but decided it might cause trouble. Then, hailing a cab and showing the driver the hand-printed address Chief Watie had given him, Amos set off to meet his Paris contacts.

The address turned out to be at the corner of a couple of narrow and undistinguished-looking streets, in what appeared to be a minor commercial district. The building, like all the others along the street, looked seedy and run-down, its once-ornate facade eroded and dirty.

Above the doorway a large, newish-looking sign announced:

CENTRE DU COMMERCE ET CULTURE DE INDIEN AMERICAIN

And, in slightly smaller letters:

AMERICAN INDIAN TRADE AND CULTURAL CENTER

Dusty display windows held a collection of pottery, baskets, beaded Plains-style moccasins and belts, dolls in more-or-less Indian dress, and the like. With a twinge of homesickness Amos recognized a Cherokee booger mask. He pushed open the door and walked inside.

The lighting within was poor; his eyes took a moment to adjust. When they did, he found himself in a narrow space between rows of glass cases full of Indian craft articles. At the far end of the aisle, behind a waist-high counter, a small, very dark young woman gazed expressionlessly at him. "*'Siyo,*" she said calmly. "*Dohitsu?*"

"*Osd*"," Amos said automatically, and then blinked rapidly several times as the gear trains of his mind momentarily slipped out of mesh. "You're Cherokee?" he said, still in that language.

"What did you expect, a Zulu?" she said in English. "And you're Amos Ninekiller. You don't look much like the picture they sent us," she added, switching back to Cherokee, "but that's just as well. You didn't hurry about reporting here, did you?"

Amos started to respond but she went on, a little less sharply, "Never mind. Come on, you'd better not stay out here."

She opened a small gate at the end of the counter and motioned him through. As he followed her down a dark musty hallway toward the rear of the building he said, "*Gado det-sado'a?*"

"Mary Wildcat." She pushed through a curtained doorway and led him into a large, brightly-lit room, furnished as a parlor. "Find a place to sit and wait here. Sam will be down soon," she said, gesturing toward the staircase at the far end of the room.

She was, Amos saw now, not quite as dark as she had looked in the poor light of the display room, but still a shade or two darker than himself: full-blood for sure, might possibly be some Seminole or Yuchi in there somewhere, especially with a name like Wildcat. She had the classic straight Cherokee nose, but there was a delicate quality to the bone structure of her face; and though she could not have stood much over five feet tall, her straight graceful carriage and slender proportions made her seem taller. Slender, Amos thought as she moved past him and bent to the small stove in the corner of the room, but plenty of round where the round needed to be. Straight thick crow-black hair, gathered in back by a beaded barrette, hung down past her waist. She wore a simple white blouse and a big patchwork Seminole skirt; her feet, he saw now, were bare. Nice feet. Amos sank onto the horsehair couch, watching her. He decided that Sam, whoever that might be, could take as long as he liked upstairs. Say till tomorrow morning or so.

Without turning around she said, "*Kawi tsaduli*"?

"Yes, no sugar." She took a pot from the stove and poured. As she brought him the coffee he said, "*Wado.*"

"*Howa.*" No question about it, there was still a definite layer of frost on her voice. He wondered what was eating her. Of course he didn't know her well enough to ask. But then even if he did she'd probably deny there was anything the matter at all, and then drop the whole thing on him later on, some time when he was least ready for it. Indian or white, Tahlequah or Richmond or Paris, they all—

"Ah," she said, "here's Sam now."

He followed her eyes and saw two men coming down the stairway: a tall, burly, middle-aged man in a dark suit, talking in low tones to a skinny little man, perhaps Amos's age, who bobbed his head in vigorous and continuous agreement with whatever the big man was saying. The effect was not unlike a bear taking a walk with a slightly anxious bird. Both men were about the same golden-brown color; both had similar high-cheekboned, short-nosed features, with short-cropped black hair, though the big man's hair was heavily streaked with gray.

Mary Wildcat said in English, "Sam? It's Lieutenant Ninekiller here."

The big man looked at Amos and lifted a hand that looked the size of a small picnic ham. "Lieutenant," he said genially. "Be with you in a minute. . . ."

Amos waited while the two men disappeared down the hall toward the front of the building. He tasted the coffee. It was French and bitter, but he tried to look pleased.

The big man was back in a few minutes, striding across the room with hand outstretched as Amos got to his feet. "Lieutenant Ninekiller! Glad we're finally meeting. Sam Harjo," he said, shaking Amos's hand and smiling. "Formerly Corporal Harjo, but that was in the Legion and a long time ago . . . you don't look much like your picture.''

"So I've just been told." Amos studied the broad, lined face for a second. "Harjo. Seminole?''

"Creek. From Tuskegee town, but that was even longer back. Sit down, sit down," Sam Harjo said, and did so himself, in a wicker chair opposite Amos. "Mary already got you some coffee? Good—get me a cup too, will you, dear child?'' He gave Amos a grin. "I suppose you two would like to chatter away in Cherokee, but I never learned more than a few words, so we're stuck with English. Unless you speak Creek?''

Amos shook his head. "Or French?'' Amos shook his head again. "Well, that's all right. Just a moment.''

He took a small silver flask from an inside pocket of his jacket and unscrewed the cap. "Drop of brandy in your coffee, Amos? No? Excuse me while I do, then.''

While Harjo poured Amos said, "That fellow who was just here—what tribe is he? I didn't know there were so many Indians in Paris.''

The big man looked blankly at Amos. He glanced at Mary Wildcat, who shrugged and spread her hands. "What are you—oh.'' Comprehension suddenly flooded his face. "I see . . . he's not an Indian, Amos. Never thought of it before, but he does look like one of us, doesn't he?''

Harjo chuckled deep in his stomach. "No, our friend there comes from a small country in southeastern Asia, a French possession—Annam, it's called on the colonial maps, but he insists on calling it Viet Nam. I knew some men in the Legion who'd been there, said it was a beautiful country but hot and wet . . . anyway, he's part of some secret nationalist movement that wants to throw the French out. Now and then he picks up information we can use; he works in a restaurant where a good many French officials dine. And now and then we're able to pass items on to him. Clever fellow, Ho. One of our good friends.''

Harjo drained his cup. "Well," he said, "what have you got for us?''

Amos took the packet of hand-written notes from inside

his uniform tunic. "It's not much," he admitted, passing the papers over. "I haven't seen much action yet, and nothing new is happening on our part of the front."

Sam Harjo laughed. "Why, what do you mean, my lad? Don't you read the papers? Your part of the front is a regular caldron of martial activity—all sorts of heroic advances and magnificent victories, the Allied troops smashing the evil Hun, dastardly enemy cracking and about to break into full retreat. To say nothing of you daring birdmen, up there slaughtering flocks and hosts of the airborne forces of evil. You aren't suggesting that the gentlemen of the press might be indulging in a teensy bit of exaggeration, are you? I mean, for shame, Amos."

Amos said, "My God, they actually print stuff like that?"

Mary Wildcat laughed suddenly, a hard cold laugh like breaking glass. "If anything," she said, "Sam's toning it down."

Amos shook his head. "Christ . . . I don't know what's going on elsewhere," he said, "but from all I can tell, and all I've heard, it's nothing but a bloody stalemate along the Somme. On the other hand, we've pretty much got control of the air over the front for the time being. None of the men in the squadron expect it to last, though."

Harjo nodded. "Yes, that's what we've heard from all our sources. Well, I'll look over these—" He pulled out a pair of rimless glasses and put them on, looking at Amos's report. "No, looks like I won't. Wrote it in Cherokee, did you? Good man. Nobody but you people can read that stuff." He tossed the packet of papers to Mary Wildcat. "You can translate it all for me later, dear."

Amos started to get up. Harjo said, "Oh, no, Amos, you mustn't think of leaving now. You'll stay for dinner, at least, won't you? And perhaps we can offer you the hospitality of our little place, here, for the night? If you've got no other plans?"

"The Lieutenant probably does," Mary Wildcat said in her dustiest voice.

"No," Amos said, "actually, I didn't have any plans at all. . . ."

* * *

Midway through dinner Sam Harjo said, "By the way, congratulations on your little victory of last week. The LVG."

Amos was so startled he almost choked on his food. "The LVG? I didn't do that. That was Yancey, and Lahaie got the other one."

"So? You don't seem to know it, Amos, but your Captain Yancey gave you credit for half shares in the kill, in his report. Interesting that he did it behind your back, so to speak."

"Well, I'll be damned. Excuse me," he said to Mary Wildcat.

"I don't give a damn," she said flatly, not looking at him.

"How," Amos said after a moment's thought, "did *you* know? About the action, let alone Yancey's report?"

Harjo smiled mysteriously. "Oh, we have our sources, we do have our sources. This isn't as primitive an operation as you might think. Another roll, Amos? More wine?"

They were seated at a massive, old-looking table in the small dining room that adjoined the downstairs parlor. It was late evening. Amos had spent most of the afternoon in the parlor, reading newspapers from home—even a two-month-old *Cherokee Phoenix* was a rare treat now—while Sam Harjo and Mary Wildcat went over his report in an upstairs room. Dinner had been brought in from a nearby restaurant with which Harjo seemed to have some sort of understanding.

Amos said, "Well, it was a pretty pointless business. About as pointless as everything else I've seen in this war so far."

The big Creek nodded thoughtfully. "The stupid mess at the front, you mean? Well, you have to remember how armies operate at the top levels. These gold-braided jackasses are merely following the rules they were taught in officers' school, rules laid down when the most dangerous thing on the battlefield was the smoothbore musket. You realize that all the Allied armies have squadrons of cavalry standing by, month after month, waiting for the big breakthrough that will let the horse soldiers gallop in, sabers flashing, to turn this into a proper gentlemanly affair at last? Charge of the Light Brigade, Jeb Stuart and all that.''

Harjo snorted. ''The French do have more of an infantry tradition—by God, they should, the way they marched us all over Africa—but even their commanders think a good old-fashioned bayonet charge is the real way to fight. Generals are like Oedipus, Amos—they figure what was good enough for Daddy is good enough for them.''

Amos stared at him. ''Excuse me,'' he said, ''but what school did you go to? You didn't learn to talk like that in the Nations.''

Sam Harjo went into another of his rumbling chuckles. ''Only fools' school, Amos. I ran away at fifteen and I hadn't been inside a classroom for a long time before that. As for the way I talk, I was in the Legion with a number of well-educated gents from various countries—you'd be surprised, Amos, we got men from Harvard and Oxford and the like, to say nothing of Heidelberg. Disappointed in love, in trouble over gambling debts or duels, or just looking for adventure —and God knows they found that, sometimes it was the last thing they found . . . anyway, I kept my ears open and I borrowed books and I picked up a bit.''

''How'd you wind up in the Foreign Legion to begin with?''

''You know what 'Harjo' means in Creek, Amos?''

''No.''

''Means 'crazy.' I must have been picked by God to prove the name fit my family. Never had a bit of sense.'' Sam poured himself another glass of wine. ''Left home, as I say, at fifteen, small misunderstanding over a certain married lady somewhat my elder. Made my way to New Orleans, shipped out as cook's boy on a Confederate freighter bound for various foreign parts. Saw quite a bit more of the world than I'd bargained for, over the next couple of years, and finally jumped ship in Marseilles after a fight with the bosun. The Legion was pretty much the inevitable next step.''

Harjo took a long swallow of wine. ''Terrible stuff, this, I've got to have some words with Raoul . . . anyway, I finally left the Legion and settled here in Paris. You might not know it, but there's quite a market for Indian arts and crafts in Europe—a basket your mother would use for dirty laundry, a buckskin dress the poorest Quapaw woman would be ashamed to wear, will bring amazing prices from these jaded art snobs. Then the war began, and, well, I diversified.''

He gestured in Mary Wildcat's direction. ''And then who should appear on my doorstep one day but this lovely child, bearing letters from your friend and mine Chief Watie, and brightening up this city beyond all measure.''

He beamed at Mary Wildcat, who gave no indication she had even heard him. After a pause he said, ''Well, well. If we are all done, I believe I would like my brandy and a good cigar. Amos, would you care to join me in the parlor?''

A few hours later, in the parlor, Sam Harjo stood up and stretched ostentatiously. ''Getting a bit late for my almost half a dozen decades, children,'' he said, and made a show of yawning. ''Time for me to turn in. No, no, now, you two young people stay here and have a visit. You must have a lot to talk about.''

He strode over to the staircase. Amos watched as he disappeared upstairs.

After a moment Amos looked at Mary Wildcat. She sat upright in her chair, not looking at him. Her face was unreadable as always but he thought he detected a slight flush. ''Well,'' Amos said.

The word seemed to trigger an already-primed response. She stood up, not hurriedly but decisively, and took a step toward the stairs. ''I'm going up to my room too,'' she said, still without looking at Amos. ''Sam already showed you your room, I'm sure you can find everything. There's plenty of reading matter, and wine there in the sideboard. If you'd like to write letters I can get you pen and paper—''

She started to walk past him. Amos reached out and took her wrist. ''Please,'' he said. ''Don't go yet. Sit here beside me on the couch and let's talk awhile. . . .''

''Talk?'' She looked at him now. It wasn't a friendly look. Her nostrils were flaring and the skin was taut over her cheekbones. ''You mean, sit down beside you while you shovel a lot of horse hokey and try to get on top of me. What's the matter," she said, "didn't you get enough last night at Dixie Land?"

His mouth opened, but no words seemed to want to come out. She laughed harshly. "Haven't you learned anything here, Lieutenant? We have contacts everywhere. We've known where you were just about every minute since you arrived in France. If I wanted to, I could find out what room you spent the night in, and what whore you were with, and what positions you did it in. Maybe I will, too, just for laughs."

She put her hands on her hips. "And by the way, Lieutenant, we aren't the only people with ears and eyes at Dixie Land. The place is an absolute gold mine of information for certain German agents. If you're going to go there, don't carry your secret reports with you—don't be too sure that the Germans can't find anyone who can read Cherokee—and watch your mouth. Which, incidentally, you ought to shut; you look such a fool sitting there with it open."

She tossed her head, making the long black hair bounce and shimmer in the lamplight. "Look, Lieutenant," she said more quietly, "come back another time and who knows, maybe we'll have that talk. But don't you *ever* come here straight from Dixie Land, still smelling of some *yoneg* whore's perfume, and try to play games with me. I won't be Act Two of your Paris adventures."

He tried again to speak, but she was already at the stairway. "Good night, Lieutenant. Sleep well. Seems to me you need it."

Next morning Amos caught the train back to the airfield.

5

"GOOD NEWS," Yancey said in a voice that carried absolutely no conviction. "We're going balloon busting."

There was a chorus of groans and curses. Lahaie said something pungent in bayou French. Faulkner punched the nearest wall with his fist and said, "Jesus Christ. Balloons. Balloons."

Amos looked curiously about him at the assembled pilots of C Flight. After a moment he said, "Am I missing something?"

"Lucky," Faulkner said morosely, "if you aren't missing parts of your body, in a few hours. Tell us you're joking, Jack."

It was early morning, the light still gray and weak, the grass slippery with dew. They had been back from Paris for three days now. The weather had finally broken, but the sky was still mottled with patches of woolly cloud.

Yancey said to Amos, "You don't know about balloons? Oh, boy." He scratched his nose with the back of his hand. "Doesn't sound like much, does it? Balloon busting, sounds like a little kid with a pin having fun at a birthday party. Pop pop pop."

He laughed without amusement. "It's a little different the way we do it hereabouts. You've seen artillery observation balloons, at least? Big fat bastards, tethered at the end of a steel cable, they let 'em up and down with a winch?"

"Of course." Amos had seen them on every flight over the lines, on both sides, hanging almost comically in the sky; he had in fact wondered now and then why no one seemed to attack such easy targets.

"The thing is," Yancey said, "since we've pretty much run the Kraut observation planes out of the sky lately, the damn balloons are just about all the eyes their gunners have left, and they protect them accordingly. Guns all around each site, ready to shoot your young ass off if you get within a mile of their precious balloon, and often as not a pack of Fokkers hanging around somewhere nearby, too. And you only get one good pass at a gasbag before they haul it down, so you've got to fly straight and get in close."

"Of course," Faulkner put in, "since it's a stationary target, it's very easy for the ground gunners to track your approach. I mean, once they see you going after the balloon, they don't have to do much guessing."

"Dawn patrol going after balloons, too," Lahaie muttered. "Crazy."

Yancey nodded grimly. "Tell me. We'll have the sun in our eyes as we make our approach, so if there are any Fokkers around they'll have us blind. But apparently orders came all the way down from the top. Probably the generals have something big and loony on the fire, don't want the Krauts peeking while they get it set up."

He sighed noisily. "All right. We're doing this together with B Flight. We'll all come in low, right down against the ground, try to take the bastards by surprise, zoom up at the last minute and everybody get in one good burst. After firing at the balloon, we all climb up to eight thousand and re-form and cover B Flight as they go in. Oh, yeah, we get the honor of leading the attack—that was how Culpepper put it—on account of I'm senior to Ashby. Can't tell you how good that makes me feel."

"Where's the balloon?" Shelby asked.

"Just south of the Bapaume road. You've seen it before. Just follow me," Yancey said. "And stay closed up. The more we get strung out going in, the easier targets the last men will be."

As they walked across the field toward the waiting Nieuports, Yancey grinned at Amos and said, "Oh, one other little thing—you want to try real hard not to come down and get captured on this mission. This incendiary ammunition we'll be using to torch the gasbag—the Krauts get very pissed off about it, call it a war crime when we use it. They catch you with it, it's possible they'll stand you up against a wall and shoot you. Probably ruin your whole day."

They crossed the lines near Bazentin, heading south of their objective, then swinging northward in a dog-leg turn that added a little time to their approach but at least kept them from having to attack straight into the morning sun. Yancey led them down to treetop level, or what would have been treetop level if there had been any trees left standing, and the ten gray biplanes slid rapidly across the blasted landscape in rough line-ahead formation, the blat of their engines amplified hugely by the closeness of the ground. They crossed the low ridge at the High Wood—a "wood" now consisting almost entirely of shattered stumps and blackened splinters—and dropped down across the lower ground beyond, hugging the earth, following the contours of the land like infantrymen under fire. A scattering of ground fire came up at them, nothing bigger than small arms so far, fired hastily by surprised German troops; nothing came close and they did not return fire.

Amos had had little experience of this sort of ground-level flying, up to now, and he found it immeasurably exciting. The closeness of the ground created a sensation of tremendous speed, such as he had never felt at normal altitudes; it was like riding cross-country on the fastest horse in the world. Rocks and fallen trees, trenches and roads and houses, all blurred and streaked past and under his nose, and he laughed aloud at the expressions on the faces of the German soldiers as he roared over their heads at pistol range. A column of horse-drawn supply wagons disintegrated into confusion and disarray, the horses rearing and stampeding as the Nieuports shot by.

And it was dangerous, so insanely dangerous; that was three-quarters of the joy of the thing. . . . A single mistake of stick or rudder or throttle, a tiny brief loss of power from the unreliable rotary engine, a bit of water or dirt in a fuel line, a German soldier luckier or more alert than the others, and there would be no chance at all to recover, only a huge smash against the French earth and an instant searing blaze. At least it would be quick; the pilot would barely have time to know what had happened.

The balloon appeared now, far ahead but growing rapidly against the morning sky, a great fat silly toy on a string, much higher than the hedgehopping Nieuports. Amos wished he could fire a quick burst to make sure his gun was clear, but there was no way to do that without shooting Faulkner's tail off. His palms were sweating inside his heavy gloves.

Yancey put the nose of his Nieuport up and came clawing toward the balloon in a wing-straining zoom climb, the others following in turn, while fire began to burst all around them. Holding his fire until the range closed to point-blank, Yancey triggered a long burst, half a drum or more, at the bloated shape that was now filling the sky ahead, and then wrenched his plane up and aside as Lahaie roared in.

Amos dragged the stick back and the Nieuport's nose rose skyward, while a sudden great force pressed him down in his seat. The ground fire was incredible; he was wholly unprepared for the solid wall of smoke and flame that exploded before him and all around him, so dense that it seemed a man might get out and walk on it. Bullets and shell fragments popped and screeched past; something tore a hand-sized hole in the Nieuport's upper wing. The plane rocked and bounced with the shock waves of nearby explosions.

There was nothing exhilarating about this; it was only stupid and terrifying. . . . He gripped the stick tightly, fighting for control, and watched as Faulkner made his run on the balloon, which was already on its way down as the ground crew frantically winched in the cable.

It was going down, in fact, faster than he had realized was possible, and he saw that he was too high. He had time for only a short burst before the gasbag vanished below the Nieuport's engine cowling, and he pulled up with a feeling of disgust: a long way to go to find the store closed. . . . Cursing, he climbed to join Yancey and the others, searching the sky now for enemy aircraft, while Shelby, who had not managed to get in a shot at all, trailed disconsolately after him.

B Flight, coming up behind them, had worse luck; the German gunners were ready now, and the rapidly-descending target forced B Flight to come in low. Ashby, the B Flight leader, got in a solid burst, as did the man behind him; but the third pilot, a Georgia boy named Pace, flew square into a bursting shell, his aircraft vanishing in a great puffball of smoke and flame, leaving only fragments to rain briefly earthward. The man behind him, dodging the debris, lost his line of attack and had to sheer off. By now the balloon was almost down, but a soft orange glow had begun to illuminate it from within, growing rapidly brighter. A little lick of flame appeared on one side.

Circling overhead, the pilots of B Flight cheered, their voices lost in the roar of their engines. While they were still cheering the Fokkers hit them.

Later, nobody could figure out where the Fokkers had come from. There were patches of cloud about, but not that many . . . they must have made a really brilliant stalk, using the cover of the clouds and then diving out of the blinding morning sun at the wheeling Nieuports. There were eight of them, or eleven, or a dozen; nobody ever agreed on that either.

Amos saw the sudden line of holes across his upper starboard wing and reacted instantly and by instinct, not stopping to look up or around, yanking the Nieuport hard to the left, while bullets snapped hungrily past his ears and the tiny windshield shattered into bright shards and blew away in the slipstream. For an instant he found himself flying straight at one of the attackers. The picture locked itself into his mind forever: a small, flimsy-looking monoplane with straight squarish wings and a boxy fuselage and a ridiculous, too-small tail, its engine shielded by an unpainted metal cowling that looked exactly like the big pot his grandmother had used to make lye for soap. The fabric covering was painted a dirty, streaky gray, with big Iron Crosses on wings and fuselage and tail. A leather-clad figure sat in a tiny cockpit above the wings, nearly hidden by a complicated arrangement of bracing wires. A pair of gun muzzles winked briefly from the nose. Amos hauled the Nieuport's nose on around and down, while the sky filled with airplanes and bullets and smoke.

The Fokkers got in a quick pass at Yancey's flight, without doing any serious damage, and fell upon the scattered aircraft of B Flight, which were still climbing away from the now-blazing balloon. Two Nieuports fell away, smoking, almost simultaneously. Ashby got a Fokker as it came at him head-on. Below, the German gunners ceased fire, but not before a wild shellburst flipped a Fokker onto its back and into a fatal spin. Shelby, diving on the tail of a Fokker, let his airspeed build too high; Amos watched helplessly as the fabric began to peel away from the upper wing and then the entire wing broke loose and folded back, the wrecked Nieuport whirling earthward like a falling leaf.

The fight turned into a wild, disorganized melee, the sort of dogfight that had not been seen over the Somme area since early summer. The Nieuports had the advantage of superior speed and maneuverability, but the German pilots were extremely good and they had shaken the Confederates badly with their surprise attack.

Amos found himself about to collide with somebody's Nieuport, pulled up just in time, and a saw a Fokker crossing his path in a shallow dive. There was no time for a clear shot but he kicked the rudder and put the stick over hard and got onto the Fokker's tail, peering through the gunsight ring and trying to line up on the German, who was now jinking violently from side to side in an effort to shake Amos off.

The weaving Fokker made a nearly impossible target but Amos fired off a long burst, giving himself a lot of lead and hoping the German would fly into it. There was no visible result. The German pilot was an absolute master, Amos thought with admiration; given anything like equal aircraft, he'd have killed Amos by now. Amos fired again at the twisting, turning Fokker. The Travis gun snapped silent.

Cursing, he hauled the Travis gun down on its clumsy rail mount—at least this plane had a pull-down gun; on the earlier Nieuports you'd had to stand up in the cockpit, holding the stick between your unsteady knees, to reload—and slammed a new drum of .303 into place. The German, he saw, was taking advantage of the brief reprieve and getting out of there. Amos knew he was about to lose this one and there wasn't a damned thing he could do about it.

But then, as Amos struggled to shove the Travis gun back into firing position, he saw that the Fokker was moving oddly, slowing down, no longer taking evasive action, its nose beginning to drop. The propeller seemed to be windmilling now, not turning under power, and the pilot appeared to be struggling with something in the cockpit.

Son of a bitch, Amos thought, maybe I hit him after all.

The two aircraft were almost clear of the general dogfight by now, the German gliding straight and steadily eastward, Amos hanging on his tail. Trying to get back to his airfield, Amos thought, but no chance in hell of making it. The Fokker was losing altitude fast, and going so slowly now that Amos had trouble staying behind him.

Amos had the sights lined up for a finishing shot when the German pilot turned and looked back at him. An arm came up and waved.

Cautiously, Amos eased the Nieuport up alongside the crippled Fokker and pushed up his goggles. The German was pointing at his engine and making an exaggerated thumbs-down motion. Now he raised a gloved hand and waved at Amos. He seemed to be smiling.

They were down close to the ground by now, their shadows flitting across the earth. Up ahead lay a broad open field, its surface clear of craters or trees. The Fokker altered course slightly and steadied on a textbook-perfect landing approach.

Amos pulled up and circled the field once, while the little monoplane touched gently down and rolled to a stop. As he came back around he saw the German pilot standing up in his cockpit, facing Amos, saluting.

Amos lined up his sights and fired. The .303 bullets walked up the Fokker's fuselage and knocked the pilot half out of the cockpit in a sudden graceless heap. As Amos pulled away the Fokker burst into flames.

The mess was full of pilots when Amos walked in. All of them seemed to be trying to talk at once; all of them seemed to be engaged in waving their arms or making airplanes with their hands. Captain Clay was seated at one of the tables, a notebook in front of him, making notes and looking even more dour than usual.

Now, though, there was a distinct drop in the talking as Amos joined the group; hands were lowered and voices fell to a low mutter. Someone said, "Christ, here he is now. . . ."

Amos saw Faulkner by the window. "Are you all right?" he asked.

Faulkner nodded jerkily. His face was very pale. "You?"

"I'm okay. What about the others?"

"All of our flight got back except Shelby. Lahaie got a bullet through the foot, they took him to the hospital, don't know how serious it is. B Flight got cut to bits," Faulkner said. "Anti-aircraft got Pace, you saw that? Fokkers got Renfro and Mizell, first pass. Barnett cracked up between the lines, but some British infantry picked him up and he's all right. Jesus, what a mess."

He paused and seemed about to say something. He was looking strangely at Amos, now, as if remembering something disturbing. But then he shook his head and turned away. Amos looked at his back for a moment, shrugged, and glanced around for Yancey.

But he saw now that Captain Clay was staring at him. Everybody seemed to be staring at him, in fact. He said blankly, "Something the matter?"

Clay pointed a stubby finger at him. "Commanding Officer wants to see you, Ninekiller. In his office. Immediately."

Amos nodded and turned to go. Behind him Clay said, "It's customary to reply, 'Yes, sir,' when receiving an order, Lieutenant. Also there's something called a salute."

Amos grunted and kept on walking. If he tries to make me salute him right now, he thought, I'll kill him. But Clay didn't push it. The pilots drew aside and let Amos pass.

Major Culpepper said, "I'd like to make sure I've got all the facts straight, Lieutenant. You disabled a German aircraft and forced it down, correct?"

"Yes, sir."

"And the Fokker was completely helpless, is that right? That is to say, there was absolutely no chance of the pilot offering further resistance? He was definitely out of the fight?"

"Unless someone was fool enough to fly directly in front of him. His engine was dead. If he hadn't been an outstanding pilot he'd have spun in."

"Ah." Culpepper nodded slowly, heavily, as if that confirmed something he'd already heard but hadn't wanted to believe. "And so you followed him down while he made a dead-stick landing, and then—" Culpepper's eyebrows came together. He gave Amos a piercing look that was entirely unlike his usual vague unfocused gaze. "Then, Lieutenant, according to eyewitnesses, you deliberately machine-gunned the German pilot as he stood in the cockpit of his downed aircraft. At least one witness says that the man was actually saluting you when you shot him."

He leaned back in his chair and put his hands on his desk. "Is that what happened, Ninekiller? Anything you'd like to dispute or add? I'm listening, sir!"

Amos winced internally. When these old-school Confederate officers addressed a subordinate as "sir"—or, in this case, more nearly "suh"—it was time to run for the hills. The CO was certainly in a state about something. Puzzled, Amos said, "No, sir, that's about the size of it . . . Major, is there some problem here? I mean, if somebody else is claiming the kill, it's not important to me—"

"Good God," Culpepper said, banging his hands on the desk top, "is it possible you don't even understand? Are you people that—"

He stopped and drew a deep breath. "Lieutenant Ninekiller," he said more softly, "you murdered a man in cold blood. Doesn't that mean anything to you?"

Amos shrugged. "Beg the Major's pardon," he said, not quite keeping the edge of sarcasm out of his voice, "the man in question had just helped murder three men from this squadron—or four, or two, depending on how you figure it. Doesn't that mean anything to the Major?"

He was tempted to add that the temperature of his blood seemed somewhat irrelevant, but he kept that to himself. This was getting ugly enough as it was.

Culpepper looked suddenly less angry. In a sad voice he said, "I see. You mean you were so . . . distraught, over the deaths of your comrades, that you lost control of yourself?"

It was a way out, and Amos knew he ought to take it. But some perverse spark of truth made him say, "No, no. I only mean, well, they were up there trying to kill us and we were trying to kill them—I was under the impression that was the *point* of it all, people trying to kill each other, isn't that why they call it a war?" He spread his hands. "In the air, on the ground, I'm afraid I don't see the difference. Sir."

He had, he realized, very nearly said "suh" himself. Starting to catch it from these people? Have to watch it, next thing he'd be drinking Southern Comfort.

Culpepper was looking wrathful again. "The difference, Lieutenant—" He stood up, an awkward angular unfolding that seemed to take a long time, and leaned across the desk. "If you don't see the difference, I'm not sure I can explain it to you. It's the sort of thing a *gentleman* doesn't have to be told."

Amazing, Amos marveled silently. He actually said it. Worse, he believes it.

Culpepper stepped away from the desk and looked out the single small window. The ground crew were lining up the Nieuports for the afternoon patrol. The clouds were all gone from the sky now.

"Certainly it's a war," he said after a moment. "And, as you say, men kill each other up there, sometimes in terrible ways. But.'' He turned and stared at Amos. ''There are things that aren't done, Lieutenant. There are rules.''

Amos said, ''Sir, I wasn't aware this was a game.''

Culpepper raised an eyebrow. ''Why, yes, Lieutenant Ninekiller, it *is* a game, a sport, if you like. Terrible and tragic though it is, war is the greatest and noblest sport of all. Oh, it's become a squalid and brutal business, down in the trenches,'' he said with a wrinkle of his long patrician nose, ''but it's different in the sky. We're the last cavaliers, Lieutenant, the last knights, if you will. We still face other gentlemen in fair combat, and, by God, sir, we keep to a code of chivalry.''

We? Amos thought but didn't say. Faulkner had told him that Culpepper had never even ridden in an airplane. But perhaps this was a royal or editorial ''we.''

''If you wanted to make sure the enemy aircraft was destroyed,'' Culpepper added, ''well and good, but you should have let the pilot get clear first.''

Amos said, ''Actually, Major, the Fokker was pretty much secondary. It was the pilot I was after. He was really good. I didn't want him coming after me, or anybody else, some other day in another plane.''

There was a long tense silence, while Culpepper stared and Amos wished he could learn to keep his mouth shut. It didn't do to tell white people the truth, his grandfather often said; they couldn't handle it.

''I wasn't happy about having you in my squadron, Ninekiller,'' Culpepper said at last. ''But they assured me you Cherokees were a civilized people, and that you yourself were a gentleman, a graduate of the University of Virginia.'' He put his hands together behind his back and bowed his head. It made him look like some sort of long-legged wading bird, a heron or a crane, looking for shellfish. ''Now, in your first important action, you behave—believe me, I dislike saying this—like a savage.''

He looked up at Amos from under thick gray eyebrows. ''This isn't a band of savages, Ninekiller.'' There was audible distaste, now, in the way he pronounced the name. ''This is a military body of Confederate gentlemen. I don't want you in my squadron," he said. "You don't belong here. I'm telling you now, so there's no misunderstanding. I'm going to try my best to have you transferred—or, if they'll listen to me, sent back to your tribe, minus that uniform you're wearing. If I had the authority, I'd make you take it off right now."

Amos had a sudden impulse to do it: take everything off, pile it on Culpepper's desk, and do an about-face and march out stark ballocky-bare-ass naked. If he hadn't been so tired, and the leather flying suit hadn't had so many clumsy fasteners to be undone, he might have done it. Instead he said expressionlessly, "Yes, sir."

Culpepper sighed. "Until I can get rid of you," he said, "I suppose I've still got to let you fly. We're short of men, after this morning. . . ."

He fell to looking out the window again. After a long time Amos said, "Sir? Anything further?"

Culpepper turned and stared at him, as if amazed to find him there. "What?" The confusion was back in his eyes and voice; the whole conversation with Amos might never have taken place. "Oh. No, that's all, Lieutenant. You're dismissed."

Yancey said, "Hell with Culpepper, Amos. You done the right thing. The Krauts got plenty of Fokkers, damn things are obsolete anyway. A pilot like that, I don't want the son of a bitch flying around my part of the sky either."

They were sitting at a table in the officers' mess, working their way through a bottle of bourbon. It was late evening. The mess was crowded and noisy as always, but it seemed quieter without Lahaie banging on the piano. Word was that Lahaie might or might not lose his foot, but he definitely wouldn't be flying again this year, maybe not ever.

"You know," Faulkner mused, "you almost have to admire Culpepper, in a way. I mean, he's one of the last of a breed. It's like seeing a live dinosaur."

Amos snorted. "*You* admire him if you want to," he said, reaching for the bottle. "I'm too busy trying to keep him from getting me killed with his God-damned Sir Walter Scott ideas. Knights of the air, for Christ's sake.''

Yancey laughed. "Yeah, the CO's a caution, all right. I remember when he first took over. Moore came in, he'd sneaked up on a pair of Rumplers and got both of them. Clay wanted to put him in for a medal and Culpepper said, 'Gentlemen don't shoot other gentlemen in the back.' He ain't quite that bad nowadays,'' Yancey said as Amos and Faulkner hooted, "but deep down he's got just about the same kind of ideas. It flat-ass broke his heart, they sent down that order we didn't have to wear spurs any more.''

"Unfortunately," Faulkner said, "he's not altogether an isolated case. The British are even worse, you know. Last year they cashiered a pilot who shot at a couple of balloon observers while they were hanging from their parachutes. The act of a cad and a bounder, old chap.''

Amos sighed. "I suppose I should have just shot the poor son of a bitch down," he said, pouring himself another drink. "While he was still in the air with a dead engine. That would have been all right.''

"Afraid not," Yancey told him. "According to the unwritten rules, as laid down by these precious assholes, you're not even supposed to do that. Once he's disabled and can't fight back, you're supposed to wave to him and go, 'Hard luck, old fellow,' and let him land.''

"Are you serious?''

"No shit. Well, hardly anybody takes it quite that far any more, except Culpepper and a few like him. What you did, though—that was a little raw, even for nowadays. Not that I'm criticizing." Yancey grinned. "Hell, I love it. Good chance, you hadn't done it, Kraut bastard might have killed me tomorrow. Gimme the damn bottle if you're done with it, Bill.''

Faulkner relinquished the bottle, a bit reluctantly. "It was the same," he said thoughtfully, "during the War of Independence. Big brave cavalry charges against Yankee artillery, infantry advancing across open ground in the face of steady rifle fire, officers on both sides playing their damned gentlemen-of-honor games while the men died like flies. You'd think somebody would remember, it's only been about fifty years. Christ, we've got generals at Headquarters who were *there*."

"Horse shit." Yancey gestured meaninglessly with the bottle. He was beginning to show the effects of the last couple of rounds. "They remember, Bill. They were a bunch of fuzz-faced shavetails then, having the time of their lives, riding their God-damned horses and waving their pretty swords and looking manly as hell while the band played Dixie. They've forgot—hell, they ain't ever *known*—that they damn near lost the war for us with that silly crap, would have lost it for sure, only the Yankees were just as stupid and we had the help of the British Navy at the right times. They think all that foolishness was why we won."

He tilted the bottle, found it empty, waved to the waiter for another. "Now if we'd lost the war," he said, "if the Yankees had whipped our ass, maybe somebody would have noticed. Then we wouldn't have all this stupid business along the Somme Valley right now. . . ."

Later, in their quarters, Amos said to Faulkner, "It's not just Culpepper, though, is it? The other pilots act like I'm carrying some kind of Mark of Cain. Don't tell me they believe in this code-of-the-air nonsense."

Faulkner sighed in the darkness. "A few, I suppose. Some of the newer ones still have illusions. They get over them quickly enough, though. Either that or they don't live long."

"All right," Amos said, "but how come I'm the Masque of the Red Death around here? And it's not just the green-horns, either."

"I know, I know. It's hard to explain . . . Amos, most fighter pilots don't think about the men they kill, you know? Maybe now and then something happens to bring it home, but generally it's something you blot out of your mind. You think in terms of destroying machines. A pilot says he got a German today, he nearly always means he shot down a German airplane. At least that's how it is with us and the British; the French take it a little more personally, and I don't know how Germans think. It's something your mind does," Faulkner said, "to keep you from going crazy, I suppose."

Amos heard him turning over in his bunk. "Then," Faulkner continued, "here you come along. First there was that business with the LVG observer, now this. They look at you and they can't help seeing a man who kills *people*. And that makes them see something about themselves, and it shakes them."

Amos thought it over. "I'll never understand *yonegs*," he said finally.

"Yo-what?"

"White people."

Faulkner laughed. "Don't feel bad. I don't understand us either, and I'm trying to write books about us."

"Anyway," Amos said, "they won't have to look at me much longer. Culpepper's going to have me transferred."

"Don't be too sure. Chances are he'll wake up in the morning and won't remember any of it. Don't pack yet, Amos," Faulkner said sleepily. "I've got a feeling you're going to be with us a long time."

6

YET, AS it turned out, it was not Amos who left the Fourth Virginia Pursuit Squadron.

They learned the news on Monday of the following week, a little before noon. C Flight had just returned from a long flight, escorting a gaggle of Confederate bombers over a minor rail junction that had not seemed to suffer much from their attentions; they had met no fighters and the ground fire had been ineffective. The flight had been brought up to strength by the arrival of new pilots: a short, hard-faced Mississippian named Bodine, transferred for unknown reasons from a two-seater squadron, and a green replacement named Henry who seemed barely to know which end of the airplane went forward.

Captain Moore, who led A Flight, told them the news as they sat at lunch. He was a thin, sallow North Carolinian who wore a stringy black mustache, perhaps to compensate for prematurely thinning hair. It was generally believed that Moore's hair was falling out because of a bad case of nerves; there was no doubt he had been in combat too long. The nervousness made him smoke too much and also made him compulsively talkative, the squadron's leading gossip. Everybody complained that Moore talked too much, but everyone bought him drinks and listened, all the same.

Now he said, "It's definite, it's official, Hawkins showed me a copy of the orders. Culpepper is being relieved."

"What happened?" Faulkner said. "Did the brass finally notice he wasn't firing on all cylinders?"

Yancey snorted. "If they started relieving all the loony commanders in the CEF, I don't know who'd be left to sign the orders."

Moore nodded and rubbed his forehead. "What I heard," he said, "there's a new order, come all the way from Richmond. All commanders of squadrons on active duty have to be qualified pilots."

"Oh, hell," Bodine growled. "You mean now we're going to have the assholes flying with us? That's the only thing I ever liked about combat patrols, getting away from those bastards for a few hours. Even with the flak and the Fokkers, it was almost worth it."

"I don't think anyone really expects the COs to fly patrols with us," Moore said. "Probably just some Richmond paper-pusher's big idea—you know, commanders who can understand what we're doing, all that." He got out a cigarette and lit it. "Still," he said, "the new CO *is* supposed to be a pretty hot pilot, so you never know. Apparently he shot down a couple of Fokkers and three two-seaters when he was with the Second Texas, last winter."

Bodine whistled. "Christ, I knew some guys in Second Texas then. They had the old Nieuport 11," he said, "any of y'all ever fly one? Son of a bitch must be pretty good if he scored five kills with one of those puny little bastards."

Yancey said, "What's this hotshot's name, Bill?"

Moore sucked at his cigarette. "I'm trying to remember. Sort of a Biblical-sounding name, you know? Right on the tip of my tongue." He frowned. "Backus? Otis? Lucas," he said. "That's it. Major James Lucas."

The new CO arrived on Thursday morning in a large gray-painted staff car that he drove himself. There was no ceremony to mark his arrival, no parade for the departing Culpepper; there was merely an exchange of salutes and written orders, witnessed only by Sergeant Hawkins and his staff of orderly-room drudges. C Flight had the dawn patrol again and missed the whole thing; the only look they got at their new commander, that morning, was a brief glimpse of a tall, erect figure in a long trench coat, standing in front of the squadron headquarters building, watching them through a pair of binoculars. But by the time they were clear of their aircraft he had already gone back inside.

An air of expectation hung over the mess during lunch. Captain Clay came in and told Moore the afternoon patrol would be starting late today. To the room at large Clay announced that everybody was to stay put after eating. "Anybody still in the billets?" he asked. "Somebody go check, get them over here right away."

"Christ," Faulkner said in an undertone to Amos, "whoever this bird is, he's got Clay shitting bricks already. That's something."

The Confederate pilots finished lunch amid a buzz of speculation. The stewards cleared the tables with nervous haste, even though Tyrone was no longer there to drive them. They could serve no drinks, they explained apologetically; orders from the new CO, no exceptions. The pilots sat and smoked and waited.

Captain Clay appeared in the doorway, shouting for attention. The pilots got to their feet with a great scraping of chairs and benches. Everyone looked at the doorway. Major James Lucas strode in.

He was not, Amos saw now, as tall as he had looked at a distance; a little above average, maybe, but so arrow-straight in his posture, and so athletically lean of build, as to give the illusion of imposing height. His face was long and hawk-nosed, with features that might have been called handsome; pale blue eyes and white-blond hair contrasted sharply with skin burned dark by sun and wind. Lighter patches about the eyes said that the man had spent some serious time wearing goggles, and not long ago.

He walked quickly to the end of the room, turned, and surveyed the pilots. "At ease," he said. "Take your seats.

And put those damned things out." The voice was rather high-pitched and almost soft, with the accents of eastern Texas. "This is a military assembly, not a social occasion."

There was a brief scattering of activity as cigarettes were hastily ground out and pipes dumped into ashtrays. Lucas nodded, once. "That's more like it. Choke and poison yourselves all you want after I leave."

He stood in a kind of parade-rest position, feet apart, hands behind his back, his eyes roaming about the room at random. "As you surely know by now," he said, "I am your new Squadron Commander. My name is Lucas. You may call me by my first name, which is Sir."

A few born suck-ups managed to make sounds of laughter. Faulkner looked at Amos and raised an eyebrow.

"I have looked at this squadron's record," Lucas said, "and it is, in nearly every respect, unsatisfactory and unacceptable. Going by the record, in fact, you have evidently been carrying the war to the enemy with all the aggressiveness of a flock of butterflies. I have added up your combined kills and I believe there have been more fatalities at the average nigger cake-walk."

He paused, smiling faintly, while a kind of ripple of wordless protest ran through the room. "Understand me, gentlemen," Lucas went on, raising a hand, "I don't necessarily mean that as a criticism of your collective or individual courage or fighting spirit. For all I know you may be a squadron full of potential heroes and aces."

He looked away, at nothing in particular, and a faint look of distaste came over his face. "It would be . . . inappropriate, and unmilitary, to criticize the policies and practices of a fellow Confederate officer. Let it suffice to say that my predecessor seems to have had a philosophy of command which is not mine."

The room was absolutely quiet now. From somewhere down the field outside came the ring of a hammer on metal.

"Gentlemen," Lucas said, "as of now, many things are going to change around this squadron. This is a fighter squadron and, by God, it is going to fight. There will be no more of these pointless little patrols with nothing to show for the waste of Confederate fuel. We will be searching aggressively for the enemy every time we cross the lines. If he doesn't come up to fight us, we will fly deeper penetrations of his territory and see if that stirs him up. We will begin knocking out those God-damned balloons as a matter of regular business—the one high point of this squadron's record over the last few months, incidentally, is the recent scrap over that balloon, even if you did handle yourselves like a bunch of French whores having a hair-pulling fight. At least it indicated some of you might have some vague idea what you're over here for. . . ."

Lucas shot out an arm, pointing a finger at them. "And if we can't find and engage the enemy in the air, then we will go down and kill him on the ground. There are, after all, thousands of German troops down there, as well as supply wagons and trucks and trains and the like. I expect every patrol," he said, "to find *something* to shoot at before turning back. Any patrol that returns with its guns unfired had better have an extremely good explanation. Any man who shows a habit of returning with his drums full is going to be out of this squadron as fast as I can arrange it—with a note in his records that I consider him a coward and a slacker."

He paused, as if to let them think about it. "Also," he added after a moment, "I will be re-evaluating Flight Leaders over the next few days. There may be well be some changes made."

He folded his hands behind his back again and stood looking at them. They sat, stunned, and stared back. The sight seemed to please him. "Good," he said, "I seem to have shaken you up. That means you damned well needed it. Captain Clay!"

"Sir!" Clay's voice was an octave higher than anyone had ever heard it.

"Have the Flight Leaders report to me in fifteen minutes. That's all. For now."

He turned and started for the door. After a frozen instant Clay bellowed for attention and they all leaped to their feet, but Lucas was already gone.

* * *

"Well," Faulkner said over dinner that evening, "you've got to hand it to him. Only this morning you had all these people asking themselves, 'Who the hell is Major James Lucas?' Now, after one brief speech, they're asking, 'Who the hell does Major James Lucas think he is?' "

"I don't know," Amos said thoughtfully. "Maybe he'll make some useful changes. You've got to admit he's got a point or two."

"Shit," Bodine said. "You ain't been doing this very long, have you? Ever fly a deep-penetration patrol?" Amos shook his head. "Bad business," Bodine said, "if you want to live to your next birthday. See, you might have noticed, the wind in this part of Europe just about always blows west to east, specially in the afternoon. You go far past the Kraut lines, you got to fight the wind all the way back—and if you've picked up a few holes in the kite, maybe used up a lot of gas tangling with some Fokkers, you just might not be able to buck it long enough to get home."

"Exactly," Faulkner nodded. "And ground strafing isn't a lot of fun either, Amos. Those poor devils on the ground —they do shoot back, you know. With all sorts of nasty weapons. And it only takes one bullet in the right place to bring you down, and then even if you survive the landing they'll probably bayonet you on the spot."

Henry said, "Well, *I* think it sounds real exciting. Didn't y'all come over here to fight?"

They all looked at him. He was a round-faced, healthy-looking boy from some small Tidewater town, and he could not have been over eighteen or nineteen; his face still wore patches of downy fuzz, and a number of pimples that he daubed unsuccessfully with various substances. Everything seemed to amaze him, including the controls of the Nieuport 17. "Like a God-damned goose," Yancey had said, more than once. "Wakes up in a new world every morning."

Faulkner said, "Tell me, Henry. Your grandfather rode with Jeb Stuart, didn't he? And told you all about it?"

Henry looked puzzled. "How'd you know?"

"Lucky guess," Faulkner sighed. "Turning into the Children's Crusade," he said to Amos. "You realize less than half the men in this squadron—pilots, I mean—are old enough to vote, back home? Anyway," he said, ignoring Henry's attempts to protest, "I didn't have any problem with the way we were fighting our part of the war. Except of course for that unfortunate fracas last week . . . it seems to me that it's altogether dangerous enough, just climbing into one of these temperamental, flimsy little things and driving it around the sky, never knowing when it's going to go into a snit and kill you for no reason at all. Letting people shoot at you—going out and *encouraging* them to do it—seems a bit much."

"You ain't just shitting," Bodine agreed. "Last outfit I was in, we had this CO, got a wild hair up his ass about—"

Sergeant Hawkins appeared in the doorway. "Lieutenant Ninekiller," he called. "Major wants to see you."

Bodine and Faulkner looked at each other and grinned. "Uh oh," Bodine said. "Any place in particular you want your effects sent?"

"When?" Amos asked Hawkins.

"Now," Hawkins said.

Major Lucas said, "Ninekiller, Amos. Lieutenant, Cherokee Flying Corps. Cherokee Flying Corps," he repeated, and shook his head. "As the Duke of Wellington said, if you'll believe that you'll believe anything. . . ."

He picked up several sheets of paper off his desk and held them up. "I've just been reading about you, Ninekiller. The good Major Culpepper left quite an emphatic and lengthy epistle concerning your conduct and character. He strongly recommends I make it an early and urgent matter to have you removed from this squadron and, if at all possible, from the Confederate Expeditionary Force. From our only meeting," Lucas said, "I wouldn't have thought the Major capable of such strong, almost violent convictions. You, he informs me here, are unfit to wear any uniform save perhaps that of war paint and feathers."

Lucas looked at Amos for a moment. When there was no reaction he said, "Yes, well, so much for that."

He wadded the sheets into a loose ball and tossed it against the office wall, where it bounced with uncanny precision into the wastebasket. "And so much for Major Culpepper, who is even now packing for his long-overdue departure, or rather dithering about, if I know anything, while his nigger packs for him. God preserve the South from its Southern gentlemen."

He leaned back in his chair and gave Amos a broad smile. His collar gaped open halfway down his chest; there was a looseness about him, now, and he seemed almost genial. "Tell you why I called you in here, Ninekiller," he said. "I just wanted to get a look at you, talk with you. After reading this report—and talking to Jack Yancey—I figured I had to meet the one man in this squadron who understands what war is about."

He reached into a desk drawer and came up with a small flat bottle and a couple of glasses. "God damn it, Lieutenant, let's have a drink."

Amos took the glass and sniffed surreptitiously before sipping. "Rye," he said, surprised.

"Old Overholt. The choice of gentlemen, and the reason this officer thanks the Almighty that Kentucky was saved for the Confederacy."

Lucas raised his glass. "Here's to Kaiser Bill, the son of a bitch."

He put his boots up on the desk. "Says in the files you went to the University of Virginia," he said as Amos raised his glass and drank. "Don't suppose it's easy for a boy from the Cherokee Nation to get into a school like that."

"No, sir."

"Which means you're book-smart *and* battle-smart. A rare combination, Ninekiller." He shook his head and took another drink. "If you were a white man I'd make you a Flight Leader on the spot. Replace that washed-up Moore. Too bad."

He looked hard at Amos. "More whisky, Ninekiller?"

Amos shook his head, held up his glass. "Thanks, I'm fine."

"Ah. You see, I'd always heard that you people were congenitally unable to hold your liquor. A race of born sots, people in my part of Texas said. Against the law to give an Indian a single taste of liquor. As usual, the wisdom of the masses turns out to be hogwash."

Amos shrugged. "Some of us can handle it," he said, "some can't. Sir."

"Yes . . . as I say, too bad, Ninekiller. Too bad about your people. A race of great warriors, with many good qualities. Often far better men than the white-trash frontier scum who displaced them. One of your tribe, I believe, invented an alphabet entirely on his own. What an amazing intellect he must have had."

Lucas shook his head sadly. "But of course you'll all have to go. Unfair as hell, but the march of history is rarely fair. Eventually, we'll have to destroy you. Ever read Darwin, Ninekiller? I know he's banned in schools throughout the Confederacy, but you must have read him at Virginia. Survival of the fittest. The strong devour the weak. It's nature's law."

He poured himself more rye. "And since, unlike the African, you won't accept servile status, that leaves you nowhere to go. Too bad." He shrugged. "You've got something we have to have, and the white man's destiny is to take what he needs. Oh, yes," he said with a wink and what was almost a smirk, "your little secret isn't entirely a secret. Some people know about your oil fields. Don't worry, nobody's going to tell—for now."

Amos gulped the rest of his whisky and held out his glass. "I believe I would like a bit more, sir."

Lucas laughed and poured. "Forget that 'sir' business in private. Christ, Ninekiller, I don't have to keep up that crap with you. You're the one man here I can talk to freely," he said, "because you're not part of the system—you're from the outside, and you'll always *be* outside."

He gestured with his glass. "Most of these alleged officers, here, aren't really soldiers—just volunteers, serving for the duration. Then they'll go back to being part of Confederate society. It's necessary," he said, "to make sure they remember their place in that society—givers of orders to the lower ranks, takers of orders from those who really run things—even as it is in the CEF. And, of course, our few professional soldiers, such as Sergeant Hawkins and Captain Clay, need and expect to be kept in their own places. You, though, will eventually go back to your people, and—since, as I say, they're a doomed people—what you do there doesn't matter. So I can say anything I want to you, Ninekiller, and, as long as it's just the two of us, you can say pretty much anything you want to me."

He grinned. His face was developing a flush under the windburn. "Unless you say something I don't like, of course," he added cheerfully. "Then I'll probably have you shot. Isn't democracy wonderful?"

Amos said curiously, "You really believe that? About the white race being destined to rule the world?"

"Of course, Ninekiller. Read Darwin, God damn it. Read history, hell, read the newspapers."

"The Japanese," Amos said reflectively, "did a pretty good job on the Russians, as I recall."

Lucas made an impatient gesture with the bottle. "The Russians are not white men, for God's sake. Ninekiller, what do you think this war is about?"

He waved a hand at the maps on his wall. "Oh, I don't mean this business here in France. I mean the whole thing, the Balkans and Russia and all that, where it really started. It's the white man against Asia, Ninekiller. Sooner or later," he said confidently, "we're going to be fighting alongside the Germans against the real enemy."

"Destiny again?" Amos didn't try to keep the sarcasm out of his voice.

"Don't laugh, Ninekiller, that's exactly what it is. Or, if you prefer, forces of historic inevitability. This is just a warm-up for the real war to come. Doesn't matter what sort of government they have in Moscow, either—whether or not those anarchist bastards manage to get rid of their useless Czar, that's all irrelevant—it's still going to be the same war that's already going on over on the plains and marshes of Russia. The East against the West, Ninekiller. 'Make ye no peace with Adam-Zad, the Bear who walks like a Man.' Not much on poetry, myself, but I love that fellow Kipling.''

He leaned forward over the desk. His face was definitely flushed now, and there was an odd glow in the pale blue eyes. ''Of course right now we're fighting the wrong people, but that's all right too. These things have to evolve with time.''

''In that case,'' Amos offered, ''why all this enthusiasm for killing Germans? I'd think—''

''Ah!'' Lucas raised a finger. ''Now this is where it gets subtle, Ninekiller. Right now,'' he said, indicating the map again, ''there are several reasons we have to beat the everlasting shit out of Germany on the battlefield. For one very important thing, it won't do for them to beat the Russians on their own—which is what they're on the verge of doing, whatever you may have read in the papers. If the white race is to rule the world, the Anglo-Saxons, not the Germans, must be the dominant branch of that race. When we finally sit down to talk terms with the Germans, we have to be able to negotiate from a position of strength.''

He paused, seeming to savor his last words. ''Negotiate from a position of strength,'' he said again, as if to himself. ''Hm, I like that . . . and,'' he said, ''we also have to put pressure on the Germans and the Austrians so they'll rise up and get rid of that contemptible gang of inbred incompetents in Berlin and Vienna and put in some strong men who can get things done.''

''So we're out gunning for Fokkers,'' Amos said, ''to help destiny along. Or historic inevitability, I think you said.''

''Go ahead, laugh up your sleeve at the crazy white man. You'll see,'' Lucas said, grinning over his glass. ''And from your recent performance, you're going to be a great help, whether you believe in this or not. Christ, if I had a few more like you we could cut through so much crap . . . you see, Ninekiller, the West isn't really ready to take on its mission against the East, not yet. That's another reason we need this present war. A necessary bloodletting to toughen our own forces up for the greater battles to come.''

Amos said, ''I'll be God-damned.''

Lucas put on a conspiratorial expression. ''Then consider this, Ninekiller. It's not just the Central Powers that are being dragged down by worn-out aristocracies and hidebound military nitwits and weak-kneed politicians. My God, we've got those liberal traitors running around Richmond, they managed to set the niggers free—going to be hell's own job undoing *that*, when the time comes—and now they're talking about letting them vote! Some things are going to have to change, Ninekiller.'' He gulped at his whisky. ''Of course, there are good, solid people, in Richmond and at headquarters, who simply don't see the big picture yet. . . .''

He fell silent, seemingly lost in thought. After a moment he roused himself and looked at Amos again. ''Point is, as I say, changes have to be made, and there's nothing like a war for making changes. Speeds up the promotion process, you know. Culls out these useless old fossils who rode with Marse Robert and haven't learned a damned thing since, and creates all sorts of opportunities for advancement for the new blood, the people who know what has to be done. You realize,'' he said, ''I'm not even thirty yet? And already a Major, in command of a squadron? And I'm not even an unusual case, these days.''

He ran his fingers through his light blond hair. ''Of course at present only a few of us really understand these things. But then most great events in history have been the work of a few men in the right place at the right time, with the brains to know what to do and the guts to do it, while the rest of the cattle—including most of the generals and politicians and the crowned heads—plod stupidly along their predestined paths and never suspect a thing.''

Amos said, ''What if I repeat the things you've just said? To, say, someone at Headquarters, or the press?''

Lucas spread his hands and laughed. ''Why, go right ahead, Ninekiller. I'll even fix you up with an appointment to see any general you choose. Who's going to believe an

Indian, against a white Confederate officer? All they'll do is have you shot for sedition and mutiny.''

Amos nodded. Well, he thought, this is going to give Sam Harjo and Chief Watie some interesting reading at last. Have to find a way to get into Paris as soon as possible. He said, ''Major, is it all right if I go now? I was on dawn patrol today, I'm pretty tired.''

Lucas waved the bottle negligently. ''Sure, sure. Been a fascinating conversation, Ninekiller,'' he said. ''We'll have to do this again some time.''

Going down the walk toward his quarters, Amos suddenly encountered a large dark shadow in his path. He said, ''Hello, Tyrone.''

A familiar basso chuckle came through the murk. ''Good evening, Lieutenant Ninekiller. I was wondering if we would meet again before tomorrow's departure.''

''Leaving in the morning?''

''Even so. The Major is to become part of the administrative staff of the training base at Tours, no doubt helping prove the proverb about those who can and those who can't.''

''You mean, 'Those who can neither do nor teach, administer.' ''

''Precisely. You were there for a time, Lieutenant. Are there many persons of my race?''

''Oh, sure. It's a big base. In fact, there's an entire labor battalion of—uh—Negroes.''

Tyrone laughed softly. ''Don't be nervous about what to call us, Lieutenant. All that matters is that one day the white people will call us 'Sir.' '' He fell in beside Amos, and they walked slowly down the footpath together. ''Well, if that is true, there should be ample opportunities for organizational work there. A richer field than this by-the-way spot, at any rate.''

He glanced at Amos. ''You were in Paris recently, I believe? How is my friend Sam Harjo?''

Amos said, ''You know him? Harjo?''

''You'll find,'' Tyrone said, ''that Sam Harjo knows, and is known to, all sorts of people. Especially people who are

. . . up to something, let us say. And Dixie Land," he went on. "Perhaps you heard the pianist, Mr. Ferdinand Morton? Known to some as 'Jelly Roll,' " Tyrone said with distaste. "An undignified name for a great genius. In a rightly run world he would be on the concert stage. In this, he provides entertainment while blue-eyed fools fornicate with whores. Well, the day is coming, Lieutenant, the day is coming."

It crossed Amos's mind that Tyrone sounded remarkably like Major Lucas at times. And vice versa.

"The new commander," Tyrone said, "you have been with him, I believe? What are your impressions?"

"Strange man," Amos said noncommittally. "Certainly different from Culpepper, anyway."

"Indeed. Lucky for us that the white people produce more Culpeppers than Lucases. An extremely dangerous man, Lieutenant Ninekiller. Be careful he doesn't get you killed in his quest for glory and advancement."

Tyrone stopped and faced Amos. "I feel I owe you something," he said seriously, "in that you were discreet about what you overheard that day, when you might have made serious trouble—if not for me, then at least for the unfortunate young man with the big mouth."

Amos started to say that it was nothing, but Tyrone cut him off. "In any case, I rather like you. If nothing else, you are a person of color who has beaten them at their own game, not an easy thing to do. Tell me," he said, "on your flights over German-held territory, do you carry items in case you should be forced down? Personal weapons, say?"

Amos shrugged, puzzled. "I haven't thought about it much," he admitted. "Probably should, too . . . of course I carry a revolver, but that's required by regulations. I don't know what good it would do me behind German lines."

"Quite so. I do strongly suggest you think about this, Lieutenant. One young man from this squadron—Lieutenant Barnett, of B Flight—has already been shot down in enemy territory and made his way back. Then, too," Tyrone said, "you are involved with Sam Harjo, I think I can guess how. So all in all, I'd like you to have this."

He held something out in the darkness. Amos took it and found himself holding a folded straight razor.

"For that matter," Tyrone went on, "you could even shave with it, if you like. No thanks due," he said as Amos tried to speak. "It was the property of Major Culpepper, an heirloom, I believe, from his grandfather. I was going to sell it, but I'd like you to have it instead."

Amos held the razor uncertainly. Tyrone said, "Don't try to use it like a knife, Lieutenant. Fold it all the way back, so that the back of the blade rests against your knuckles and your thumb holds the curved tang in place. Use it somewhat like a knuckleduster. You can open a throat before the other man sees it coming. Go for the side of the neck, under the ear, rather than the Adam's apple. There are major blood vessels through which a man's life will drain in seconds."

Amos bounced the straight razor thoughtfully on his palm. The idea seemed farfetched, yet no more so than anything else about this war. Anyway, Tyrone obviously meant the gift as a kindly gesture. He said, "Thanks, Tyrone. Really."

"You are most welcome. I doubt if we will meet again, at least for a long time," Tyrone said, extending his hand, "so good luck, Lieutenant, and be careful."

Amos took his hand. "You too."

He watched the big dark figure vanish into the night. Then he walked on to the pilots' billets and his cubicle. Faulkner was lying on his bunk, reading.

"Nice visit?" he said when Amos came in. "Shall I inspect your ass for tooth marks?"

Amos plopped down on his own bunk. "Tell you some other time," he said, tugging at a boot. "I'm tired of talking, right now. And—"

"Let me guess," Faulkner said, raising a hand. "It's a long story."

"You could say that," Amos said, yanking off his other boot and stretching out and staring at the ceiling. "You could definitely say that. . . ."

7

THE NEXT day Lucas began making changes.

He sat them down on the grass in front of the headquarters building like a schoolboy sports team. Behind him a blackboard had been set up by Sergeant Hawkins. In one hand Lucas swung a leather-covered riding crop.

"Gentlemen," he said, "you are now about to begin learning what it means to be a fighter squadron. Up until this time you have operated as no more than a gang of irresponsible adventures and reckless aerial desperadoes. I have seen more organization and cohesion in a Georgia lynch mob getting ready to string up a nigger. If you fornicate the way you fight I feel sorry for the girls at Miss Rhetticia's."

He waited, one eyebrow slightly raised, for the murmur to die down. "Not, mind you, that I am singling out this particular squadron," he said. "You've merely been following the accepted style. It is a style that originated when pilots floated around in airplanes that were not much more than powered kites, and took shots at each other with pistols to break the boredom. Like all the pilots in the CEF, you think you're all heroes, much too brave and daring to bother with things like discipline and organization."

He slapped the riding crop against his palm. "Gentlemen," he said, "playtime is over. The day of the individual is finished in warfare and damn near everywhere else. You are now going to become, not merely the best fighter squadron in the CEF—that goes without saying; God help the man who *doesn't* think it goes without saying—but the first genuinely effective fighter squadron in the history of the world.

"You are going to work your fine Southern asses off. You will learn to fly in formation, so tight you can smell what the next man had for dinner last night. You will learn how to use your formation in defense and in attack. You will learn to look out for each other like a squad of crooked policemen in an election year. Expect to find yourself practicing basic flying and gunnery skills as if you were still a cadet, if I find you deficient in these. To answer the question in your churning little minds, yes, I will indeed be flying patrols with you from time to time, and observing you at all times."

His cold blue eyes combed their ranks. "Now on the other hand, I'm not a spit-and-polish man. Within reason, and as long as we don't have the brass visiting us, I don't give a damn what you look like, unless it interferes with your efficiency. Eubanks, there's no way in hell you can operate a rudder bar properly in those silly boots, and if you're forced down you won't be able to walk half a mile, let alone run if someone's shooting at you. If you want a transfer to Buffalo Bill's Wild West Show, I'll see what I can do."

He swung the riding crop and pointed at a diagram on the board. "Now this is the basic formation you will be using. As you see, it has obvious advantages—"

He spoke for over an hour, without pause except to ask or answer questions. He showed them the formations to be used on patrol, on full-squadron sweeps, when attacking from above and below, and when attacked by superior force. Almost all of it was as new and alien to them as a lecture on the geography of Mars, and they listened with more amazement than comprehension. The riding crop whacked the blackboard with pistol-shot impacts; he lectured them in short fierce sentences, his high soft drawl laced with acid as he pointed out what they had been doing wrong, which was almost everything.

At the end of his talk, as they got to their feet and started to move away, he called out, "Henry!"

Henry turned, looking confused. "Sir?"

"I watched you land your aircraft yesterday, Henry. Or rather I watched you grapple the poor thing to the ground, with all the grace and delicacy of a trainload of Mexicans going off a cliff. I do not see how you ever qualified as a pilot." He peered anxiously at Henry. "You *did* qualify as a pilot, didn't you? I mean, you're not just some poor cracker—say the trooper who shovels up after General Pinckney's horse—that these boys put into a pilot's uniform to play a little joke on the new CO?"

"No, sir." Henry blinked. "I mean, yes, sir. I mean, I'm a pilot, all right, sir."

"And I am the Archduke Ferdinand. Well, Henry." Lucas smiled warmly at him. "Tell you what you do, son. You take your aircraft up and you give me ten of the best landings you can manage, one two three, like that, all right? And, of course, that will mean ten takeoffs, which I'd also like you to give your best effort. Do that for me, will you? I'll be standing right here, watching."

Before Henry could respond Lucas added, "One little point that might help clear things up for you." He swung the riding crop gently. "This, Henry, is your elbow. This, on the other hand, is your ass. There seems to be some confusion in your mind . . . go, Henry. Ten landings. Do your best."

Henry's plane sailed in over the trees, wobbled, smacked the ground hard, bounced, and rolled raggedly down the field. Lucas, standing in front of headquarters, said something under his breath. The half-dozen pilots who had stayed to watch winced almost in unison. Henry gunned his engine and lurched into the air again.

He made three landings, all clumsy. As he rolled past the watchers, they could see him hunched grimly over the controls, a look of desperate determination on his face.

On the fourth takeoff, just as he cleared the far end of the field, his engine quit. There was no miss, no hesitation; it just stopped running.

Henry, like every other pilot, had been taught early and often the iron rule: if the engine quits on takeoff, keep straight ahead and bring the aircraft down wherever possible, but *never* try to turn back downwind to get back to the field. It was probably the most-repeated rule in a pilot's training.

Henry, however, was by now wholly beside himself with confusion and frustration. Panicking, forgetting everything but the need to regain the familiar safety of the field, he jammed rudder and stick hard over. The Nieuport's wings groped for lift and found none.

The watchers at the field saw Henry begin to turn. A couple of men said, "No," as the gray-painted Nieuport went into a helpless stall and then disappeared behind the screen of trees. A second later they saw a great puff of smoke and flame erupt above the treetops.

The noise of the crash drifted back to them. By now most of the pilots were already running.

Amos stood, seeing no reason to rush to the site. There was undoubtedly nothing to be done for Henry now, and he had seen crashes before. He looked at Lucas.

"Classic case," Lucas said calmly. His face had not changed its expression. "Textbook example, Ninekiller. The non-survival of the unfit."

He turned toward the headquarters building. "C Flight has the afternoon patrol, I believe?" he said without looking back. "Tell Yancey I'll be flying with you today. Since this leaves you a little short-handed."

During the days that followed Major Lucas lived up to his word. He drove and harried them beyond anything they had ever imagined. Leisure time became almost unknown; when they were not flying their regular patrols, they trained.

"Spending a few hours on a routine patrol," Lucas told them, "does not necessarily entitle you to spend the rest of the twenty-four drinking, playing cards, singing old songs, or masturbating. The men in the trenches often go for days without sleep, let alone rest, under appalling conditions and steady artillery fire—of a kind much more accurate and heavy than the haphazard sort you occasionally fly through. Why should you be privileged?''

They learned to fly in the peculiar and revolutionary style he demanded. The Flight Leader, as before, flew the lead aircraft; but now the second man flew off to one side—the side toward the sun—and a little behind, covering the Flight Leader against attack. The third and fourth planes, paired off in a similar manner, followed on the rear flank of the Flight Leader and his partner—''wingman'' was the term Lucas insisted on—and covered each other, as well as the other two. At all times the flight arranged itself to guard against attack from the direction of the sun, since this was where trouble usually materialized.

This, Lucas told them, should have been the basic formation for a single flight: a pattern not unlike that of the fingertips of a man's hand. ''However,'' he said, ''our superiors in their wisdom have decreed that each flight shall consist of five aircraft, and I have had no luck changing their minds. So the fifth man in each flight will take up a position astern of the other four, and tag along and try to protect them from getting jumped from behind. This man will therefore be allowed to weave and slide around quite a bit more than the others; in fact he had damn well *better* do it if he wants to go on living, and he had better have a swivel neck like a hoot owl.''

The basic arrangement, which he called the Lucas Formation (''I invented it, so I get to name it''), could be combined with other flights for larger operations, or could break apart in a dogfight to pursue individual planes. The wingman, however, had to cover his leader at all times.

''If you find yourself alone in a fight,'' Lucas said, ''hook up with somebody, anybody. If you can't, get the hell out of there and come home. A single plane is dead meat in a dogfight. Remember that in attacking, too. Like wolves—break up the herd, cut out the individuals, and rip their throats out one at a time.''

He drilled them unmercifully in every aspect of their work. Pilots considerably more experienced than Henry found themselves flying practice landings and takeoffs, after a mistake under those eerie blue eyes. He marched them to the butts where the armorers test-fired Travis guns and made them fire hundreds of rounds at silhouettes of aircraft and men; while they fired, he stood behind them and tossed firecrackers at random among them and fired over their heads with his revolver. "Any fool can shoot straight if he's got time to think it over and take careful aim," he said, when they cursed and protested. "You'd better learn to do it even when all hell is breaking loose around you." From somewhere he acquired half a dozen shotguns and a clay-target thrower and had the pilots practice a sort of skeet shooting in which they did not get to call "Pull!"; instead Lucas launched the clay pigeons without warning from impossible directions and hurled more firecrackers at those who missed.

"He's insane," Faulkner said with feeling. "You'll see. Any day now some men in white uniforms will show up and take him away, and they'll find the *real* Major Lucas in some cellar where this escaped lunatic tied and gagged him."

Amos said, "I don't know." He did know, privately, but he had not told Faulkner about his conversation with Lucas. "He's got some good ideas," he said. "At least I like the idea of having other people helping keep me alive, rather than that every-man-for-himself business we used to do."

"You're just saying that because he excused you from gunnery practice. God *damn*, where'd you learn to shoot like that?"

"Putting meat on the table for a big family of hungry Indians since I was big enough to lift a gun—or a bow. And I do have pretty good eyesight," Amos admitted. "Anyway, I didn't get out of anything. I had to spend that time with the mechanics, learning things I didn't want to know about how an engine works. God knows why."

"No good's going to come of this," Faulkner predicted. "Just watch. We had a pretty nice little war going on here. Now, the way he's going at it, somebody's going to get hurt."

Lucas made good his promise, or threat, to fly with them. He led a patrol in strength, all three flights together, with himself leading A Flight. It was the first time Amos had seen the entire squadron in the air at once; from his position on Yancey's wing he had a fine view of the whole formation as they droned across the lines, the little biplanes rising and falling and rocking slightly in the air currents, a scattering of shellbursts decorating the sky about them as they reached enemy territory.

Beyond the lines, by prearranged plan, they split up: B Flight holding altitude, C Flight dropping down to low level to look for ground targets, while Lucas led A Flight up to eleven thousand feet. With any luck the enemy would try to do something about B or C Flight, and then the high flight would pounce on them.

C Flight shot up what it could find, in a friendly sort of way; they were too far from home to use up much ammunition hosing down rear-area troops and supply wagons. Amos fired half a drum into a collection of parked vehicles, without notable effect, and caused widespread consternation and despondency among several flocks of chickens. He saw a couple of German soldiers raise their rifles, aim at him as he roared toward them, and then think better of it and dive into a ditch. That was all the opposition he encountered.

The German airmen, at any rate, were having none of it. No Fokkers rose up to meet them or dived on them out of the sun; the only aircraft in the area were a flight of British bombers in the distance, on some mission of their own. Amos pictured Lucas grinding his teeth in frustration. That was not how he himself felt about the situation, but then he and Lucas had already established that they did not have much in common.

On the way back, Eubanks spotted a single German aircraft, a Roland two-seater, a long way off and close to the ground. Forgetting that he was supposed to be covering Moore's wing, Eubanks yanked his Nieuport out of formation and went after the Roland in a long diving pursuit curve. By the time the others had figured out what was going on, he was on the Roland's tail. The woodpecker knock of machine guns drifted briefly up to them. They saw the Roland fall off sharply and plunge into the ground. Eubanks struggled back up to them, waggling his wings triumphantly as he rejoined the formation.

Back at the field, Lucas verbally disemboweled Eubanks before the assembled squadron.

"You irresponsible braying jackass," he said softly. "You prancing tinhorn moron. God ruined a perfectly good penis when he gave you ears and a nose, didn't he?"

Eubanks grinned. "Hell, Major," he said, "I just—"

"Shut up. Shut *up*. If you utter another word I will kill you, here and now, do you understand? Jesus *Christ*." Lucas ground his teeth audibly. "What the hell do I have to do to get your impermeably stupid attention? After I talk myself crosseyed about teamwork and discipline and formation integrity, after we practice this business day after God-damned day till you should be able to do it asleep, hell, *dead*—then a God-damned shit-kicking cowboy from Houston drops cheerfully out of formation, in enemy airspace, and goes diddling around on his own . . . and for what? A fleet of Zeppelins bound for Paris? Kaiser Bill's personal staff car? Hell, no, just a God-damned Roland that wasn't even doing anything but going home. God almighty."

Eubanks was deathly pale now. "Sir—"

"Do it again, Eubanks," Lucas said intensely, "and I suggest you keep going, land at a German airfield, and tell them you want to change sides. That would be your best chance of survival. Otherwise, I swear I'll shoot you out of the sky myself."

The weather stayed hot into September. The German fighters continued to refuse fight. No one had seen a Fokker in days. Word was that other squadrons along the front had been having the same inexplicable lack of contacts. Nobody knew what to make of it.

"It's weird," Faulkner said. "It's as if the Germans have all joined some new religion that doesn't believe in airplanes."

One of B Flight's new replacements, a Kentuckian named Yarbrough, said dubiously, "Maybe they've just realized we've got them whipped. Maybe they've given up."

Everyone hooted. Yancey said, "Krauts don't give up that easily. If it was our brave French allies you were talking about, now, maybe. I been fighting these bastards since spring of '15, and they'll fight till hell freezes over and then fight you some more on the ice.''

Headquarters, in tones of polite skepticism, ordered ''aggressive patrolling'' and ''maximum effort'' to find and engage enemy aircraft. Lucas, furious and raging, sent the squadron to attack front-line ground targets. ''If they won't come up to protect their own infantry,'' he said, ''I don't know what the hell will raise them.'' The Nieuports rampaged at will across the blasted landscape east of No Man's Land, searching trenches with machine-gun fire, turning roads into killing grounds where men and horses ran and screamed and died. Some of the pilots began carrying grenades, bartered from infantrymen in exchange for bourbon, and lobbing them by hand from the cockpit at the men below. Lucas devised a new trick: road strafing in three-plane elements. The center plane drove men to take cover in the ditches on either side of the road, where the other two Nieuports raked them.

Hedgehopping one afternoon near Courcelette, Amos came over a low ridge and found himself swooping down on a battery of artillery, its gunners still digging emplacements. He triggered a long burst into their midst, kicking left and right rudder in gentle alternation to swing the Nieuport's nose from side to side, sprinkling them with .303 bullets like a man hosing down a lawn. The gunners dived for cover, throwing aside their shovels and picks, and here and there a man threw up his hands or simply fell across a howitzer's trails. Amos circled, came back, and finished emptying the drum into what he could see of the battery, hoping to disable a gun or two.

He pulled up, while someone in a nearby emplacement opened up on him with a machine gun, and pulled the Travis gun down and changed drums. Down to his last drum, and even Lucas had said to save that, just in case enemy aircraft finally put in an appearance. He climbed skyward and pointed the Nieuport's blunt nose toward home.

He was not disappointed to be done with the day's work. He had found that he positively loathed trench strafing. Never mind that the Nieuport 17 wasn't particularly well suited for ground-attack work—being too lightly built to take much ground fire, and fitted with only one machine gun and no way of carrying bombs—and it wasn't even the danger, though God knew strafing was risky enough; Hatfield had been killed by ground fire two days ago. No, Amos would cheerfully have taken on any number of enemy aircraft rather than strafe another trench.

What bothered him was the incessant killing. It was odd, perhaps; in the air, he had no compunctions about the men who died under his guns, and an enemy pilot on the ground was likewise fair game. And he would have killed, with equanimity, for personal reasons—and had done so, in another time and place—or under various other circumstances, in or out of war. It was not even a thing he gave much thought to.

Anyone who voluntarily climbed into an airplane—and no country he was aware of drafted its airmen—and went up into the skies of a war zone, it seemed to him, had accepted death as a possible consequence. As Faulkner had once said, anyone crazy enough to do this deserved whatever he got— and, Amos thought, that applied just as well to himself; if a German should one day shoot him in the back in a dogfight, he would have no right to feel bitter or ill-used by fate.

But this on the ground was butcher's work, and it sickened him. What quarrel did he have with a farmboy from Schleswig-Holstein in an ill-fitting new uniform, or a middle-aged conscript driving a supply wagon? Let alone the poor damned horses who fell, thrashing and kicking, as he strafed the roads . . . it wasn't, after all, as if this had anything to do with him; it wasn't even his nation's war. Much more of this and he was going home, and Chief Watie could find himself another spy. . . .

Yancey climbed up alongside Amos and waggled his wings. C Flight closed up its formation and headed homeward.

Back at the field, yet another surprise was waiting.

As Amos clambered from his cockpit and dropped tiredly to the ground, Sergeant Hawkins ran up and said, "Lieutenant? You're supposed to wait by your plane till some people get here. CO's orders.''

Amos stood leaning on the Nieuport's oil-streaked fuselage, wondering what fresh madness Lucas had devised. Then he saw, coming around the end of the hangar, two men in civilian clothing. One carried a large camera, the other a folded tripod and a leather case that appeared to be pretty heavy. He said, ''Oh, Christ.''

The man with the camera said, ''Lieutenant Ninekiller?''

Amos nodded. ''Ah,'' the man said. ''Could you give us just a minute, here? . . .'' He handed the camera to the other man, who had set up the tripod a short distance away. ''We're going to take your picture, Lieutenant.''

''I'll be damned,'' Amos said, poker-faced. ''I'd have sworn you were getting ready to build a chicken house.''

''What? Oh. Ha ha.'' The photographer watched while his assistant finished setting up. ''Right, this won't take long. Um, let's see, try leaning against your aircraft, there—you might try folding your arms, yes. No, no, don't smile. We want you to look as Indian as possible.''

Stifling an impulse to knock the man down and see if his camera would fit up his rectum, Amos sighed and positioned himself as requested. ''You're sure,'' he said, ''Major Lucas approved this?''

''Oh, yes. Said to tell you it was a direct order. Now, then.'' The man disappeared beneath the black fabric hood of his camera. ''Ah, very good. If you could turn your head a few degrees to the left? And raise your chin ever so slightly? Now hold quite still—''

Several pictures later, the photographer indicated the session was over. ''Thank you, Lieutenant,'' he said as his assistant packed the plates and the rest of the bulky equipment. ''We'll send you a print, after the picture's published. For your mother, perhaps, or your sweetheart?''

Sergeant Hawkins said in an undertone, ''CO said tell you he wants you over to his office, sir. If these fellers are through.''

There was another civilian in Lucas's office, a tall, almost theatrically handsome man with iron-gray hair and a thin, meticulously clipped mustache. He wore an expensive-looking light-brown suit, cut in a modified military style, with a yellow silk scarf at his throat in place of a tie. He stood up and gave Amos an almost blinding smile. "Lieutenant Ninekiller. An honor to meet you." He put out his hand. "Gabriel Cassidy."

He said it as if he assumed the name would mean something to Amos.

From behind the desk Lucas said, "Mr. Cassidy is a very prominent correspondent, Lieutenant. His reports on the war are printed and read all over the Confederacy. Even the Yankee magazines sometimes run his stories."

The name did sound vaguely familiar. Amos said, "Sorry, I'm afraid I don't follow the newspapers very regularly." He took Cassidy's extended hand. The newsman's grip was almost painfully strong; Amos knew that white people considered this a sign of great manliness and sincerity, though Indians generally regarded a crushing grip as the mark of an aggressive bastard looking for trouble. "Is there something I can do for you, Mr. Cassidy?"

Then he remembered the photographer. "Oh, my God. You've come to interview me."

"Well, I hope to do that, yes. Did Loudermilk get your picture all right? You see," Cassidy said, with just a touch of condescension, "you're a remarkable human-interest piece, Lieutenant Ninekiller. God, the name alone. . . . Cherokee warrior stalks the Hun in the clouds, counts coup on the Boche. Red birdman fights alongside his white brother in the great cause. Et cetera, et cetera. Have to work out the details later, of course."

Amos looked at Lucas. "Major, do I have to do this?"

Lucas laughed. "Oh, horse shit, Gabe, climb down off your lecture stage and talk straight, will you? I told you, this Indian's no fool." He looked at Amos, grinning. "Don't let Gabe put you off, Ninekiller. He just shovels so much shit for a living, he doesn't always know when to quit. Look, give him the interview. It'll be all right."

And, when Amos started to protest, he added, "But yes, Ninekiller, it *is* something you have to do."

Amos looked Cassidy up and down. "Understand this," he said to the journalist. "If the word 'redskin' appears anywhere in this story—or 'buck,' or 'brave,' or 'chief,' unless you're talking about a genuine chief such as Chief Watie—or if you make me out to speak broken English," he went on, riding over Cassidy's attempts to speak, "if you pull *anything* like that, and you know damn well what I'm talking about, I'll hunt you down and I'll kill you."

Lucas was pounding the desk top and guffawing. "God damn it, Gabe, didn't I tell you? And he'll do it, too, you bet your inkslinging ass. Don't worry, Ninekiller," Lucas said, "he'll behave himself. Gabe and I go back a long ways. Now answer his damn questions."

The interview went better than Amos had feared. Cassidy asked intelligent questions, listened closely to the answers without interrupting, and seemed genuinely interested. Amos had little experience with newspaper correspondents, but it was obvious this man was an expert at his profession. If he also had a high opinion of himself—and it was clear he did; the egotism radiated from him in waves—maybe he had some right. Amos found himself getting interested against his will. After all, he thought, a little favorable publicity right now wouldn't hurt the Cherokee Nation; from what Chief Watie had told him, they could use any good will they could generate.

Besides, it had occurred to him that Mary Wildcat might be a little friendlier to a man who'd had his picture in the papers.

At the end of the interview Cassidy folded his leather-covered notebook with a flourish and a snap, put away his expensive-looking pen, and smiled broadly. "Well, Jim, by God, you weren't exaggerating. You've got yourself an original here. He'll be twice as interesting to my readers as some grunting comic Indian. I can see my slant now." He made lines and blocks in the air with his hands. " 'No Fenimore Cooper savage, Lieutenant Ninekiller is an educated and polished young man, a graduate of the University of Virginia, whose people have long been known as the most civilized of Indian tribes. Yet he still keeps the fierce warrior spirit of his ancestors,' blah blah blah. Oh, it'll sell, it'll sell. I just wish you had a few more kills," he mused, looking at Amos. "No chance we could, ah, adjust that, Jim?"

Lucas shook his head. "I'm afraid that's one thing I can't help you with, Gabe. The scoring system is pretty much sacrosanct. Oh, once a pilot becomes a big hero with a lot of recognized kills, then sometimes they get a little helpful in boosting his count—flexible about things like confirmation—but for someone like Ninekiller, no. The one Fokker, that's it. Sorry."

Cassidy shrugged. "I'll work around it. Nobody's scoring anyway, the last few weeks, anywhere along the line. Maybe that's my angle." He looked thoughtful. " 'Having driven the Hun from the sky, the gallant aviators of the Confederate Flying Corps are now carrying their work of winged destruction to the Teuton hordes on the ground, strafing and bombing wherever the Kaiser's minions show their spike-helmeted heads. Dangerous work, where a single slip can bring instant death—' "

"Nieuports don't carry bombs," Amos pointed out, "and the Germans don't wear spiked helmets any more."

Cassidy waved a hand. "Who's to know? What matters, Lieutenant, is not what is true, but what is believed. My function is to tell the good people of the Confederate States of America what to believe. For which, God bless them, they pay me very well."

Lucas said, "Remember what I told you, Ninekiller? About the historic forces at work, and the need to prepare the nation for its mission? Gabe, here, is in a position to be of great help." Seeing Amos's expression he added, "Oh, it's okay. Believe me, we can talk freely with Gabe."

"The Confederacy," Cassidy said to Amos, "like any other nation at war, needs heroes to inspire the masses. And heroes are pretty thin on the ground in France right now. We try, God knows, but even the press has a hard time putting a good face on this shambles on the Somme. Sooner or later people start to think. Can't have that, where would we all be?"

He gestured at Amos and Lucas. "But you aviators, now, you're another story. Not only is your work genuinely dangerous and exciting—Christ, even I'd have a hard time exaggerating that—but you're the only people along the front nowadays who are actually accomplishing something. In fact you've almost accomplished too much, from my point of view; you seem to have kicked the Germans clear out of the sky. What the hell's going on, Jim?"

"Damned if I know. See anything today?" Lucas asked Amos.

"Not even a carrier pigeon. Well, there was a balloon, but they hauled it in before we got within range."

Cassidy was nodding. "Exactly what I meant. Still, you people will always make good copy. Even before the war, aviators were intrepid daredevils; everybody wanted to read about them. And you look sharp, in your flying suits and scarves and boots, leaning on your airplanes—so much prettier than those poor bastards at the front. The people don't want to see pictures of their boys all covered in mud and blood and bandages. It depresses them, and it makes them ask too many questions."

"You see," Lucas said to Amos, "this isn't just about selling newspapers, or even keeping the civilians worked up and ready to lynch anybody who criticizes the war. As I told you that first evening, there are changes that have to be made. The people who understand what has to be done, and have the guts to do it, still have to be gotten into positions. Not always positions of authority—sometimes a minor clerk can be the hinge-pin of great events—but that, too. Some new leadership is definitely needed."

"Right," Cassidy agreed, "and who better to lead the new Confederacy than its heroes? Such as, let us say, the leader of the most successful and daring fighter squadron in France?"

"Modesty forbids me," Lucas said, digging out a bottle of Old Overholt and three glasses. "And all that."

"So," Cassidy said to Amos, while Lucas poured, "it is important, in the big picture of things, that the Fourth Virginia

Pursuit Squadron should distinguish itself, and that the public should be made aware of its feats—and, of course, of the outstanding qualities of its heroic commander.''

Lucas nodded. "I will drink to that," he said, raising his glass. Cassidy raised his own. "To the free press."

Faulkner said, "Gabe Cassidy was here? And he's doing a story about you? Good God."

"You know him?"

"Oh, hell, no—not personally—but of course I've read his stuff. Who hasn't?" He looked at Amos. "Evidently you, for one."

"I doubt if he's ever written for the *Cherokee Phoenix*," Amos pointed out. "Highly improbable he can write Cherokee, in fact. And it's been a long time since I read the Confederate papers. Is he any good?"

"He's good at what he does," Faulkner admitted. "A master propagandist. I've never known whether he does what he does out of conviction—you know, necessary evil in a good cause and all that—or cynical opportunism."

"From what I saw of him, I'd guess a mixture, leaning heavily toward the latter. Christ, I'm starting to talk like you," Amos said. "But I mean, is he any good as a writer? You ought to be qualified to judge."

"Amos, I'm a writer—or trying to be one. Gabriel Cassidy is a journalist."

"And isn't a journalist a type of writer?"

"If the Lord High Executioner was a type of surgeon, yes. Or if Miss Rhetticia is a type of Mother Superior. Don't mind me," Faulkner sighed. "I'm just jealous. I'll never make as much money as Cassidy does, or be read by as many people. As to your question," he added, "Cassidy's style is at least a bit less florid, and considerably more literate, than the usual From-Our-Man-Over-There swill—most of these hacks just take the official statements handed out by the relevant HQ and regurgitate them, with a few extra adjectives and adverbs to bring out the subtle yet piquant flavor of the day's lies. Now and then he comes up with something really hair-raising, like his proposal, last year, that Andersonville prison be reopened to house pacifists and anti-war agitators.''

"He actually said that?''

"Among other modest proposals. Was he merely playing to the cracker gallery, you might ask, or is he really six points to the right of Ivan the Terrible? I'm damned if I know—you've met him, I haven't, your guess is probably better than mine. What's he doing here, anyway? Somehow I don't think he's come just to chronicle the adventures of the great Amos Ninekiller.''

Amos hesitated. "He and Lucas are . . . friends, apparently. Old friends, I think.''

"So? Men like that, Amos, are friends only when they can be of service to one another, usually in some way that wouldn't stand public scrutiny. Hm.'' Faulkner looked pensive. "Now what can this mean? Lucas is clearly a man of vaulting ambition; in fact I'd bet money he has at least one ancestor named Snopes. Can it be that Gabriel Cassidy is out to promote the rise of the Lucas star, by publicizing the daring exploits of a certain squadron and its noble CO? And, in the process, further his own career?''

Amos said noncommittally, "I got the impression it might be something like that.''

He was strongly tempted to tell Faulkner the whole story. The little Mississippian would probably have some valuable insights; in some ways he had the subtlest mind Amos had ever encountered. But Faulkner also talked too much when he drank, and drank too much too often. Better not confide in him just yet.

Faulkner said, "Like that, is it? Then watch yourself, Amos. We'd *all* better watch ourselves, if we're to be the heroes on whose heroics they depend. For Cassidy's purposes, there's no hero like a dead one. . . .''

Later, just before falling asleep, Amos said, "Wonder where the German planes have all gone.''

Faulkner said something indistinct into his pillow.

Two days later, they found out.

8

C FLIGHT WAS supposed to have the dawn patrol that morning, in the normal order of rotation. But then, the evening before, Lucas announced a change.

"High Command's got something going on in the morning," he said. "Naturally they won't tell us what, probably another suicidal attack to try and gain another few hundred square yards of bloody mud. At any rate, they want this road junction bombed, here, to keep the enemy from rushing up reinforcements. The First Georgia Bombardment Squadron will be doing the bombing. We're to provide cover, just in case the Fokkers finally decide to get back into the war, and afterward we're to strafe targets of opportunity along the road."

He pointed here and there on the map with his riding crop, outlining the details of the mission. "C Flight," he said, "will do the honors, with B Flight replacing them for the dawn patrol. B Flight has too many green men right now. If the Fokkers do show up—and a bomber formation is going to be one hell of a tempting target—I want some experienced men up there. A Flight is still on for the afternoon patrol."

He did not say what everyone knew: that he wasn't sending

A Flight because he regarded Moore as dangerously undependable.

"Watch out," he told them. "It's been too God-damned quiet for too God-damned long. I don't like it."

C Flight took off before the dawn patrol, in what was only technically classifiable as daylight, the runway marked by sputtering flares in the gray murk. Over the valley of the Ancre they climbed into bright sunlight, picking up the bombers a few minutes later and wheeling toward the front at eight thousand feet.

Weaving through broad arcs and S-turns to stay with the slower bombers beneath them, the pilots of C Flight scanned the skies for the unaccountably absent enemy. Amos saw a number of specks in the distance and for a second his pulse began to accelerate, but then he recognized the distinctive bulky silhouettes of a flight of British F.E. 2b's, heavy two-seater fighters on some mission of their own.

Exhaling a little unevenly, cursing himself mildly for his nerves, he glanced down at the bombers: Voisins, French-built single-engine two-seaters, well-built aircraft but too small to carry much of a bomb load. They looked fine, though, with their long square-tipped wings spread kitelike to the wind and the Stars-and-Bars insignia catching the morning sun. Chief Watie, Amos thought idly, should have gotten him into bombers rather than fighters; not much glory there, but they must surely see a lot more of the overall war. . . .

He looked up just as the German fighters came out of the sun. It was possible, in fact, that he was the first to see them. No one ever knew.

There were half a dozen of them, coming straight toward the Confederate formation, and at first they were no more than the usual featureless black dots against the blinding sunlit sky. But then he saw that the shape was not the familiar boxy Fokker outline, but something entirely unfamiliar, some sort of biplane, and that they were moving faster than anything he had ever seen in his life. That was all he had time to see; then the Germans were there.

He fired a quick short burst to clear his gun and warn the

others, and pulled the Nieuport's nose up and around to meet the attack, not waiting to see if the others were doing the same. The nearest German's nose lit up with twin muzzle flashes and bullets popped and sang all around Amos. He fired back without aiming, just hoping to throw the German's aim off, and rolled half over and dived to one side, out of the line of fire, as the German roared past just above him.

He had a brief but clear look at the enemy: a sleek, predatory-looking biplane, considerably bigger than his Nieuport, with angled-back wingtips and a broad, efficient-looking tail. The fuselage was streamlined, shaped rather like a shark's body, with a pointed spinner over the propeller boss; the cylinders of a big and obviously powerful in-line engine protruded above the nose, flanked by twin machine guns. The wings and tail were covered with a multicolored lozenge pattern; the fuselage was a soft grayish blue.

Even in that moment, he had time to marvel: it was easily the most lethal-looking airplane he had ever seen, and the most beautiful. Then his stunned mind snapped back to the realization that the thing was trying to kill him. He said involuntarily, "*E-e-e!*" and yanked the Nieuport around to counterattack.

The German fighters ripped through the Nieuport formation, brushing the slower Confederate planes aside, and fell upon the bombers like sharks in a feeding frenzy. A Voisin was already trailing smoke; as Amos watched, it flipped over and went into an out-of-control dive. Another gray two-seater staggered and fell away in flames. An observer slumped dead over his gun, hanging half out of the plane. The Voisins were scattering rather than bunching up to give each other covering fire, and the German biplanes were savaging them ruthlessly.

C Flight was not having much luck doing anything about it. The Confederate fighters were fighting mostly to stay alive. Faulkner's new wingman, a green pilot named Moss, died in the first pass, his airplane and his body riddled by 7.92mm. bullets. Bodine, in the rear-guard slot, took a long burst in his engine and dropped away, smoking. Faulkner managed to get onto a German's tail, only to have the sleek biplane pull away from him in a dive that would have ripped the wings off a Nieuport; seconds later he was struggling desperately to shake another German off his own tail.

Amos saw a German going after Yancey—the white markings of the Flight Leader's aircraft stood out even in the confusion and the smoky air—and laid his sights on the long torpedo shape and fired, a long burst and then a short, more careful one, and the German pilot jerked visibly in his seat and then bowed his head as if in prayer. Amos had no time to see if the German went down; bullets were ventilating his own wings and fuselage and he broke right without waiting to look around.

It was only the briefest reprieve. He felt the Nieuport stagger as more gunfire chewed at its tail. Another burst popped close over his head and there was a horrible whanging noise; he looked up to see the Travis gun smashed halfway off its mount, the muzzle pointing crazily at empty sky.

He shoved the stick forward and dived, the rotary engine in the nose raising its voice to a shriek, the wind in the wires wailing a witch chorus, a couple of snapped wires flailing wildly in the slipstream. Diving her too hard, he knew, the wings could come off any second, but he was going to get them shot off anyway if he didn't get out of there. . . . A glance over his shoulder showed a German biplane, this one with a yellow nose, hanging easily on his tail, following him down with almost casual grace, its guns still flickering. A strip of fabric, perhaps the width of his hand, began slowly to peel off the center of the top wing.

Below, not far away, a Confederate bomber was going down in flames, trailing a great dense cloud of black smoke. Desperately, without much real hope, Amos put the stick over and aimed the Nieuport astern of the dying Voisin. More bullets punched through his wings. A strut splintered. The controls began to feel very loose.

The smoke was thick and oily and very black; it was like diving into a pool of ink. He had cut it closer than he had intended; flames from the blazing bomber licked back around him for a moment as he dived past. He got a brief lungful of choking, stinking smoke, and he coughed violently as he pulled clear into the air beyond. The German, he saw, had pulled up rather than risk hitting the burning Voisin.

At that, he could have caught Amos again without much trouble. But he didn't try. Probably, Amos thought, he didn't see any need to bother. Even at a distance it must have been obvious that the Nieuport was coming apart. More fabric was starting to peel off the wings and another wire broke with a nasty ping.

Amos pulled gently back on the stick, torn between the need to level off while he still could and the knowledge that the Nieuport wouldn't stand the strain of a hard pull-out. The engine was now vibrating violently, shaking the whole aircraft. The vibration made the compass unreadable, but Amos saw that he would have no trouble finding his way: in the near distance, great boiling clouds of smoke and fire marked the location of the front lines, where all hell was clearly breaking loose.

The Nieuport leveled off, after a fashion, and staggered westward. Behind Amos the dogfight had scattered all over the sky by now. Not really a dogfight, he realized, more a turkey shoot. He wondered if any of C Flight had survived. Off to the north, the flight of British two-seaters appeared to be tangling with more of the mysterious biplanes, and getting the worse of it; they had gone into a defensive circle, covering each other from attack, while they worked their way gradually toward the safety of their own lines. On the ground below, various piles of wreckage smoked and flamed.

The engine was sounding really terrible now, and the Nieuport was losing altitude rapidly. There was no question of making it home; it was going to be all he could do to reach friendly lines and get down alive. At least there was no fire. So far, his mind added before he could shut off the thought.

The racket from the engine got worse, and he began to fear it might tear the weakened aircraft apart. Reluctantly he shut off power. As the propeller windmilled slowly in the rushing air, he saw that the wooden blades were holed by bullets. A wonder the blades hadn't shattered. Too bad Cassidy's photographer couldn't be here, get a picture of this, send it to the factory, where they could hang it up: *This aircraft actually flew in this condition, after being demolished by homicidal German maniacs in infinitely superior machines. Not bad for an underpowered, undergunned little piece of shit. Buy War Bonds.*

By now two things were obvious: one, he was going to come down in the area of the front lines, and, two, this was an extremely bad time to do that. The whole front, on both sides, was all but obscured by smoke and dust and leaping fountains of earth. With the engine off, he could hear the rolling thunder of the artillery with terrible clarity, the sound almost painfully loud even at this distance. He should, he knew, land here, behind the German lines, and take his chances; with all that confusion at the front, it shouldn't be hard to hole up somewhere and wait till dark and then make his way to Confederate or British lines. And even if they captured him, would it be that bad? He might still be able to escape; at worst, it wouldn't be such a bad way to spend the next couple of years.

But some perverse impulse made him keep the Nieuport on course, still wobbling doggedly toward the holocaust at the front; and he even threw his remaining drums of ammunition over the side to lighten the Nieuport and perhaps gain a few yards of glide distance.

He was down low now, sailing over the German artillery emplacements and reserve trenches within easy shot, but no one fired at him; they all seemed to be absorbed in the work of the battle. He saw gunners laboring furiously, bent from the waist, loading and firing amid the swirling smoke, shells bursting among them; here and there a gun pit lay silent and blackened from a direct hit. No one even looked up at the Confederate biplane sliding past above their heads.

Too late, Amos realized that this was easily the craziest thing he had ever done. He was heading straight toward an incredible maelstrom of fire and steel, a wall of billowing flame-laced smoke that towered higher than his line of flight. The noise was deafening and now he could hear the scream of the shells themselves; for an instant he actually saw one, a huge oblong thing hurtling past him on its mindless trajectory of destruction, and he flinched, irrationally, as it went by. Below, he could make out the zigzag lines of trenches, the shapes of men firing rifles and machine guns, and the glint of great belts of barbed wire. Barbed wire, he thought, oh, God, please don't let me come down in that. The blast of shellbursts rocked the Nieuport violently, almost flipping it over. A strut cracked with a sharp rending sound. It didn't matter; the ground was very near.

The Nieuport had seemed to be barely moving, on the verge of a powerless stall; but now as the ground came up at him there was a sudden sensation of great speed and he braced himself as best he could, wondering whether he should undo his straps before the impact. The harness would protect him, perhaps, in the crash itself, but if the Nieuport caught fire it might slow his escape and cause him to be broiled alive. But it was too late to worry about that, too; it was too late for everything.

The Nieuport touched down, rather neatly at first, and rolled rapidly across the wasted earth, seeming to ignore the storm of shot and shell that laced the air around it. A wheel struck a minor hole and dropped in, and the Nieuport went into a ground loop and then stood on its nose. The wings crumpled and folded back over the riddled fuselage.

Amos was jerked and tossed madly forward and back, from side to side, up and down and through several dimensions that seemed to have no names, the straps cutting and wrenching him but preserving him from being hurled to the ground or beheaded by rigging wires. His forehead hit the instrument panel a sharp crack and he almost passed out, but then the Nieuport stopped moving and he yanked violently at the buckles and clawed his way clear of the ruined cockpit and dropped to the ground, while bullets and shell fragments whanged past on all sides. There was a shell crater nearby and he dived in without pausing to think about it.

And lay there in the muck, taking long shuddering breaths, while his senses struggled to orient themselves, to make sense of a scene out of the nightmares of the damned. . . .

The noise was worst of all; it nearly blanked out everything else. "Noise" was not really the word; the sensation had little to do with any normal concept of sounds perceived by the ear. Rather the enormous crescendo of the battle struck with physical force against the entire body, shock waves pounding continuously in a cataract of invisible blows, while the earth jumped and bucked underneath. The shellbursts came so close together that there was no separating the blasts, only a constant gigantic roar of excruciating intensity, through which came the screams and whistles and monstrous whirrings of the shells themselves as they descended. Very faintly, under the bombardment, came the occasional cracklings and rappings of rifles and machine guns, sounding tiny and silly amid the huge din.

The racket drilled clear through the skull and pounded up and down the spine; it paralyzed the mind and fried the nerves. Even a few minutes, and Amos knew torture beyond anything he had ever experienced. To lie under such a bombardment for hours and days, as he knew men regularly did—he could not conceive of it. Surely a man would go mad.

But gradually a kind of shocked numbness set in; the pain was no less, but he could stand it. He began to take stock of his surroundings.

He was in a hole about six feet deep and perhaps eight or ten feet across, roughly funnel-shaped, like a doodlebug's ant-trap hole. There was a foot or two of greenish-yellow water in the bottom, in which his feet rested; but when he yanked them upward in surprise and disgust, he found himself starting to sink into the mud, and he froze, afraid to move at all.

The mud was like no mud he had ever encountered before. It was not so much mud in the usual sense as a kind of clinging black slime, somewhere between glue and quicksand in consistency, with a gagging, fetid stench that was the solidest thing about it. Up near the top of the hole the stuff was solid enough to support his weight, carefully distributed on chest and arms; but near the bottom, where it was wetter, there was only a bottomless goo into which a man could sink without a trace. Cautiously, moving very slowly, he wriggled his way as far upward as he dared, until the top of his head was barely below the crumbling lip of the crater. Bullets and shell fragments were coming over in a steady sleetstorm of metal, but he dreaded the thought of being buried alive in that muck worse than a bullet through the head.

He looked down into the hole, shuddering with revulsion, and saw something that turned his stomach inside-out. Sticking out of the mud, about halfway down the side of the crater and perhaps two feet from his legs, was a hand. Frozen by rigor mortis into clutching claws, its fingers grasped horribly at the smoky air. Where the wrist disappeared into the mud, a bit of rotting uniform cuff showed; but it was impossible to identify the nationality the thing had worn.

Amos started to jerk away, instinctively—the hand almost seemed to be grasping at his leg—but a tremor and a sucking underfoot reminded him to stay still or become another buried corpse. He stared, fascinated. What impressed him most, for some reason, was how *clean* the hand looked. Something— last night's rain, perhaps—had washed the mud away from the discolored skin, leaving it the only thing in sight that did not bear a coating of muck.

He tore his eyes away, fighting to keep from vomiting; but even when he looked away, he could feel the damned hand there beside him, its decomposing fingers still clutching. . . . He knew with sick certainty that that hand was going to figure in many, many bad dreams for years to come.

If, of course, he lived long enough to have them; the matter did seem to be in considerable doubt. He had obviously come down in the middle of a serious attack. The artillery barrage had moved on a little way—toward the German lines, he thought, but he was now badly disoriented—but plenty of shells were still coming down in his vicinity, and the small-arms fire was continuous overhead. Now and then he saw vague fleeting shapes of men, advancing with rifles across the open ground, moving at a ponderous lumbering walk; he wondered why they didn't move faster, then realized it must be barely possible to move at all in the sticky soft mud. He thought he recognized the butternut gray of Confederate uniforms, and considered calling out for help; but they must surely have all they could do as it was, without further risking their lives to help a feckless pilot who was uninjured and probably in a safer spot than they were. And anyway, what could they do for him? Drag him out of his hole and escort him back to their lines, through a hurricane of machine-gun fire and shrapnel? Amos decided he could stand it where he was, just a little longer.

He lay there for hours, while the battle moved back and forth across No Man's Land and the sun rose high in the French sky. The shellfire at last slackened as the two armies came to grips, too close for either side to fire without hitting its own men. The roar was replaced by a weird cacophony of small-arms fire, grenade explosions, and shrieks of wounded and dying men. Once, for just a moment, Amos saw an airplane, a black speck slowly droning across the circle of sky above the shell crater, but he could not make out what kind. From all he could tell, from his occasional quick glances over the edge of the hole, his own Nieuport had simply ceased to exist, its wreckage pounded into shreds and mixed with the mud.

It was a long day. He had no water, and his throat burned. He had no food, either, but he could not have eaten. The stench was incredible, a gut-turning mix of cordite smoke and decomposing bodies and traces of poison gas left over from the last gas attack. There was water at the bottom of the hole, but nothing, not boiling, not chemicals, not Jesus Christ himself, could have made that evil liquid fit to drink.

A rat, gray and fat and incredibly big, ran along the edge of the hole, looked at him, and scurried away in no great hurry. Amos wondered what it found to eat out here in this wasteland; and then his gorge rose again as he realized what the answer must be.

Finally, knowing he was reaching his limits, he closed his eyes and withdrew into himself, as his grandfather had taught him: shutting everything off and out, making himself the center of a great circle and then drawing the circle closer and closer about himself until the world, and time, and space, all ceased to exist. Empty and untouchable, he waited in utter stillness for whatever would come.

* * *

He came back into himself as darkness began to settle over the battlefield. His mouth and throat burned from thirst, his stomach was an empty knot, and his entire body ached from lying all day in the mud; and yet he felt, in a certain sense, almost refreshed. He looked at the darkening sky and said softly, "*Wado.*"

Moving very carefully and slowly, he managed to haul himself up onto more or less solid ground—at least he sank only six inches or so—and sat up, his head and shoulders above the top of the crater. Nothing was moving in his vicinity; no weapons were being fired, and the nearest artillery fire sounded a mile or more away.

He dug his revolver out of his mud-choked holster and examined it. An unlicensed Confederate copy of a Smith & Wesson .45, it was in many ways an excellent weapon, but it seemed unlikely to be much use under the present circumstances; even if the mud-clogged thing would fire, which was doubtful, a shot would probably bring down a withering crossfire from both sides.

Not that there seemed to be anyone to shoot. No Man's Land was living up to its name now; the muddy plain was deserted.

Or rather it was deserted by the living. The dead were present in multitudes. They lay everywhere: singly, in bunches and windrows, whole or in pieces, their limp soggy shapes barely distinguishable in the dim light from the mud into which they had already begun to sink.

Amos studied the distant lines of barbed wire that marked the positions of the opposing armies. As best he could tell, nobody on either side had gained or lost an inch from the day's struggle.

He gazed for a little while over the darkening battlefield, and at last he said to himself, in a barely vocalized whisper, "*Sgiduh nusdi.*" Which meant that that was the way it was and there was no point in thinking any more about it. . . .

He watched the sky, waiting for enough stars to come out that he could get his bearings; he was fairly sure he knew which way was which, but he did not entirely trust his sense of direction after the beating his nervous system had taken.

Just his luck, he thought, to survive all that and then get up and walk straight into the German trenches. It was worth taking a few more minutes to be sure.

Now it grew almost completely dark except for the faint light of the stars. Amos eased himself silently out of the hole, wondering if he should lie flat and crawl on his stomach, or scuttle along on all fours, or just get up and make a dash for the lines and trust the darkness to cover him. It occurred to him that he was probably going to be in far more danger from nervous Confederate or British sentries than from the Germans.

It was then that he heard the sounds of men moving across the muddy ground nearby. They were pretty good, he thought; considering the conditions, they were doing a really professional job of trying to move quietly. Probably no white man—at least no ordinary white man—would have heard them at all.

He went flat on his stomach, clutching the .45—it would still make a good club; he wished he had brought Tyrone's razor—and slithered silently toward them on an interception course. Six of them, he was nearly sure, but whose? Then he heard a faint but unmistakable whisper: *"Shit fire, Billy, watch it—"*

Amos sighed silently in relief and crept forward. As the leader of the patrol crawled by, Amos reached out and put a hand on his shoulder.

Later, he reflected that this was probably not the best way to go about making contact. There was a violent flurry of startled movement, and Amos found himself surrounded, his arms pinned. A number of shiny, unpleasantly sharp-looking implements glinted in the starlight, very close to his throat.

He said in a low but frantic whisper, "Jesus Christ, I'm a Confederate pilot!"

There was a pause. One of the men holding him whispered, "Might be. He's wearin' one of them leather flyin' suits."

"This here's a Griswold .45," another offered.

"That airplane that come down this mornin'," the first man said. "Hit was right about yere."

A big bulky man thrust his face close. "Name General Lee's horse," he hissed. "No funny answers, either."

"Traveler, God damn it." Amos ground his teeth. "Are we going to lie here and bullshit until the Krauts shoot our asses off?"

The soldiers seemed to recognize the logic in this. With a warning not to try no funny shit, they began moving slowly back toward the Confederate lines, an exhausted Amos in tow.

The Confederate trench was considerably deeper than Amos had expected, its sandbag parapet well above even a tall man's head. Firing steps had been cut in the side of the forward wall in order to allow men to look and shoot over the top. "Trench" was a misleading term; because of the boggy soil, only about half of the depth was actually dug into the ground, the rest of the earthworks being made up by piles of sandbags. Even so, the bottom of the trench was a slippery, slimy, waterlogged mess into which men sank to their ankles. Amos, in his cumbersome thick leather outfit, could barely move at all. The rear wall of the trench was riddled with scooped-out holes, soggy burrows where men curled up and tried to sleep. As the patrol led Amos along the trench, there were curses from men whose protruding legs had been tripped over or stepped on. The cursing sounded automatic, as if the men were too far gone with exhaustion to feel real anger.

The soldiers turned down a narrow communication trench, herding Amos wordlessly along, and, a few minutes later, pushed aside a hanging scrap of canvas and led him down into a dank dugout, lit by a single candle. Boards covered the floor, after a fashion; a roughly-made bunk occupied one wall. Most of the remaining space was taken up by a raw-wood table, covered with maps and books and papers, at which a husky-looking man sat on a folding stool and glared at the visitors. His eyes were red, his face heavily lined, even though he could not have been much over thirty.

One of the soldiers said, "Captain, this here's the pilot of that airplane that come down. Says he is, anyway."

"God damn it, Corporal." The voice was higher than Amos would have expected from such a big man. "Why didn't you report to your Lieutenant? Don't you know about chains of—''

"Lieutenant Hicks got killed this morning," one of the men said quietly. "We're all that's left of the whole damn platoon."

"Son of a bitch. That's right." The Captain ran a hand across his eyes. "This God-damned mud must be getting into my brains. Well, we better let HQ know we've got their pilot alive and well." He picked up a sheet of paper. "Name and unit?"

"Ninekiller. Amos Ninekiller." He saw a flicker of interest in the big Captain's eyes. "Fourth Virginia Pursuit Squadron."

The Captain scribbled rapidly and held out the paper. "Corporal, go find Sergeant Cash and tell him to get this off. The rest of you, dismissed, and good work."

When they were alone he said, "Suppose you'd like a drink?"

"Some water," Amos croaked, "would be good."

"Christ, yes; you've been out there since morning, haven't you? I saw the crash, never saw you get out though." He felt around under the table and handed Amos a canvas-covered canteen. "Here, help yourself."

The water was heavily treated with some sort of chemical, but at the moment it tasted wonderful. "Hungry too? This isn't much but it's all there is. They didn't get any food up to us today because of the attack. Supposedly we were going to help ourselves to the Germans' supplies after we occupied their positions."

"This" consisted of an open can of some sort of salty meat—either very bad corned beef or fairly good boot leather—and a few stale biscuits, the shape and general consistency of buffalo turds. Actually Amos could barely taste anything; the stench of the battlefield had left his taste buds temporarily dead.

"Ninekiller," the Captain said, studying him. "You some kind of an Indian?"

Amos nodded, his mouth full. Swallowing with great difficulty, he said, "Cherokee Flying Corps. Temporarily attached to the CEF."

"Cherokee Flying Corps?" The Captain laughed, shaking his head. "Well, hell, anything's possible in this God-damned war." He stuck out a hand. "George Patton."

It was like shaking hands with a polite bear. Patton said, "I suppose you're something of an outsider among these white Southern bloods. I know how it is. I'm an outsider myself."

He leaned back and adjusted his broad leather belt. Amos noticed that he wore a large, old-fashioned revolver with carved white handles. "Born in California," he explained, "which makes me a damn Yankee, but my grandfather was with Lee and my father went to VMI before moving out to the West. They wanted me to go to VMI too, so I went back to Virginia. Wound up staying on, taking a commission in the old prewar Confederate Army, chased border raiders down in Texas for a while and then the shit hit the fan over here. Never did take out Confederate citizenship, so I'm still running an infantry company. They tell me there'll be an oak leaf for me pretty soon, though."

He paused, lost for a moment in some private thought. "So," he said, "how'd you come to be shot down in the middle of our little party?"

Between intractable mouthfuls, Amos told him the story. He kept it short and as clear as his ragged mind allowed; there was something in that unwavering, penetrating gaze, an intangible force that reached Amos at levels he had not known existed. He suspected the big Captain had that effect on other men, too.

"Son of a bitch," Patton said, when Amos was finished. "So the Krauts have finally decided to take back the sky. Can they do it?"

"If they've got more of those new fighters. And more pilots of that quality to fly them. It wasn't just the aircraft," Amos said. "They had tactics and organization beyond anything I've seen so far, on either side. As if—" He started to say as if they had a Lucas of their own, but stopped, realizing Patton wouldn't know what he was talking about. "I don't know if they can drive us out of the sky, the way we drove them out for a while," Amos finished, "but one thing for sure, it's not going to be a one-sided game any more."

Patton nodded. "Son of a bitch," he said again. "So there goes the one God-damned bright spot in the picture, the one area in which we were actually whipping their asses. Should have known it was too God-damned good to last."

He gestured with his thumb. "You saw the action today. Just a minor attack, a probe in force, not even a major assault. Over the God-damned top, through the God-damned mud, into the God-damned Kraut machine guns, same as all the other times before except that sometimes it gets worse. I'm a professional soldier," he said. "War is my trade and I'm not ashamed of it. But hell, Lieutenant, this isn't war—and, unlike what the Frenchman said about the Charge of the Light Brigade, it isn't magnificent either. As a trained officer I'm ashamed to have to order men out to get butchered on a stupid God-damned plan of attack that any Mexican bandit could have improved on."

He gave Amos a crooked grin. "Of course, if you think this was bad, you should see the poor damned British infantry in action. Our boys are trained to advance as fast as they can— not that that means much in this shit—and use any available cover, support each other with rifle fire, operate in small groups or even as individuals; the Confederate Army at least absorbed that much of the lessons of places like Shiloh and Sharpsburg. The Brits," Patton said scornfully, "just line their men up shoulder to shoulder and send them off at a slow walk, straight into the machine guns—with their God-damned bayonets fixed, because the only way they can bring up replacements to keep up with the casualty rate is to rush the poor sons of bitches through training so none of them know how to shoot." He snorted angrily. "All of which is why the Confederate Expeditionary Force is now the second largest Allied army on this front, after the French; the British High Command has managed to murder its own army and most of a generation."

He flung up his hands. "But our own God-damned Headquarters is still hopelessly in thrall to the Brits, hypnotized by that flag the sun never sets on—a French Colonel told me that was because God doesn't trust the British in the dark— so they all line up and kiss Haig's ass and come back happily waving another of his suicidal God-damned battle plans, and here we go again."

Amos said, "How would you do it?" He wasn't really that eager to hear more of the lecture, but Patton seemed to feel a need to unload. "Break this stalemate, I mean."

"Ah!" Patton's eyes gleamed briefly. "Mobility, Lieutenant. Mobility, concentration of force, and technology. People like Stonewall Jackson and Jubal Early knew about the first two, and you should know about the third. I've seen those new 'tank' vehicles in action. Crude right now, but they're going to be the key, if anybody ever has sense enough to use them properly—mass a whole shitload of them opposite your target point, attack suddenly without a preliminary bombardment to alert the enemy, send in fresh infantry behind the tanks—with decent training in skirmishing and open-order fighting—and keep control of the air, so you've got eyes and the enemy doesn't." He was banging the table now for emphasis. "Hit the other son of a bitch with everything you can, fast, and then kick him in the balls while he's off balance. Hell, your people wrote the book on mobile warfare, long ago."

Patton sighed, looking suddenly very tired. "But I don't know how many more good men are going to die uselessly before those dinosaurs at Headquarters wake up. If ever."

He leaned back against the dugout wall. "Tell you something, Lieutenant. Wouldn't say this to just anybody, but you're an outsider like me . . . the real irony of all this," he said, "is that we probably wouldn't be bogged down like this if the Confederacy hadn't won their War of Independence. Think about it," he mused. "A United States that was still united could have come into this thing—either in the beginning or later on—with enough forces to overpower the Germans, no matter how badly they were handled. Or, if they didn't come in at all, the Krauts would gradually overwhelm the British and French and bring the thing to an end . . . but as it is," he said, "the Confederate Expeditionary Force has been just enough to balance out the odds but not enough to throw the scales. So here we sit. Stalemate."

"The Union may yet come into the war," Amos observed. "A lot of people think so."

"Oh, sure. No doubt about it. Right after the next election, is my guess. They'll have to talk themselves around to it,"

Patton said, "convince themselves they're doing it to help their old friends the French and never mind the wicked British and the nasty Rebs. But even when they do, it won't be enough to alter the situation much. Without the Southern states, they don't have the numbers—and, anyway, by then this bloody shambles will have gone on too long. Everybody will be exhausted."

Amos said, "You don't seem to have much hope."

Patton shrugged, heavily. "Not unless there are some major changes at CEF headquarters, and in Richmond. . . ."

He gave Amos a hard look, as if suddenly thinking of something. "God damn. The Fourth Virginia Pursuit, didn't you say?"

Amos nodded, puzzled. "That's right."

"Ah. Then you're under James Lucas, by God. Don't know why it didn't register," Patton said. "Of course I haven't slept in two or three days, maybe that has something to do with it."

Amos said, "You know Major Lucas?"

"Oh, hell, yes. Of course he's got himself an oak leaf now and I'm still wearing these railroad tracks, even though I'm three years older than him, but that's the Flying Corps for you. Has some interesting ideas," Patton said thoughtfully. "Some very interesting ideas indeed . . . well." He stood up, bowing his head beneath the low ceiling. "If you want to try and get a little sleep, Lieutenant, help yourself to my bunk, such as it is. In the morning we'll see about getting you back to your squadron."

The Corporal driving the truck watched as Amos Ninekiller struggled to climb into the cab, his mud-caked leather suit making him clumsy as an armored knight. After a moment the Corporal reached down to help him. He said, "Here, Lieutenant. Let me give you a hand."

Amos stared for a moment at the extended hand. Then he bolted around the side of the truck, out of sight. The Corporal sat listening in blank bewilderment to the sounds of helpless vomiting and dry retching.

"Now what the hell," he said to himself, "did *I* say? Pilots. . . ."

9

"CONGRATULATIONS," LUCAS said. "It appears that Lieutenant Amos Ninekiller is not only the one man in this squadron to shoot down one of the new German fighters in yesterday's scrap, but possibly the first man in the CEF to get one of the bastards. There is some talk of a minor but attractive medal."

Amos said, "You mean I actually got that one? Are they sure?"

Lucas nodded. "Jack Yancey saw him go down. So did the pilot and observer of the one surviving bomber. Went straight into the ground, power full on, even though the aircraft appeared undamaged. Sounds like a dead pilot," Lucas said, "which sounds like a certain sharp-eyed Indian, doesn't it?" Lucas grinned at Amos. "I like your style, Ninekiller. An aircraft can fly with its wings and tail full of holes, it can sometimes land safely with the prop shot off or the engine dead, a few men have even gotten a plane down in flames —but kill the pilot and it's all over. Wish I could get the rest of these people to understand that. Not that any of the others can shoot like you, although Bodine's close."

He put his hands on his desk and looked down at them.

"Christ, what a day. All of a sudden I've barely got a squadron left here."

Amos had already seen the roster board, with its sudden gaps amid the chalked-up names, and talked briefly with Faulkner. The writer had gotten away from the fight unharmed, as had Yancey, though both had badly riddled aircraft; Bodine had somehow managed to stagger across the lines, his engine barely running, and crash-land at a British artillery-spotter base. B Flight, on dawn patrol not far away, had been jumped by more of the mysterious fighters—or perhaps the same ones—and shot to rags, its inexperienced replacement pilots hopelessly outclassed before the fight began. Only Ashby and Lynch had gotten home. That afternoon, A Flight had had slightly better luck, but only slightly: a pair of the new fighters had made a single pass, killed Rogers and wounded Duvall, and departed in a high-speed dive no Nieuport could follow.

And, rumor had it, things had been pretty much the same all up and down the line. At least in the British and Confederate sectors; as usual, the French might as well have been on another planet.

Amos said, "Anything yet on those new German fighters?"

"Not yet. Headquarters Intelligence—there's a contradiction in terms for you—is working on it. Supposed to have something soon."

Lucas stared past Amos at nothing. "Right now, though, I've got eight pilots left—nine counting me—and from four to six serviceable aircraft, depending on how many of the shot-up crates the mechanics can patch up. Until we get more planes and pilots, it doesn't much matter if the Krauts fly Curtiss pushers, this squadron can only make a token effort."

He reached in his desk and pulled out a sheet of paper. "This came in just now, Ninekiller. You have to go to Paris and report to some bureaucrat at the Confederate Embassy. Something about some missing papers, they need your signature or something. Hell of a time for me to have to let a pilot go, but the orders are clear. So," he said, "you can take care of something for the squadron too. When you're through with your business at the Embassy, go out to Orly airfield, report to Major Littlefield, and collect a new aircraft he's got for us. You'll also collect a couple of alleged pilots, fresh from our fine training program, God help us all. They'll fly with you. Try not to let them break their aircraft, which we need badly. Carry a supply of toilet paper to wipe their noses and their asses. If they're typical replacements, you'll need it.''

Sam Harjo said, ''More chicken?''

''Thanks,'' Amos said, reaching. ''Very strange business,'' he remarked, after a moment. ''At the Embassy, I mean. Supposedly some papers got lost, something to do with my status as a non-citizen serving with the CEF, I don't know. But all they wanted was my signature on a couple of forms. You'd think they could have just sent them up to the squadron for me to sign.''

Sam Harjo was chuckling; Mary Wildcat's shoulders were shaking in silent accompaniment. ''Amos, Amos. Didn't you figure it out?'' Harjo smiled widely. ''Word came to me that you had a new commander, a man with a certain reputation and some interesting friends. It was also made known that the noted journalist Gabriel Cassidy had paid your squadron a visit for the purpose of interviewing you. For these and other reasons, I thought it would be a good idea to bring you to Paris for a little talk. If nothing else, I figured you could use a good meal.''

Amos said incredulously, ''You arranged that business at the Embassy?''

''A simple enough matter. A minor clerk with a weakness for certain illicit drugs, for which I happen to have sources . . . never mind the details.'' Harjo dismissed the matter with a wave of one big hand. ''As it turns out, we were almost too late, weren't we? Thank God you did survive that terrible business yesterday. My information is that a lot of pilots did not live to see the sun go down.''

''I should have known.'' Something struck Amos. ''You know about Lucas, then?''

''Only by association, as you might say—has connections

in some surprising quarters, of which Gabriel Cassidy is merely the most flamboyant. And, of course, I've read his service record."

"Of course," Amos said drily.

"Whether he represents an actual conspiracy," Harjo went on thoughtfully, "some sort of cabal with sinister plans, or merely a loose association of ambitious malcontents among the Confederate officer corps—that I don't know. Your description of the man, however, is fascinating. I had pictured a humorless fanatic."

Amos shook his head. "Not humorless, no." He chewed slowly, thinking. "Actually," he said at last, "he can be downright likable. And yet he *is* a fanatic, all the same. He really believes it's the historic destiny of the white race—which, in his definition, stops at the border of Poland—to conquer the world, starting with Russia. With," he added, "the Confederate Americans, and I suppose the British, in charge of the crusade, closely supported by Germany. I get the impression he doesn't think much of the French."

Harjo chuckled. "Does anyone in the CEF? Not that they're far wrong, on a purely military basis. The French Army is rapidly approaching the point of collapse. The *poilu*, unlike his Anglo-Saxon counterpart, will only stand for so much useless slaughter and suicidal stupidity. Then, being a logical person, he simply sits down and refuses to go on with the farce any longer—which is why France has always found the Legion so valuable, with its Germans and Britishers and the like. Push the French infantryman too hard, and he shoots his officers and mutinies. It's already happening," Harjo said, "in some of the units around Verdun. Going to get worse, too, if it's a bad winter."

He reached for the wine. "Between that," he said, "and the slow inexorable destruction of the British Expeditionary Force by its own commanders—as noted by your Captain Patton—the burden of the war is beginning to shift heavily to the Confederate forces."

"There's Russia," Amos pointed out. "Lots of Germans tied down on the Eastern Front, I understand."

"Ah, yes." Harjo waggled a finger at him and smiled mysteriously. "Watch for a little surprise or two there, *unhisse*. Not soon, perhaps, maybe not until next year, or even the next, but watch for it. We are on the verge of astonishing events, Amos, events that will change the world as utterly and terribly as our own world was changed when the first white men came ashore in Florida."

Amos studied Harjo's broad bland face and made a mental note never to play poker with the big Creek. "You sound," he said, "as if you believe in these fantasies of Lucas's. About the Allies and the Germans uniting to fight the Russians."

Harjo shrugged massively. "I don't necessarily believe or disbelieve in anything," he said. "But it's no fantasy. In these times, is anything impossible? Mind," he chuckled, "I doubt that the outcome will be seriously affected by the machinations of a few obscure Confederate officers and political adventurers. Might as well expect the destinies of the great powers to be changed by our little friend Ho Chi Minh."

Later, Sam Harjo made a considerable show of having to go out for the evening.

"Business calls," he said, "and business, as the Yankees say, before pleasure—which is the sort of thinking that causes your Southern colleagues to put the prefix 'damn' before 'Yankee,' but never mind that. I'll probably be gone all night," he added pointedly, picking up his hat, "but I'm sure you two will be all right, won't you? If you need anything, Amos, Mary here can take care of you."

Amos sneaked a glance at Mary Wildcat, but she was looking off into an empty corner of the room. There was a certain set to her shoulders, however, that was not encouraging.

"Brandy and cigars if you like," Harjo went on. "Good cigars, too, real Havana. Can't understand how those Cubans find time to make such fine cigars in between attacks on the Spanish occupation forces, but we're all blessed that they do. Oh," he said at the door, "we've got a new gramophone and some records. You might enjoy that."

When he was gone Amos sat for a moment watching Mary Wildcat, thinking, well, here we go again. Should have just gone on to Dixie Land.

But then she turned and looked at him, and her face was not unfriendly. She said, "Help yourself to the brandy if you like. I'm going to get myself some wine instead."

At the foot of the stairs she paused and said, "Put on some music. I'll be right back."

Wine? Put on some music? Amos poured himself a quick brandy, nearly spilling it, and drank it fast. Then, after a half-second's review of the prospects at hand, he poured another and drank that too.

The gramophone stood against the wall, its lid already open, its big morning-glory-blossom horn in position. He cranked the spring motor tight and looked through the stack of records on the little table nearby. All the titles were in French, Italian, or German, and most were classical—Sam Harjo appeared to be fond of Wagner—but Amos picked out an unfamiliar French number and put it on. There was a moment's hissing and scratching and then the sound of dance music, not exactly hot but reasonably warm, filled the parlor. A typical weak-voiced French tenor began to sing. Amos nodded to himself and went over and turned the lights down a bit.

The overall effect, he decided, was pretty damn romantic. He poured another brandy but did not drink it yet, only sniffed, as he had seen the rich boys do in the fraternity houses at the University of Virginia, and watched the stairway, his pulse running a bit faster than usual.

Mary Wildcat appeared on the stairs, holding a bottle of wine. Halfway down, she paused and looked about the room, and then at Amos.

She said in Cherokee, "How much of that have you had to drink?"

Amos's burgeoning hopes collapsed. So did something else. He sat down limply in the nearest chair. "Huh," he grunted, unable to think of anything to say.

She laughed. "*Gusdi nusdi*," she said. It was a double-edged expression; it could mean either "Something is wrong," or "What's your problem?" and, as with most spoken Cherokee, there were shadings and nuances that had no exact parallel in English, Cherokee sarcasm being a murderously sophisticated art form.

She came down the stairs without waiting for an answer. "I like that," she said, setting the wine down and nodding toward the gramophone. "Do you know that song?"

"I don't know that much French," Amos confessed. "I just picked it at random."

She nodded her head in time with the music. "Can you dance?" she said suddenly.

He stood up, setting his brandy glass aside. "Sure," he said. "Did you want to . . . ?"

She came toward him, holding her arms out, a little uncertainly. "Teach me how," she said. "I don't know how to dance *yoneg* style. All I know is stomp dance."

He took her hands and positioned her and showed her a simple box step. "Like this," he said. "Then of course you can get fancier if you want—"

She picked it up quickly, her small bare feet moving with light sure steps on the deep carpet. "I like this," she said, moving in closer to him. "My parents were strict Cherokee Baptist, didn't believe in dancing at all. Then when they died I lived with my grandmother. She was old-fashioned, didn't think we ought to learn *yoneg* ways. So I never learned."

Amos looked down at her. "You're doing very well. You're light on your feet."

She laughed. "I told you, all I know is stomp dance. You dance all night with a bunch of turtle-shell rattles tied to your legs, you can do nearly anything after that." She laid her head against his chest. "I didn't go to a fancy Eastern school like you, Amos. I'm just a Bird Clan girl from Goingsnake District, went to the Baptist missionary school enough to learn to read and write and speak English, and if Chief Watie and his wife hadn't taken an interest in me—they knew my parents—I'd be living in a log cabin back in some hollow, pounding corn and nuts for *kenuche* and having babies, right now."

The record came to an end. Mary Wildcat retrieved her wine and poured herself a glass, while Amos looked through the records. "Never mind," she said, "play that one again. I'm just starting to get this."

They danced for a long time, playing the same song again and again, changing at length to something by Strauss so she could learn the waltz. Amos realized suddenly that this was something he hadn't done in a couple of years. The last time —it came to him, after very little thought—had been at that ball in Charlottesville, with the beautiful red-haired girl whose brother captained the football team. He had heard her, afterward, giggling excitedly with a group of crinoline-rustling friends by the punch bowl: "—*told* you I'd dance with that Indian, now that's five dollars you owe me, Jo Beth—"

He said to Mary Wildcat, "What changed your mind? I thought you'd made up your mind you didn't like me."

She shook her head slightly, burrowing into his lapel. "Tell you some other time," she said. "Don't talk right now."

Finally, when the electricity between them had become almost too strong for him to stand, she pulled away. Holding on to one hand, she moved toward the stairs. "Come on," she said. "*Nula.*"

He followed her up the stairs, letting her lead him like a child. Her room was small and austerely bare, only a bed and a single chair and a shelf with a few books. There was a colored lithograph on one wall, a portrait of Sequoyah; another wall bore a small oil painting of some flowers. There was not even a mirror.

She was already undoing the buttons of her plain white blouse. "I'm not going to try to tell you I've never done this before either," she said quietly, "but it's only been a couple of times and I don't think it was done very well. So you might have to show me how to do this too."

As it turned out, he had no complaints.

They lay in the darkness, comfortably naked against each other, under a single sheet. Amos said, "I guess I'd better get up and get out of here before Sam comes back."

She made a low gurgling laugh. "Don't worry about that. I know where he is. Believe me, he won't be back tonight."

"Oh?"

"There's this woman," she said. "Dutch, I think, but she pretends to be Javanese or something. Dances practically naked on stage. Sam's been doing it with her. He claims it's just because she's a German spy and he's getting information from her, but I've seen her dance and I know what he's getting, just like all those other men. I can't think of her real name," she added. "Calls herself—what is it? Some phony Asian name, sounds more like Seminole to me . . . Mata Hari, that's it."

She squirmed against him. "She's supposed to be really beautiful. Got a good shape, even though she's older than me. But even when she takes everything off, she always covers her chest, and her maid told me it's because she's got nothing at all up here." She took Amos's hand and pressed it against one of her firm hard-pointed breasts. "Like a couple of fried eggs, Yvette said, or pears gone bad. Of course mine aren't all that big, the way the *yoneg* men like. What do you think?"

"They're, uh, just fine." He gave a squeeze to emphasize his words. "Listen," he said, "what changed your mind? About me?"

She sighed and put an arm across his chest. "Oh," she said, "I thought at first you were a cold person. Inside, I mean. You don't show much, Amos. I think I could live with you for a hundred years and never really know what you were thinking. You play your cards close to your chest," she said in English. "It's like part of you is always standing off to one side, watching and not getting involved. Probably a good way to be in a war, probably keeps you alive sometimes, but no woman likes it."

He considered the idea. "I suppose it's true," he said slowly. "I never really thought about it."

"Tonight, though," she said, "when you were telling Sam about the battle, about the men dying and suffering in the trenches, and that hand—God, that's the scariest thing I've ever heard, I don't see how you kept from going insane—a little something showed through, Amos. There's somebody with some feelings under there somewhere."

He said, "So you decided you were wrong about me?"

"That's part of it . . . but mostly," she said, "I just got to thinking about how close you came to getting killed, how easily it could happen to you, any time. And to any of us," she went on in a different voice. "You do realize, Amos, the French would stand Sam and me up against a wall and shoot us if they knew some of the things that go on here? And there are Union agents in Paris by the scores, and they'd love to find some way to betray us. So would the Germans —Sam had to kill a man in that parlor, downstairs, less than a month ago," she said calmly, "a German agent who was trying to blackmail us, and I had to help get rid of the body."

"Christ," Amos said involuntarily, in English.

"It's all too uncertain," she said, "to waste time and opportunities. Here we both are, and no telling where we'll be tomorrow. You know what I'm saying?"

"*Carpe diem*," Amos said, running his hand along her back.

"What's that mean?" she said suspiciously. "What is it, Choctaw?"

"Latin. Means 'seize the day.' "

"Is that right? I'm about to seize something in a minute or two here, college boy, and it's not going to be the day . . . just one thing," she said. "No stupid talk about love. We don't love each other. We don't even know each other."

She slid along him and took hold of him as he rose to meet her. "But," she said, her breath quickening, "I love us when we do this—"

At Orly, next day, there were only two new Nieuports waiting for the Fourth Virginia. One of the replacement pilots, Major Littlefield informed Amos, had made a small error in landing yesterday, and had spread himself and the third Nieuport over a remarkably large area.

Amos studied the other new pilot without much joy. He was a skinny, ridiculously tall boy—Amos wondered how the hell he managed to fit that elongated structure into the cockpit of a Nieuport, and what genius had assigned this human derrick to fly the smallest fighter in the entire Allied arsenal. He had wavy, unruly red hair, freckles, and a comical nose; large blue eyes gazed back at Amos with an expression of total trust.

"Cobb, sir," he said. "Lieutenant Steve Cobb."

"Don't call me 'sir,' for Christ's sake," Amos said, more harshly than he had meant. "I'm just a God-damned Lieutenant like you."

Cobb, he noticed, winced visibly at each profanity. He sighed, deep and long. "Tell me, Cobb," he said, "is there any chance at all of getting you to forget this whole thing, right now? You know, is there any sort of chronic illness or physical discomfort you haven't told the Medical Officer about? Headaches above five hundred feet, say? Back pains?"

"No, sir," Cobb said cheerfully. "I feel fine."

"Hm. And you wouldn't want to reconsider? Convert to the Quaker religion, maybe, or tell them you've been having lustful thoughts about your mechanic, or just run like hell off this airfield and hole up in some seedy quarter of Paris and live off the earnings of a lady of easy virtue, if any? I've got friends who might help."

Cobb grinned happily. "You can't kid me," he said, in a voice that still had a trace of adolescent cracking here and there. "I can't hardly wait to get to do some real flying over the front." He stuck out a large knobby hand. "Listen," he said earnestly, "I ain't got a thing against Indians. My grandmother was part Shawnee. I'm proud to be flying with you."

Amos groaned inwardly. "All right," he said to Cobb. "Just follow me. And watch out for large birds."

Major Lucas stood before a large three-view plan drawing and tapped it with his riding crop.

"Gentlemen," he said, "meet the Albatros D I. Some of you have already met the bitch, but haven't been formally introduced . . . this is the reason life has gotten so interesting lately."

"Wait a minute," Bodine objected. "I know what an Albatros looks like. I shot one down last year. That ain't an Albatros."

Lucas shook his head impatiently. "Not the Albatros two-seater you're used to. This is a whole new beast. Right now it may just possibly be the best single-seat fighter in the world. *We* sure as hell don't have anything in its class, and God help us if the Krauts have anything better.''

His riding crop pointed out the salient features. ''You've already noticed the streamline design, which accounts for much of its speed. Big in-line water-cooled Mercedes engine, we believe it's good for over 150 horsepower.''

Yancey whistled. ''Christ, our old Le Rhône rotaries only crank out 110 when they're brand new.''

''Right. And, as I don't have to tell those of you who've danced with these bastards, they're faster than a Nieuport in level flight and one hell of a lot faster in a dive. Though a few reports indicate they may have our old problem of the top wing coming off in an all-out dive, but I wouldn't count on it . . . being heavier than a Nieuport,'' he said, ''thanks partly to that big engine, they can't climb as fast, which is something you might want to remember if you care to go on living. Ceiling is at least as high as ours—they bounced a photo-reconnaissance plane at sixteen thousand yesterday and they did it from above. As you'll recall, the old Fokkers had all they could do to get up to eleven thousand.''

Somebody groaned. Lucas said, ''The best is yet to come. Two Spandau 7.92mm. machine guns, synched to fire through the prop, and all new pilots *will* report to Master Sergeant Harlan down at the repair hangar, immediately following this briefing, for a good look at what an airplane looks like after one of these flying buzz-saws gets a few bursts in. I know, I know, the late-model Fokkers had two guns too, but they could barely get out of their own way for the extra weight. These things have enough horsepower to haul a French seventy-five cannon around, damn near. You will also note the broad tail surfaces and generally well-balanced layout, and consider that an in-line engine does not develop the torque of a rotary, which means—what? Anyone, children?''

''Stable gun platform,'' Shoemaker said. ''Oh, Christ.''

''Just to make everyone really happy,'' Lucas added, ''there are two more new fighters in the opposing line, though not much is known about them and they don't seem to be too common—the Halberstadt D I, and an entirely new Fokker design, a biplane, the D II. Supposedly neither of these is quite as nasty as the Albatros, but you'll all recall that Anthony Fokker's products gave us a very hard time last year, so I'd expect this one to be something of a handful too.''

Moore said, ''Great God, do they expect us to fight those things with these worn-out, underpowered little one-gun wonders? Can't we get anything better?''

''Not without changing sides,'' Lucas said sardonically, ''at least right now. The Brits have been having just about as much trouble as we have, with their Sopwith Pups and the old pushers, and the French haven't come up with anything better than the Nieuport so far—and I don't have to tell you, this is the only fighter the Confederacy has managed to produce in its own plants to date. Unless the Russians or the Japanese have a secret design for us, this is it.''

''Shit.'' Moore looked even more unhappy than usual. ''Any chance of modifying what we've got, then? Mount a second gun?''

''They tried that,'' Ashby said. ''The French did. Too much weight. Anything you pick up in firepower, you lose in performance.''

''And we don't exactly have performance to throw away,'' Faulkner remarked. ''You know, I think I know how the German pilots felt when we started making planes that outflew the old Fokkers.''

Lucas shook his head. ''Don't exaggerate, Faulkner. The difference isn't *that* great. Probably no more than a ten-mile-per-hour difference in level speed . . . and,'' he went on, ignoring several groans, ''we do seem to have an advantage in maneuverability. Doesn't matter if the son of a bitch has a dozen guns, if he can't hit you. And it doesn't matter if he's got the fastest plane in the world, if you get behind him and shoot him before he knows you're there.''

He tapped the drawing. ''That big powerful engine is water-cooled, remember. A bullet or two through the cooling jacket and it dies. See this rectangle on the top wing? Exposed radiator, another vulnerable point. That pretty streamline fuselage is plywood; it'll burn like a match. The whole plane is bigger than yours, so it's a bigger target.''

He hit the drawing hard, the riding crop splitting the paper with a loud, tearing crack. "And, God damn it, that's exactly how you've got to think. You've got to see the son of a bitch *as* a target, if only because it's the best way to keep him from making a target out of you. Sound like a bunch of old ladies,'' he sneered, ''pissing your drawers because the Krauts finally come up with something good enough to make you work for a living for a change. Been having a fine time, haven't you, parading around the sky in your pretty little airplanes, shooting up a few worn-out old crates flown by men with more balls than you—Christ, if they ordered this squadron to start flying Fokker monoplanes, you'd all run and hide under Miss Rhetticia's bed! Now they finally get to fight back, you don't know whether to shit or go blind.

"The purpose of this squadron," he said with heavy sarcasm, "and of the Confederate Expeditionary Force, is not that of getting your pictures in the hometown newspapers so you can come home afterward, with your nice uniform, and the local girls will all let you pull down their pants. This squadron isn't even here for the primary purpose of keeping you alive. But if you *want* to stay alive,'' he went on, jabbing at them with the riding crop, ''you'd better quit pissing and moaning about how good their planes are, and start concentrating on outflying and outfighting the sons of bitches.''

"How?" Moore said. "Sir," he added, after a barely detectable pause.

Lucas stared at him. "You do everything I've been telling you to do all along," he said, "only you do it better. Keep your formation intact, watch out for yourself and each other, pull your head out of your ass and look around. Get up to altitude before you cross the lines, use clouds and the sun, and attack them before they know you're around. Difficult as it may be for some of you, *think*.''

He pointed at Amos with his riding crop. "Now one man in this squadron kept his head, the first time he ever saw an Albatros, and remembered what he was supposed to be doing—protecting his Flight Leader—and shot the son of a bitch dead, even though he was under fire himself at the time. Why the hell can't all you lily-white Southron boys do the same? Right now I'd trade all of you for two more Indians from the Nations. Hell, one.''

He stopped, glaring. Cobb sat grinning happily, arms folded. ''Jesus Christ,'' Lucas said. ''What the hell is this elongated object in the midst of my squadron? Is it a new pole for the wind sock, or what? You there. Identify yourself.''

''Lieutenant Cobb, sir.'' Cobb rose to his feet, a somewhat lengthy business. ''The Major was out when I got here, sir, so I reported to Captain Clay.'' He resumed his goofy grin.

''Cobb. Cobb. Does this mean—'' Lucas closed his eyes for a moment. ''No, no, it's too easy. Cobb, you seem to find all this amusing.''

''No, sir.'' Cobb blinked repeatedly, still grinning. ''I mean, I thought the Major's talk was *entertaining*, but—''

''Silence.'' Clay held up a hand. ''Be quiet, Cobb, before I go irrevocably mad. All right, A Flight is dismissed. B and C Flights, I'm making some changes. Bodine goes to B Flight—sorry, Yancey, but Ashby doesn't have an experienced man except Lynch right now. Faulkner, I want you to take over as Yancey's wingman. Ninekiller.''

''Sir?''

''Ninekiller, you will take charge of this . . . this Cobb, here. Try your best to turn it into some semblance of a combat wingman. If you can't, you have my permission to draw a rocket from the armorer—one of those Le Prieur incendiaries we were supposed to use against balloons—and stick it up Cobb's ass and launch him in the general direction of the German lines. The sight should at least cause alarm and despondency in the enemy ranks. God knows it alarms *me*.''

Amos said bitterly, ''Thank you, sir.''

Lucas waved a hand. ''Don't mention it, Lieutenant. Always glad to be of service to our allies of the Cherokee Flying Corps.''

10

DURING THE days that followed, more replacement pilots arrived, together with more aircraft, until the Fourth Virginia Pursuit Squadron was again brought up to something like normal strength. They came none too soon. The fighting was now brutal and continuous all along the Somme front.

The new Albatros and Fokker and Halberstadt fighters were up in force and spoiling for a fight, every time a patrol entered their territory. Made bold again by their new protectors, the artillery observation aircraft were up in record numbers, too, and balloons dotted the sky. German artillery fire began to strike with terrible precision, while Allied spotter aircraft found their already dangerous task had become virtually suicidal.

All of which was bad news for the armies on the ground, where High Command had launched yet another offensive. Having at long bloody last taken the high ground—such as it was—of the low ridge east of the Somme, the weary infantry were now ordered by Haig and Pinckney to push on down the exposed far slopes. This ensured that they would spend the approaching winter in the boggy lowlands beyond, in freezing flooded trenches, but Headquarters was adamant:

the offensive must be maintained. Frantic orders came down to the squadrons, demanding "aggressive action" to recapture control of the skies.

Meanwhile the Confederate pilots had begun to take the measure of their new opponents. The big German fighters, they learned, were indeed less maneuverable than the nimble little Nieuports. Ashby, tangling with an Albatros, managed to out-turn the German and get on his tail and shoot him down, then climbed rapidly into a patch of cloud before the other Albatroses could catch him. Bodine got one of the new Fokker biplanes in a fight that went clear down to treetop level. A new man named Hill picked off a Roland observation plane under the noses of its Albatros escort.

Amos, however, barely saw anything of his next couple of engagements. He was too busy trying to keep Cobb alive.

"It's incredible," Amos said to Faulkner. "How the hell did they let him become a fighter pilot? I think my grandmother would be better at this."

"Poor Amos," Faulkner said with a sadistic grin. "Kaiser Bill has the Austrians and you've got Cobb. Is he really that bad? I haven't been watching."

"Oh, hell. . . ."Amos sighed and stretched out on his bunk. "The truth is, he's not actually that bad a pilot, in a ham-handed sort of way. Nothing like Henry, anyway. He gets the plane off the ground, he stays more or less in formation, he lands without breaking any major components. I suppose," he said, "he wouldn't be too bad flying observation or reconnaissance, or maybe even bombers. But he's just the most unimaginative, unaggressive person I think I've ever met, and he's got the reflexes of a dead catfish."

"Can he shoot?"

"Who the hell knows? He never seems to remember he's *supposed* to shoot—it's as if he forgets he's even got a gun with him. Christ, did you see that Albatros that went right through us this morning, the all-black one that nearly got me? Cobb had a clear shot at it and I don't think he ever fired." Amos sighed. "I told him to stay on my wing and by God, you can't fault him there, he stays on my wing as if I had him tied there. I think I could dive straight into the ground and he'd smash in right alongside me. It just doesn't seem to occur to him that he ought to *do* something while he's hanging on to my wing. Maybe he thinks I just want him along for company.''

''Get rid of him,'' Faulkner suggested. ''Tell Lucas you can't operate with him there, he's slowing you down. Lucas is crazy for more kills. He'll take him off your hands.''

''I tried. Lucas just grinned and said sure, he'd assign him to Eubanks. Put Cobb with Eubanks and you might as well shoot him out of hand. That Texas son of a bitch will fly off chasing medals and leave the kid to get killed.''

''Well, is that your problem?'' Faulkner gave Amos a curious look. ''Come to that, I'm a little surprised you haven't simply let nature take its course—that Fokker you took off Cobb's tail the other day, for example.''

''The one he never even saw.''

''Right, and when we got back it was news to him that he'd been under attack. Why didn't you let the German solve your problem for you? You could call it self-defense,'' Faulkner pointed out. ''Because there's an excellent chance Cobb is going to get you killed, sooner or later.''

''I know,'' Amos said helplessly. ''But hell, Bill, just look at the kid. Could you do it?''

''Probably not,'' Faulkner confessed. ''He's just a big good-natured fool waiting to fill a coffin, isn't he? The one I'd really like to have in my sights is the bastard who signed the orders to send him up here in the first place. God damn them,'' Faulkner said with sudden viciousness, ''the sons of bitches who sit at desks back where it's safe and murder these kids with their pencils.''

A Flight went after a couple of two-seaters over Rancourt and were promptly jumped out of the sun by a flock of Albatroses that had been patiently waiting for someone to strike at the bait. Eubanks stood his Nieuport on its tail and, almost stalling, put a burst into the engine of an Albatros before kicking away into an evasive spin. Shoemaker damaged a German and got damaged in return, neither fatally. The fight broke off inconclusively when a pack of British Sopwith Triplanes happened along and drove the Germans away.

It was then that everyone noticed Moore was missing. No one had seen him go down; no one had seen him since the start of the fight. They formed up on Shoemaker and flew home. Moore's Nieuport was already parked in front of the hangar.

Lucas took their reports in a darkening silence. At the end he said, "Shoemaker, on your way out, tell Sergeant Hawkins to go get Captain Moore for me."

He said it calmly, almost casually, as if he wanted to ask Moore to make up a fourth for bridge.

Hawkins was back in a few minutes. His face looked very bad.

"Major Lucas," he said, "you better come. It's Captain Moore, sir. He's shot himself."

Moore half-sat, half-lay on his bunk, still in full flying suit, except for leather helmet and goggles. His heavy revolver hung from one hand, its muzzle almost touching the floor. There was not much left of the top of his head.

Lucas pushed through the excited crowd of babbling pilots in the corridor and viewed the body with no particular sign of emotion. "Get Captain Clay," he said to Hawkins. "And go ahead and start the paper work, Sergeant. You know the routine."

He glanced at the white faces in the doorway. "Shoemaker, take over A Flight. Remember you've got the afternoon patrol tomorrow." He turned and moved toward the door. The pilots drew aside to let him pass.

"Another case for the books, Ninekiller," Lucas said to Amos, much later. "The unfit not only fail to survive, sometimes they even weed themselves out. The first worthwhile contribution Moore makes to the progress of the war, and his last. That's the great thing about warfare, Ninekiller. Cuts out the weak and useless, improves the breed."

Amos said with careful formality, "If the Major says so. Sir."

Lucas snorted. "Oh, for Christ's sake, Ninekiller, don't tell me you're going sentimental on me. I thought you were the one man around here who understood the realities of the world. Next thing you know you'll be feeling sorry for the Germans."

He tilted his head and gave Amos a long searching look. "Which reminds me. You've been babying Cobb. I told you to show him the ropes, not hold his trembling little hand— no, strike that, Cobb doesn't have sense enough to know when to tremble. You've been leading him around, anyway, being his guardian angel, watching over him when you're supposed to be concentrating on killing Germans. That's what you're up there for, you know, not to protect the squadron idiot."

"I got a Fokker Wednesday," Amos pointed out.

"So you did. So you did, in your usual efficient style, and I commended you for it at the time. But you only went after that Fokker because your simple-minded white brother was about to become the Fokkee. I was there, remember?"

Amos remembered. Lucas had flamed the leading Fokker before anyone else had even begun to react, and damaged another, which Yancey had finished off, minutes later.

"God damn it, Ninekiller," Lucas said, "I've told you every way I can: there's no more time for the old humanitarian bullshit. This is the Twentieth Century. Time to throw out all those weakling notions that were never anything but prettied-up lies. We're entering a world where the only rules are the old hard ones of survival or destruction and the only kinds of people are winners and losers. Moore was a loser. So is Cobb. You'd better decide which you want to be."

Amos said tonelessly, "If that's all? Sir?"

Lucas sighed. "All right, Ninekiller. If that's the way you want it." He swung around in his chair, turning his back. "Get out of here."

It was still dark next morning when Amos awakened and groped his way to the mess for a cup of coffee and a couple of undersized eggs. They had been starting early lately, trying to get across the lines and into German territory before the sun was high, hoping to get a favorable position with the sun behind them before the first enemy planes appeared.

Yancey was already there, holding a cup of coffee under his nose and sniffing the steam. Beside him, Cobb was working his way enthusiastically through an enormous breakfast: eggs, biscuits, enough bacon and sausage to account for a small herd of pigs, even grits on the side. Amos shook his head in wonder. "How the hell can you eat like that at this hour?"

Cobb grinned, chewing. "This is about when I always got up back home," he said, after a mighty and visible swallow. "Heck, we had to milk the cows and all like that."

Yancey looked at him with red-rimmed eyes. "Where are you from, anyway?"

"Sugar Grove, North Carolina," Cobb said proudly. "I love this food, though. I could eat it just about any time. These niggers can really cook, can't they?"

Yancey buried his face in his coffee mug, muttering indistinctly. Amos said to Cobb, "You don't drink coffee, do you?"

"Naw. My church, we don't believe in drinking coffee or liquor or smoking cigarettes. My grandma dips snuff," he admitted, "but Daddy says it's all right because she's too old to change. Daddy's a preacher," Cobb added. "Holy Ghost Apostolic Tabernacle In Christ."

"Don't think I ever heard of it," Amos said politely.

"Daddy started it. Right now there's just the one."

Amos was saved from having to think of anything to say; Faulkner came in, along with the newest replacement, a Tennesseean named Blankenship who had transferred into fighters from an observation squadron. "Morning," Yancey grunted.

"Morning hell, this is the middle of the night," Faulkner grumbled. To the mess steward he said, "Just coffee. My God, Cobb, how can you do it?"

"Don't get him started," Yancey said hastily.

"This isn't so bad," Blankenship remarked. "We used to get up earlier than this when there was a big artillery shoot scheduled. I'm just getting used to only flying one patrol a day. They kept us in the air as steadily as they could get us refueled and pointed east.''

"What were you flying?" Yancey asked curiously.

"B.E. 2c's. Flimsy old pieces of shit," Blankenship said with feeling. "So slow you could just about get one to hover in one place with a headwind. One machine gun, set up so the observer couldn't possibly hit anything with it.''

"B.E. 2c's? Christ, I didn't know anybody but the Limeys were crazy enough to fly those things.''

"I think we were the only Confederate outfit to have them. Rumor was we inherited them from a British squadron that converted to Sopwith One-and-a-half Strutters.''

Yancey nodded. "Probably the only pilots ever to be glad to get into Strutters, then. Even the old Fokker monoplanes used to eat them for breakfast.''

"I guess our Nieuports look pretty good to you," Amos offered.

"You better believe it. The old B.E. might be good enough to train a virgin pilot on. In a fight it's as out of place as a queer in a whorehouse.''

"Speaking of whorehouses," Faulkner said, "did you hear about the new girl at Dixie Land? Supposedly she—''

"Shut up, Bill," Yancey said crossly. "I woke up with a hardon that wouldn't go down. Makes it hell trying to get into a flying suit. Don't get me going again.''

Cobb was turning bright red. Faulkner said, "Oh oh. We're embarrassing Cobb.''

"Don't mind me," Cobb said stiffly. "I just wonder how you men would feel if your mothers could hear the way you talk.''

There was a short silence, while nobody looked at anyone else. Finally Blankenship got out a pack of cigarettes and offered them around. "Smoke?''

Yancey and Faulkner accepted cigarettes. Amos tilted his head in polite refusal. Cobb said, "Those things are bad for you, you know.''

"What the hell," Blankenship said, "so what if they are? You really think any of us will live long enough to die from smoking?''

"The Germans can't hurt me," Cobb said seriously, "unless it's the Lord's will."

There was another pause in the conversation. Faulkner made a considerable operation out of lighting his cigarette.

"Well," Yancey said finally, "they're not holding the war up for us. Let's go do it."

They took off and flew through near-darkness, keeping formation by the reddish flares of their exhausts. They met the first sunlight as they crossed the lines at eleven thousand feet, still climbing. The sky was clear except for a few small patches of cloud just to the north. A few shells burst well below them, fuses set far too early, the gunners thrown off by the tricky light.

They crossed the Bapaume-Peronne road, where men and horses and wagons already streamed along toward the day's business. A little way beyond, they swung in a great arc toward the northeast and then north. Amos scanned the sky in all directions, his eyes flicking from side to side, up and down, his neck constantly in motion—that was why the pilots all wore silk scarves; the alternative was a chafed and bleeding neck from the steady friction against the collar—as they swept over the German-held fields and villages. Ahead and to his left, Yancey's Nieuport hung on the morning wind, with Faulkner tucked neatly into position off the Flight Leader's right wing. Amos could see their heads, too, rotating and swiveling above the open cockpits, their goggles occasionally catching a flash of the bright early sun.

To the rear, Blankenship flew a graceful weaving pattern, covering the flight's collective tail. Amos saw him only in brief glimpses, but he knew Blankenship was on the job, with that intense alertness learned in over a year of flying hopelessly slow, virtually unarmed observation aircraft in hostile skies.

And, off to Amos's right, Cobb plodded doggedly onward, trusting whatever inscrutable God his father served. As far as Amos could tell, Cobb took no more than a tourist's interest in his surroundings. Once, when Amos glanced his way, Cobb raised a hand in a friendly wave.

They were almost at their point of maximum penetration, about to turn for home, when they saw the two fast-moving little flecks in the distance, sliding westward across the patchwork landscape. Rumpler two-seaters, headed for the front, down around eight thousand feet or so. . . . Yancey was swinging his arm and pointing, but Amos had already seen the eight Albatros fighters that hung above the Rumplers, strung out abreast and climbing steadily.

There was a methodical look to the whole setup; the Germans were clearly up to something, and it was not hard to guess what. The Rumplers were too low for effective observation work, but they would make splendid bait for any fighter patrol, with the Albatroses waiting to slam down from above.

Yancey waved, signaling. C Flight wheeled, putting the sun at their backs, and nosed down steeply, their engines howling excitedly into the wind. Just before they got in range an Albatros pilot twisted around and saw them and yanked his plane over into a dive, and the other Germans began to break, but C Flight was on them like a quintet of angry wasps.

Amos had his sights on an Albatros but the German broke hard to the right as Amos fired, the .303 bullets nibbling harmlessly at the fabric of the graceful wings. Cursing, Amos yanked the stick back and climbed sharply into a chandelle turn, to come back down in a second attack. He was vaguely aware that he had lost Cobb at some point, but there was nothing to be done about that now.

The German formation had broken up into singles and pairs, the bright-painted Albatroses whirling and milling about under the shock of the surprise attack. Amos saw an Albatros going down, smoking, but there was no time to wonder who had done that one; the air was full of roaring airplanes and popping bullets. Discipline and tactics forgotten, the Confederates and the Germans slashed madly at each other like crazed razor fighters.

A red-nosed Albatros was coming almost head-on at Amos, its nose guns flickering. Amos hauled the stick back, standing the Nieuport on its tail. As the German shot by underneath and the Nieuport began to lose speed, Amos kicked hard right rudder and laid the stick over and dropped into a stall turn to latch on to the Albatros's tail.

The German pilot jinked hard left and right, trying to throw Amos off, but he did it a shade too regularly; Amos found the rhythm, waited till the big Iron-Crossed rudder banged the other way for a zigzag, and fired. There was no immediate reaction, but then the Albatros began to weave oddly. The pilot seemed to be having trouble with the controls.

Amos fired again. The German pilot jerked convulsively in his cockpit and Amos thought he had killed him, but he sat up again, still fighting the controls. A long flame licked back from the engine. The Albatros burst into a bright smoke-trailed blaze and headed earthward.

He pulled up in a climbing turn, checking his tail. There was nothing after him for the moment, but he saw that two Albatroses were chasing a Nieuport off to his right. He kicked over and fired a long burst at extreme range, meant only to throw the Germans' aim off, and then half-rolled and went after the nearest Albatros in a tight inside pursuit curve. The range closed and Amos steadied the Nieuport and fired carefully, leading the German and letting him fly through the pattern. The Albatros staggered visibly and fell off in a spin, smoking.

Amos watched, considered following it down to finish it off, but remembered that pilots often got killed that way. He saw, then, that a pair of Albatroses were coming at him. He fired hastily at the nearest one, missed, and put the Nieuport into a flat spin as 7.92mm. bullets cut the air where he had been.

The sky and the ground whirled sickeningly as the Nieuport spun downward, the horizon turning at crazy angles, while Amos fought to keep his stomach contents down. Pulling out of the spin at last, he found that he had left the dogfight, which had now spread out all over the sky above him.

He was about to start climbing back toward the action when he saw, just below him and a little to his right, the two Rumpler two-seaters that the Albatroses had been covering.

The observers opened fire on him with their rear-mounted guns as he moved in, setting up a professional and very dangerous crossfire as they covered each other. He dropped back and dived under the nearest Rumpler, coming up beneath its pale-blue belly and pulling the Travis gun down on its swinging mount for an upward shot.

The other Rumpler tilted its wings sharply as its pilot tried to give his observer a clear shot at the Nieuport, but Amos kept the first two-seater in the line of fire, denying the observer a clear shot. He aimed the Travis gun upward at a 45-degree angle, like a duelist's pistol, and fired, the .303 bullets stitching a long line down the length of the Rumpler's underside.

The Travis gun snapped empty and Amos pulled hastily away, followed by streams of bullets and, no doubt, imprecations. As he yanked the empty drum from the machine gun and banged a new one into place, he saw the first Rumpler slanting steeply downward in a power dive. The observer seemed to be trying frantically to reach the pilot, who was slumped down in his cockpit. Amos watched as the two-seater plowed into the ground far below, the impact inaudible at this distance, the brief fountain of earth and smoke only a minor detail against the broad French plain.

The other Rumpler had gone down close to the ground now, barely clearing the trees, where it would be dangerous to follow. Amos watched it flee eastward and felt no particular desire to do anything about it.

Looking around, he saw that he was now pretty much alone. He aimed the Nieuport back toward the lines, wondering how the others had made out.

But as he approached the front he saw another aircraft a little way to the south and made for it, thinking it might be one of C Flight's Nieuports.

It wasn't; it was a lone German two-seater, a DFW, almost certainly on an artillery observation mission. Suspecting a trap, Amos scanned the sky carefully, but there were no fighters anywhere in the area. The DFW's crew did not seem to have spotted him.

He looked at the two-seater for a moment and considered letting it go. But then he remembered the artillery bombardment he had endured, and the Confederate infantrymen who had rescued him, and he put the stick over and started down.

At the last instant the DFW's observer woke up and fired a wild burst at the oncoming Nieuport, but by then the pilot was already dead and the engine on fire.

And that, Amos decided as he watched the DFW smash into the black mud of No Man's Land, would definitely have to be enough for one day.

Back at the field there was pandemonium. Men ran toward his plane from all directions, even before he had rolled to a stop. As he dropped to the ground, hands pounded his back and shoulders. Yancey appeared in front of him, poking him in the ribs, a huge grin spread over his weathered flat face.

"Two Krauts in one fight," Yancey said happily, "or maybe three, we can't get confirmation yet on that one you took off Bill's ass. But you got the other Albatros and the Rumpler for sure."

Amos said, "I got another one on the way back." He wondered why he bothered telling anyone about it; it didn't seem important. At the moment nothing seemed very important. "Another two-seater, a DFW. Up at the front."

"Holy shit." Yancey looked around. "Somebody get on the phone and see if any of the front-line units can confirm. Ought to be easy enough."

Amos said, "Is everybody all right?"

"Yeah, yeah, we all got back okay. Blankenship got a little nick on his leg but it's nothing. Few holes in my plane and Bill's. Man, we're the big heroes right now," Yancey said. "I got an Albatros, Bill got one too—he's waited long enough for that—and Blankenship may have gotten a third, that's another one we can't confirm. And then you with your one-man massacree. Hot damn."

"Cobb?"

"Lumbered through the whole thing, seems like, blind as a bat. Said everything just happened so *fast*." Yancey laughed. "Armorer says he fired off half a drum, but he probably did that by accident. And not a single hole in his plane. Maybe he's right about God looking out for him. I always heard he watches over idiots."

Yancey shook his head and clapped Amos on the shoulder. "Jesus Christ, that was the God-damnedest fight I *ever* saw."

"Incredible, Ninekiller," Lucas said. "Absolutely incredible. I'm genuinely impressed. And I'm not a man who impresses all that easily, as you may have noticed."

He leaned back and regarded Amos almost fondly. "I was starting to wonder about you, Ninekiller. Thought maybe I'd misjudged you. But you came through, didn't you? Four enemy aircraft in one day. In one *patrol*. Two of them fighters, too. Not bad at all."

Amos said, "At least one unconfirmed, so far."

"Details, details." Lucas made brushing-away motions. "We'll worry about that later. Even if—"

There were footsteps in the orderly room next door, and sudden voices. Lucas said, "Ah. I believe that may be someone I've been waiting for. . . ."

The door opened and Gabriel Cassidy walked in. "Jim," he said to Lucas. "Your phone call caught me just about to leave for the front. Good thing I was so close."

To Amos he said, "Lieutenant Ninekiller. Congratulations. Four enemy airplanes in a single patrol. Hard to imagine it."

Amos said again, "Only two confirmed—"

Cassidy swung around to look at Lucas. "Is that true?"

"Relax, Gabe. We'll get confirmation, one way or another. If worst comes to worst, we can pull a few strings, exert a little pressure." He looked from Cassidy to Amos and back again, smiling sardonically. "Right now Headquarters wants something like this as bad as we do. For one thing, morale's been lousy ever since the Krauts hit us with the new planes. Ninekiller just proved it's possible to kick their asses in, with the aircraft we've got right now."

Cassidy nodded, looking relieved. "As long as it can be fixed. I can print almost any fantastic crap I want, but they're sticky about reporting a pilot's score—I can't go beyond the official count."

He rubbed his hands together, pacing the floor. "Man, man, this is going to make one hell of a story. Indian aviator downs four Huns in one flight—a little trick wording, it'll sound like he did it in one fight.''

Lucas said, ''Is this a record? I don't remember anyone else doing it, but you keep up with these things better than I do.''

Cassidy looked thoughtful. ''Well, let's see. That Englishman, Ball, may possibly have gotten four in a day—the Brits will probably claim he did, anyway, they've just about made it official that he walks on water and his shit doesn't stink. Nungesser or Guynemer, perhaps; I'm not up on French pilots.''

''Doesn't matter,'' Lucas said. ''Nobody gives a damn about them anyway.''

''Then there's the other side—Immelmann could have pulled off a quadruple, back when the Fokkers were the only fighters in the world with forward-firing guns. But he's dead . . . there's supposed to be a new Hun pilot, some sort of nobleman, flies an all-red Albatros, but I'm pretty sure he hasn't done anything like this yet.''

Cassidy smiled at Amos. ''But in the Confederate Flying Corps, I'm fairly certain it's never been done. You're the first, Ninekiller.''

Amos said, ''Technically, I'm not in the Confederate Flying Corps.''

''Technically, technically, my ass.'' Cassidy waved his hands impatiently. ''Technically you're not even here. Who cares? Of course,'' he said to Lucas, ''it might be better if he were white, especially from some respected old Confederate family. Or even a pine-hill cracker, we could make pretty good poor-but-honest-patriot material out of that. But the Indian angle will work fine, and I've already laid the groundwork with that feature piece.''

He raised an eyebrow significantly. ''And, of course, we'll be sure the readers know he did it all under the leadership and guidance of a certain outstanding Confederate officer.''

''Of course,'' Amos said, deadpan.

Lucas grinned cheerfully at him. ''Go ahead, Ninekiller, mock away. You can't ruin this for me, it's too damn good.''

Cassidy said, "Now what about medals? You've got to get him something good, Jim. And not only for now—when the time comes, I'll be able to tell the readers how many medals were won by the pilots in your command. Reflected glory and all."

"Well," Lucas said, "of course the French will want to give him the Croix de Guerre—"

"Jesus Christ, Jim." Cassidy looked annoyed. "Of *course* he'll get the Croix de Guerre, I'll fix that myself. Hell, the French hand out the Croix de Guerre the way the Heinies hand out the Iron Cross—the only way to avoid getting one is to desert and fight for the other side. I'm talking about serious medals," Cassidy said. "What can we get for him? The Southern Cross?"

Lucas rubbed his jawline. "I don't know, Gabe. If it was a white man, in a minute. But I don't think they'd give it to an Indian. Hell, there's probably a regulation says you have to be white to get it."

"There's a regulation," Cassidy pointed out, "that says you have to be white to be an officer in the Confederate Army."

"Yeah, but as he says, he's not, really. And that's another thing, I don't think you can give the Southern Cross to anybody but a Confederate citizen. I'll see what I can do," Lucas said. "The Medal of Valor, maybe. Or the new Distinguished Aviator's Star. You sound out your friends at Headquarters, work on it from that end."

Amos said, "Don't I have anything to say about this?"

They looked at him. Lucas said affably, "Not a thing, Ninekiller. As one pilot to another, you've got my respect. But right now you're also something we can use."

"Besides," Cassidy added, "it'll be good for your own people. Who, I understand, could use some good publicity right now."

"Let me guess," Amos said. "At least once, in this piece, you're going to use the words 'a credit to his race.'"

Cassidy laughed. "Jim said you were a quick study. Now let's see—shall I use the same photo as before, or get Loudermilk back up here for a fresh one—"

* * *

That night the mess went mad. Bourbon and beer and brandy flowed more than copiously; glasses crashed into, or at least near, the fireplace, and stewards sweated and gasped as they ran to try to keep up with the demands for refills. The air grew downright viscous with tobacco smoke. One of the replacements, a fat boy from Florida named Weaver, claimed to be able to play the piano; with shouts and ragged cheers, the piano was dragged from the corner where it had rested since Lahaie's departure, and Weaver sat down and began pounding the keys with really spectacular imprecision. A couple of pilots began trying to sing, their efforts hampered somewhat by their failure to agree on what tune Weaver was playing. Nobody else seemed to mind.

Hill dropped a lighted cigarette on his lap, burning a hole in his butternut trousers before anyone noticed the smoke. Shoemaker grabbed a pitcher of beer and poured it over the endangered area as Hill leaped to his feet. Enraged, Hill swung wildly and then grappled with Shoemaker as both men rolled under the table. Minutes later they were sharing another pitcher of beer, passing it back and forth and drinking directly from it, while Hill began a long tearful story about his mother.

At the corner table Amos looked at Faulkner. "The Children's Hour," he offered.

Uncharacteristically, Faulkner did not rise. "Uh huh," he said absently, and took a drag on his cigarette. The ash tray in front of him was choked with butts. Amos had lost track of how many drinks the Mississippian had had. His face looked very tired.

Amos said, "You all right, Bill?"

Faulkner shrugged, blew out his breath in a long uneven sigh. "Sure. Hell, I'm fine." His voice was flat. "Got me a German today. I'm a God-damned hero. Not as big a one as you, of course, but a hero. Don't you see me celebrating?" He raised his glass and drained it. "Innkeeper, another of the same."

"It's eating you?" Amos said quietly. "The German you shot down?"

"You could say that. My first," he said, looking at a point just past Amos's eyes. "Been here over a year, flew more patrols than you've had women, Amos old aboriginal sport, and never before actually got one of my own. Shot *at* a good many, knocked bits and pieces off here and there—who knows, maybe one of the poor bastards crashed later on with no one to see it. But this was the first I got to see go in."

He got out a pack of cigarettes and put one between his lips. "Got a match?"

"You've already got a smoke going," Amos pointed out. "About to fall off the table there."

"Oh. Sorry. Don't want to see a good smoke go up in smoke, eh? That's reserved for the dear old German." He retrieved his cigarette and clipped it between his lips, putting on an expression of desperate jauntiness. "Also known as the Hun, the Boche, the Kraut, Heinie, Fritz, Jerry—did I leave any out? How do you say 'Germans' in Cherokee, Amos?"

"*An'dachi.*" Amos lifted his own glass. "Probably comes from hearing white people call Germans 'Dutch'—'*ani*' means a people, a tribe."

"Ah. Well, here's to the *An'dachi.*" Faulkner slurred the word badly, not taking his cigarette out of his mouth. He looked into his empty glass. "Shit, I can't drink to the enemy until I get something to drink. Very important, drinking to the gallant foe," he said, waving for a steward. "Tradition of us glorious birdmen, you know. Gentlemanly as all hell. When not frying each other in flaming gasoline."

"He burned?" Amos set his glass back down without drinking. "The one today?"

"Like a Roman candle on Robert E. Lee's Birthday." Faulkner looked straight at him. Amos realized suddenly that the eyes in the lined young face were wholly and terribly sober. "Lucas was right about that plywood fuselage, you know. Blazes right up, with the pilot in the middle. Very festive effect. The Spanish Inquisition would have been impressed. Regular auto-da-fé in the sky."

Amos could think of nothing to say.

"And they call you a killer and a savage," Faulkner said, "for shooting at the pilot. Christ, you're the most humane man here."

Amos shook his head and reached again for his own drink. "I got a flamer today," he said. "Then there was that two-seater. The observer was alive, all the way to the ground, with a dead pilot for company. I'm not too happy about that one either."

A steward appeared with another drink. Faulkner took it with faintly trembling hands. "I'll be all right," he said, seeing Amos's face. "Just the first time, you know."

He downed a large swallow and set the glass on the table with both hands. "I wouldn't mind so much," he said, "if it meant anything. But Christ, Amos, even granting that the war has any purpose in itself—let's not get into *that* one just now—what the hell does killing one man accomplish?"

His eyes took on a slightly dreamy expression. "Now," he said, "if that were Kaiser Bill in front of your gun, or the Emperor Franz Josef—or, by God, the Czar of Russia or the King of England or even—" He gave Amos a foxy look. "Don't worry, I'm not going to say it. Although who'd hear me in this din, I'd like to know."

There was a crash and a thud from a far corner of the room, and the splintering sounds of a chair breaking. Someone gave a wordless yell.

Standing beside the piano, Blankenship sang:

> *"Oh I wish I had someone to love me,*
> *Someone who would be mine alone,*
> *Oh I wish I had someone to play with,*
> *Cause I'm tired of playing with my own."*

"On the other hand," Faulkner said, "one of your own Albatri perished in a very fine cause, namely keeping one William Faulkner alive. In the general confusion I seem to have forgotten to thank you. He was getting unconscionably close."

Amos inclined his head. "Glad to oblige."

Eubanks's voice cut through the racket: "Weaver, what

did you do with the money your mama gave you for piano lessons?''

Blankenship sang:

> *"Just before the battle, Mother,*
> *I was drinking mountain dew,*
> *When I saw the Yankees coming,*
> *To the rear I swiftly flew."*

Faulkner stood up. "I think I'm going to bed now. To sleep, perchance to dream—but Christ, I hope not. Not tonight."

11

"AND THEN," Amos said to Sam Harjo and Mary Wildcat, "this French General or Field Marshal or whatever he was, with the white mustache and the eyepatch—with absolutely no warning, he grabbed me and kissed me on both cheeks. My God, why didn't somebody warn me so I'd be ready for it?"

Mary Wildcat was laughing uncontrollably, wiping her eyes. Sam Harjo said, "Yes, yes, the custom does come as something of a surprise to a stranger. I remember it was the same for me."

Amos said skeptically, "You got the Croix de Guerre too?"

Harjo shrugged. "Little affair in North Africa, in the Legion. Fort Zinderneuf, that was the name of the place. Very strange business." He raised his glass and sniffed. "What a perfectly execrable Pinot. Mary, inform Raoul that this simply will not do. The wine improves or his wife gets those letters, *toute suite*."

"The breath," Amos said, shuddering in recollection. "That old man's breath when he kissed me. Like some sort

160

of small animal crawled into his mouth and died. They should have given me one of those new gas masks.''

Sam Harjo looked thoughtful. ''You know, it's only been a couple of weeks since your quadruple victory. That's pretty fast even for the Croix de Guerre—not to belittle your accomplishment, Amos, but Cassidy was right, they have been rather casual about handing them out lately. Two weeks? And a full award ceremony here in Paris, with a flag-rank officer making the presentation, for an ordinary Croix de Guerre? I think I detect the fine hand of Mr. Cassidy in this.''

''He did imply he had connections,'' Amos admitted.

''Well, nothing new about that. Even in the so-called War of Southern Independence, the people who handed out the decorations—on both sides—were widely known to be hand-in-hand with the gentry of the press. Never mind,'' Harjo said. ''Believe me, our people back home can make good use of this sort of thing. It may soon be that the people of the Confederacy will need to be reminded that Indians fought at their side.''

''Cassidy was there,'' Amos said. ''At the ceremony. Had that Goddamned photographer with him, taking pictures— oh, my God, if there's a picture of that old goat kissing me I'll kill him. . . .'' He ground his teeth and gulped his wine. ''And then the bastard had the gall to come around afterward and ask how long it was going to be before I got the other two.''

Mary Wildcat wrinkled her nose. ''Other two what?''

''That's what I said. What Cassidy wants,'' Amos said, ''is for me to get two more kills so he can run the headline NINEKILLER LIVES UP TO HIS NAME. Says he's already got most of it written—fill in the details and file it and presto, another attention-grabber. I quote,'' Amos added, ''more or less directly.''

''My God,'' Mary Wildcat said. ''He wants you to go kill two more people just so he can get a cute headline?''

Amos nodded. ''That's about the size of it. I said some things, I don't remember the exact wording, and he just gave me that cynical grin and walked away. I know one more I'd be glad to kill," he said, "only I don't think they count *yoneg* reporters."

Sam Harjo cleared his throat and lifted his glass. "Never mind the sordid ancillary details. After all, we too have a tradition of honoring the warrior. To Lieutenant Amos Nine-killer," he said, "the most decorated officer in the Cherokee Flying Corps."

Mary Wildcat said, "There's something we've got to get straight."

"It's already straight," Amos said in a slightly strained voice. "If it gets any straighter it's going to be painful. I mean, just *look*——"

"Not that. Well, in a minute. Amos," she said, "I don't want you thinking I'm doing this because you got that medal."

It was close to midnight. Sam Harjo had gone off to see his dancer again. They had not gone upstairs this time; they lay naked on the rug in the parlor, in front of the small fireplace. The dying coals cast reddish highlights on their skins.

"Men always think women get excited over heroes and all that stuff," she said. "Maybe some women do. Not me, Amos . . . ohhh, that's nice, but wait a minute . . . Amos," she said sharply, "I don't want you taking chances, getting yourself killed, doing something you think is going to impress me."

"I'll try to remember." His voice was muffled.

"You do whatever you feel like you have to do," she said. "Go kill all the Germans single-handed, or give these *yonegs* back their airplane and walk away from the whole thing, it's all the same to me. Amos, stop that." Her breathing became ragged. "No, not yet. Do that last part some more. . . ."

"Balloons," Yancey said. "Jesus Christ. Not balloons again."

"Headquarters was very explicit. They want balloons," Lucas said. "Specifically," his finger tapped the map, "they want this one here."

"God," Faulkner groaned. "First the bastards get fighters that make ours look like cheap box kites. Now our own people want us to commit suicide going after balloons again. This is Hell, nor am I out of it. . . ."

Yancey said seriously, "Major, those things were the most dangerous targets in France even when they were only covered by ground fire and the old Fokkers. If they've got Albatroses watching over them too—"

"Save the arguments," Lucas said. "Headquarters isn't listening. It's all-out war on balloons, effective now—they've decided the reason their grand plans of attack keep failing is that the Krauts are detecting all their movements from the observation balloons. And this one in particular," he indicated the map again, "is in fact in a peculiarly nasty position. You can see for yourselves; the observers have a perfect view of all the key areas in that sector."

"Which means," Blankenship pointed out, "the Krauts know it too, and they'll have this one protected like the crown jewels of Germany. Why don't we just go after the Kaiser in person? Be just as safe."

"All very true," Lucas agreed. "And all completely irrelevant. Orders, as the Krauts say, are orders."

His mouth twisted sourly at the corners. "Son of a bitch. Here we are in the second decade of the Twentieth Century, and we're having to fuck around with observation balloons. Christ, Stonewall Jackson used the damned things in the siege of Washington, didn't he? It's stupid, but there it is."

He smiled slightly at them. "And it's what you get for being heroes. This squadron has distinguished itself lately— some of us more than others," he said with a glance at Amos, "but our overall scores have also impressed Headquarters. Seems they figure the Fourth Virginia is the obvious outfit to wipe out the balloon menace."

Faulkner looked at Amos. "See what a mess you've gotten us into."

"Now I've read the reports on your last balloon-busting effort," Lucas said, "just before I assumed command, and the tactics were simply idiotic. Two flights coming in, one after the other, from the same direction—at low level at that—I'm amazed any of you survived. One flight is enough, or else it can't be done at all. In fact two planes should be able to do the job, but we won't go that far yet.

"C Flight," he said, "will go after the balloon, using the ground-level approach. It would be better if you could dive straight down at the balloon from above—the balloon blocks the ground fire off, that way—but these Nieuports won't take that kind of vertical dive. If we had Sopwiths or something . . . but, as they say back home, if a frog had wings he wouldn't bump his ass when he lands."

"What do we use," Yancey said, "gunfire?"

"Oh, sure. Those Le Prieur rockets aren't worth a damn. I think rockets are going to be a major aerial weapon some day, but they'll have to do better than those silly things. Now," Lucas said, "as you go in, A and B Flights will be up at altitude, covering you. Each of you, as soon as you've finished your run on the target, climb up and help cover the others."

He gave them his predatory look. "With any luck," he said, "we'll flame the balloon and get a few Albatroses as well."

Yancey said, "Beg the Major's pardon—"

"Horse shit," Lucas said. "Spit it out, Jack."

"You said 'we,'" Yancey said. "Does that mean you're coming?"

"Oh, certainly." Lucas smiled warmly at them. "I'll be up above with the covering flights, watching the whole thing. Wouldn't miss this for the world."

When Faulkner was asleep, Amos got quietly out of his bunk and pulled on his uniform trousers and blouse. Kneeling, he reached under his bunk and pulled out his old leather kit bag. Groping in the darkness, he pawed aside socks and scarves and letters until at last his hands found what they were looking for.

Still barefooted, moving in total silence, he eased out the door and down the corridor. There was a full moon and the damp grass of the airfield shone like silver powder beyond the hangars. The guards were easy to evade; in minutes he had cleared the far fence and was moving through the trees beyond the end of the field. The leaves and grasses felt soft and pleasant beneath his bare feet. It was very quiet.

When he had put enough distance between himself and the airfield, he sat down and untied the thongs that bound the small buckskin bundle his grandfather had given him.

He had never opened it before, but he had a fair idea what it contained; he fingered the contents, lifted a few items to his nose and sniffed, and nodded to himself. Leaving the buckskin spread out on the ground with its contents piled in the middle, he stood up and removed his clothes.

Squatting, he cleared a little space on the ground and made a tiny heap of dry twigs. It took a few tries to get a spark from the flint and steel in the bundle—he had not done this in years—but at last a small flame licked up, throwing sudden red lights across his hands and face. He grunted unconsciously and reached for the things on the buckskin.

A sprig of cedar went on the little fire, just as the flame was almost out. As the cedar sparked and sputtered, Amos laid a bit of white sage, from the Cimarron country, across it. Thick aromatic smoke began to curl upward in the darkness. Amos began to sing softly, a high-pitched ancient song without words.

Singing, he fanned the smoke over himself, fanning with his hands, holding his hands repeatedly in the heart of the smoke and rubbing them together as if washing. He turned slowly in the smoke, letting it touch him all over, as he continued to sing.

At last he bent again to the bundle. His fingers found the long buckskin-thong loop and, suspended from it, the little bag of soft thin hide. The bag was not much bigger than his thumb. It was tied tightly at the neck; he did not open it. He did not know what it contained; he was not supposed to know.

Singing without pause, he hung the thong loop around his neck, feeling the little bag resting against his chest, almost weightless. It felt very warm, almost as if it gave off an internal heat of its own. He put his hand over it for a moment and whispered briefly in Cherokee.

The bundle also contained a small pouch of tobacco: good

Carolina tobacco, the native plant, grown from seeds carried by the people all the way from the eastern homeland, carefully cultivated in the hill soil of the new Nation ever since. He had no pipe, but it was not important. He blew the fire to life again and put the tobacco on it in a little mound, singing again, fanning the smoke to the four directions with his hands.

Then he simply sat there, for quite a long while, staring into the darkness, so still that a field mouse ran across the little clearing without noticing him. Finally he rose, put on his clothes, and padded silently back through the trees and across the field. The guards still did not see him.

There was little of the usual banter in the mess that morning; the pilots' faces were taut and gray over their coffee. Hardly anyone except Cobb and Weaver managed to eat anything, and Weaver seemed to stuff himself more from nervous compulsion than any real appetite.

Amos walked back to the pilots' quarters alone, not waiting for Faulkner. His flying outfit was already laid out on the bunk. There was a lot of it; it was still early fall, but already the air was painfully cold at any altitude at all.

He got into the clumsy fur-lined leather suit, dragging the stiff brown shell on over his uniform trousers and blouse, thinking that soon it would be necessary to add a couple of layers of wool underwear too. If the birds and plants of France were anything like those of the Cherokee hills, all the signs pointed to a brutally cold winter. . . . He pushed his feet into the tall flying boots, pulling the tops up over his thighs, and stood up and buckled on his wide belt with the holstered .45 revolver, wondering why he bothered. The saying among the pilots was that the gun was to shoot yourself if your aircraft was on fire, but Amos doubted whether anyone had actually done it. A big sheath knife, now, would be a useful thing to have, and he made a mental note to buy one next time he was in Paris—it might be good for getting clear of a wrecked plane, and if a downed pilot did have need of a weapon, it should be a silent one. . . .

Remembering, he rummaged among his personal kit and found the straight razor Tyrone had given him. He tucked it into the top of a boot, more as a kind of good-luck charm than anything else, and grinned at himself in the mirror.

Sweating already under the layers of leather and wool and fur, he started for the door as Faulkner came in. Faulkner said, "Christ, why wear all that stuff? We're going in at zero altitude."

"But we'll be climbing up to eleven thousand afterward," Amos pointed out. "And it's cold up there."

"I can stand it. We'll be heading home by then." Faulkner pulled on a long leather coat with a fleece collar, wrapped a silk scarf about his neck, picked up his helmet and goggles and gloves, and said, "That'll do. If I go down and have to get out of a burning wreck, I don't want anything slowing me down. Certainly not that damn cannon."

They walked together out of the field. A and B Flights were already in their planes, warming up the engines, mechanics crouched against the propeller blast as they held on to the wingtips. C Flight was to leave slightly later, to give the others time to climb to their covering altitude. It was hoped that the covering flights, by arriving first, would distract German attention while C Flight came in at treetop level.

They watched while A and B Flights took off, the gray Nieuports flitting through the dim light like shadows, the racket of their engines the only substantial thing about them. Lucas led, lifting off with a grace that almost made the thing look easy. Then Shoemaker, Eubanks, Barnett. . . . Weaver did something awkward as he began his roll and almost ground-looped, but he got it straightened out at the last second and wobbled off after the others. Yancey said, "Son of a bitch flies the way he plays piano. Wonder how he ever got them to let him in flight school, fat as he is."

"His daddy's a banker in St. Augustine," Blankenship said. "He pretty much admitted there were some bribes involved."

Captain Clay stood holding a watch. As the last Nieuport vanished eastward he moved his lips silently, looking at the dial.

They stood shifting from one foot to another, waiting. Blankenship sang softly:

"When John Henry was a little baby,
No bigger than the palm of yo' hand,
He jumped off his high chair and busted his head,
Said, John Henry gonna be a fighter pilot man,
  Lawd, Lawd,
John Henry gonna be a fighter pilot man."

Captain Clay said, "It's time."

Down low, the light was still dim, the hollows and dips of the landscape holding pools of near-darkness. It was a dangerous time to be hedgehopping; it was difficult to judge heights and distances, and easy to miss a tree or a steeple until it was too late.

And there was more to have to miss now, Amos realized. The lines had moved eastward through the last couple of months, the Germans yielding gradually and grudgingly to the constant pressure of Allied attacks, and in consequence they were now flying over land that had not yet felt the full effects of steady bombardment. There were actual trees, not just soggy splintered trunks but whole groves of living, leaf-clad trees, and hedges and bushes and patches of green. It was pleasant to see, but nasty to fly over at this height; Amos wasn't used to treetop-level missions that included real treetops. A couple of times he thought he felt branches brush his wheels.

They flew in twos, Yancey and Faulkner side by side in the lead, then Amos and Cobb—who was, surprisingly, managing the tricky flying without too much trouble—and Blankenship bringing up the rear. The old line-ahead attack, Lucas had pointed out, ensured that the last men would be shot at by gunners who were fully alert and ready. More than two abreast, on the other hand, would get in each other's way.

Amos saw the balloon now, a small oblong black spot against the lightening sky, growing very fast as the distance closed. It was still on its way up, he noticed; they must just now be sending it aloft. He raised his free hand to his chest and pressed for a second, feeling the small warm lump of the little bag.

Now the balloon was a great fat obscene thing blotting out the morning sky, the three inflated vanes at its tail holding it steady in the breeze. Amos could see the basket dangling beneath, where the observers rode with their telescopes and maps and telephone, and their parachutes that they might be using soon—unlike the Confederate and British pilots, whose High Command considered that parachutes might tempt them to acts of cowardice. Now he could even see the steel cable that tethered the balloon in place.

Yancey's Nieuport tilted its nose sharply upward in a full-throttle zoom, aiming straight for the gasbag, while beside him Faulkner followed suit. As the two Nieuports rose into full view, the air in front of them exploded in sheets and billows of fire and smoke and metal. Amos could barely see them as they charged through the barrage, their wings rocking violently from the blasts. The sound rolled back to him, drowning out even the all-out bellow of his own engine. My God, he thought, this is worse than before, this is the worst yet. . . .

He hauled back the stick and watched his own engine cowling rise up and cover the belly of the balloon, the size of the target making the ring-and-post sights almost irrelevant. Out of the corner of his eye he saw that Cobb was still with him. At least, he thought, this is a target even Cobb can recognize. He gripped the stick and fingered the trigger, wishing he could take off his gloves and wipe the sweat from his hands and face, and then the first bursts of ground fire exploded all around him and it was impossible to think at all.

It was like being caught in a tornado, or diving into a huge waterfall. The enormous sound battered at him from all directions; shock waves slapped the Nieuport about like the paws of a great unseen cat in a playful mood. Something came through the side of the cockpit and the compass exploded in his face, drenching his flying suit with liquid. A shellburst under the tail almost wrenched the stick from his grasp. He felt the Nieuport shudder under various impacts and knew he was getting a beating, but it was impossible to know how bad it might be, and impossible to turn back now anyway. The gasbag swam into range and he opened fire, holding the trigger down and keeping the Nieuport pointed at the balloon almost to a collision: safer to wait till the last instant to pull up, so the balloon blocked some of the ground fire while the fighter climbed away. He thought for a moment that his wheels were actually rolling along the top of the huge gasbag.

Climbing away, using the balloon for cover but still hearing a few long shots searching for him, he looked back and saw Cobb and Blankenship rising after him. There was a big hole in Blankenship's upper right wing, but the damage didn't seem to be fatal. Cobb's appeared to be all right. Cobb's mouth was open.

The balloon was being hauled in. It did not appear to have suffered any serious damage. The gas had not ignited. As often happened, the explosive and incendiary bullets had simply flicked through the thin fabric envelope and out the other side without going off.

Yancey was waving his arm as the flight formed up on him, and Amos thought at first he was telling them to go around again, but then he looked up and saw the flashing specks in the sky overhead. The rest of the squadron was engaging enemy fighters, how many and what kind he could not tell. Yancey pointed upward and C Flight began to climb to join the action. Lucas, Amos thought, wasn't going to like this—undoubtedly he would say that they should have gone back for another pass at the balloon—but the hell with Lucas; nobody in the world ought to have to fly into that hellstorm a second time in the same day.

The Nieuport felt funny, the controls sluggish, though Amos couldn't see any major damage. Of course he had only a limited view of the aircraft, from the cockpit, and he wasn't about to stand up to have a better look. The engine, at least, was running smoothly, and there was no smell of gasoline.

An Albatros appeared, coming down at him on a head-on course, and he fired a quick burst to keep the German honest, half-rolling out of the way as the gaudily painted Albatros roared past at pistol-shot distance. More Albatroses were coming now, and a couple of Halberstadts, swarming in from above and all around, more enemy aircraft than Amos had ever seen at once. He snapped a burst at the nearest one and thought he might have hit it, but there was no chance to find out. A black-crossed shape rose into his sights and he steadied the Nieuport and triggered.

The Travis gun jammed.

Amos screamed "*Shit!*" and kicked the Nieuport into a spin as streams of fire came at him from above and behind and, it seemed, everywhere else. Supposedly you could clear a jammed Travis by pulling it down and hammering on its breech—he had no hammer, but the butt of his revolver might work—but trying that in the middle of a fight like this would be like trying to shoe a horse in the path of a buffalo stampede. The only chance of survival was to get clear of the whole scene, as fast as possible. . . .

Sky and earth blurred and the horizon canted and Amos's stomach threatened to mutiny. The Nieuport spun downward, an impossible target, obviously out of the fight anyway. The altimeter, Amos noticed, had been smashed. He watched the earth whirl up toward him, decided this was close enough, and hauled on the stick and kicked rudder to pull out of the spin.

The Nieuport declined to comply. In fact it began to spin harder. Amos could feel some sort of strange oscillation building in the controls; somewhere, part of the airplane was tearing itself to pieces. The green-and-brown blur of the ground was getting far too close. The engine started to shake and rattle.

Desperate, now, he kicked and yanked at the controls, trying everything he had ever heard of and then a few original ones. The Nieuport ignored his efforts completely. The controls felt slack and useless. He was tempted to simply push the stick forward and get it over with.

But he reversed the rudder bar and threw the stick over one more time, acting now out of no more than automatic random reflex, and the Nieuport suddenly slowed its rotations, leveled off, and straightened sluggishly into something resembling normal flight.

For a moment Amos sat still, getting his breath, afraid to move anything. The Nieuport was flying very strangely, one wing lower than the other, with a sort of crabwise yawing movement that suggested it would rather start spinning again. The engine was banging and missing now. Strips of fabric hung fluttering from the trailing edge of the upper wing.

But the airplane was still flying, more or less level. . . . Amos looked unthinkingly at the wrecked compass and then up at the sun, and realized that he was heading straight east, deeper into German territory with every shaky second.

A brief nervous experiment determined something else: the Nieuport wasn't going to turn around and go the other way. Only the single weird combination of stick and rudder positions kept it flying at all; the least deviation and it started trying to go into a spin once more.

For a couple of very long minutes Amos tried to decide what he should do. Keep going and try to regain control of the damaged Nieuport, in the hope of flying back? Or go ahead and try to land before he got any farther from home?

The engine solved the problem for him by stopping dead. Suddenly he was piloting a heavy and badly damaged glider.

The ground appeared fairly level, where he was heading, with large open fields dotted here and there with clumps of small trees. He could see no people at all. He braced himself as the earth came rapidly up to meet his battered airplane.

At the last second he realized he had not fastened his seat belt. There was no way to do it now; it was taking both hands on the stick to keep the Nieuport from dropping a wing and cartwheeling in.

There was a row of trees ahead of him, and a long narrow depression, perhaps a streambed, filled with underbrush and willows. He tried to turn to miss the trees but the Nieuport would not respond. He shut his eyes and put his head down and covered his face with his arms as the Nieuport's wheels hit the ground and bounced. The fuselage shot between a couple of trees, wiping the wings clean off on either side with a horrible splintering crackle. The wheels hit something and stopped and the nose went down and dug into the soft sod.

Amos was thrown violently from the cockpit, narrowly missing a tangle of wires and broken struts that would have decapitated him in another second. Flying through the air, he heard beneath and then behind him the sounds of the Nieuport breaking up; but then he smashed into the bushes and tumbled down the slope of the gully, and then something hit him hard on the head and the world flashed red and then went out.

12

WHEN AMOS regained consciousness the sun was shining directly on his face through a gap in the trees, and when he opened his eyes the sudden bright light made him blink and fling up an involuntary hand. His arm encountered twigs and leaves and then he remembered where he was and how he had gotten there. He froze, listening, for a little while, but there were no sounds except those of the wind and a couple of birds and, far away, a low grumble of artillery fire.

He was lying in a low thicket, his feet almost touching the dark water of a tiny sluggish stream. The ground beneath him was soft and mossy but not muddy; beside his face was a protruding root on which he guessed he must have struck his head. That was all he could see of his surroundings from where he lay.

Very slowly and cautiously, he sat up, raising his head until his eyes barely cleared the tops of the bushes. The movement sent ugly pains through his head for a moment and he winced slightly, but the pain went away after a second and he looked around, nerve-ends tingling, ready to duck back under the bushes.

But the area seemed deserted. He saw only the trees and

bushes and, sticking up nearby, the blackened remains of his airplane.

Getting to his feet, ignoring the fresh flashes of pain that drilled through his head, he waded through the streambank thicket that had broken his fall, the twigs scratching at his thigh-high flying boots with an unpleasant small sound. At the top of the embankment he stopped and looked around again, keeping close to a tree trunk, but there was no one.

The Nieuport had burned, standing on its nose; there was nothing left but a blackened pile of metal fittings and wires and charred bits of wood and, half-buried in the soft earth, the ruined engine. The machine gun was gone. Nearby, impaled on a tree, a ripped-off piece of wing remained unburned, but much of the fabric, including the big Stars-and-Bars insignia, had been stripped away.

Amos moved slowly about the immediate area, studying the ground. There were plenty of tracks and other signs to tell him the story. A patrol of infantry—troops on foot, anyway; he did not know much about German boots—about twenty in number, had come across the field to the crash site. They must have come for the specific purpose of investigating the crash, because they had gone back the way they had come. They had stood around the crash in a rough circle for several minutes—there were stamped-out cigarette butts to tell him that—and he guessed they had been watching it burn. They had made no attempt to search the area; possibly they had simply assumed the pilot must have burned up with the plane. An indentation in the soil, and a set of footprints that were deeper going away, showed him where the Travis gun had been ripped free in the crash, landed on the ground nearby, and been picked up by a soldier and carried away. A cluster of tracks indicated that stripping fabric from the piece of wing had been a popular activity. Amos shook his head and grinned to himself. Souvenir hunters always amused him.

He went back and looked at the wrecked Nieuport for a moment. Whatever arrangement the Cherokee Nation had with the Confederate Expeditionary Force, he hoped it didn't require them to pay for the airplanes he crashed. This was getting monotonous, and expensive.

His head still hurt, but it had settled down to a dull throbbing ache. He took off his gloves and fingered his scalp and forehead, but there did not seem to be any cuts. Well, his father had always said that you couldn't hurt a Cherokee by hitting him on the head.

Amos became aware that he was sweating profusely. Sitting down, he took off the boots and then peeled away the heavy flying suit with a feeling of enormous relief. He considered going barefoot, but it had been a long time and his feet were probably too soft for that now. Reluctantly, he put the boots back on. Standing, he buckled the pistol belt over his uniform; if nothing else, the heavy .45 might do to hit someone over the head with. Besides, if he came back without it, Lucas would probably make him pay for it.

He was about to move off, but then he gathered up the flying suit and the gloves and the leather helmet with its attached goggles, and pushed them all out of sight under the bushes. Other soldiers might come along, and there was no point in advertising the fact that a Confederate pilot was alive and on the loose in the area.

He checked the sky. It was late afternoon, judging by the angle of the sun. He struck out across the fields, working his way roughly westward, keeping close to whatever cover there was, not really sure what he planned to do, but moving anyway.

He walked for perhaps a couple of hours, working his way from one patch of cover to another, creeping bent-over along hedgerows, and now and then going well out of his way to avoid crossing too much open ground. He knew he was not making much progress, but it was dangerous enough moving about in the daylight at all. He knew he should have waited until dark, but he wanted to put some distance between himself and the crash, in case a more alert patrol came along.

He did not know how far he had to go. The balloon site had not been far back from the front lines, and he could not have flown very far before the crash; the sounds of artillery fire suggested that the front shouldn't be many miles away. Nothing much to it, if a man could walk unhindered down a straight road, but under the circumstances even a mile might be a tremendous distance.

Twice he had to hide while German troops passed close by, marching along the country lanes in loose formation, evidently heading for the front themselves. Once he saw a German dispatch rider in the distance, tearing along a road on his motorcycle; he considered setting some sort of trap and getting himself a motorcycle to ride, but dismissed the idea as stupid and dangerous. He saw no civilians at all.

It was in the last hour of daylight that he came upon the cluster of farm buildings. By now he was barely making any progress at all; it was clear that he was getting into an area of heavy German activity, and he had begun to consider holing up in a ditch or thicket until dark. When he saw the buildings he went to ground and lay for a while studying them, thinking over the possibilities.

There was a small house, a barn, and a couple of outbuildings, as well as a stone-walled pigsty and what looked like a beehive. The house was partly in ruins, the roof blackened and shattered, apparently the work of a stray shell or bomb. A dead cow lay blocking a gate nearby. The beehive, if that was what it was, lay on its side.

The whole place looked abandoned; obviously nobody was doing any farming here for now—even if the original owners hadn't been killed by whatever had hit the farmhouse—but the barn still appeared solid, its roof intact, and Amos knew that such a place would be a popular bivouac spot for soldiers coming up the nearby road. It was possible the place held a whole platoon of infantry, in fact; there was no sentry in evidence, but they might not bother, in a rear area like this. Or there might be deserters hiding out here, far more dangerous than any fighting troops. . . .

Yet the place would be perfect to hide in for the rest of the daylight time, and Amos badly needed such a place right now. He moved closer, ready to run at any sign of movement, but there was no one and nothing.

Standing at the corner of the wrecked house, ready to duck into its shadow, he threw a couple of rocks at the barn door. There was no response. He took out his revolver, reconsidered, and put it back—if he did walk in on armed soldiers, his only chance of staying alive would consist of raising both hands instantly and having them visibly empty of weapons —and walked toward the barn.

There was a small side door, partly open, sagging on its hinges. He slipped inside, eyes struggling to adjust to the gloom. The barn was warm and musty inside, filled with the smell of rotten hay and animal manure. As his eyes adapted to the near-darkness, he saw that he was indeed alone. He had not been excessively cautious, though; the floor was littered with cigarette butts and food wrappers and bits of paper bearing Gothic print. German troops had used the barn, more than once, and not too long ago; he could still smell traces of cigarette smoke. He picked up a piece of newsprint and tried to read it, but one year of university German proved to have been inadequate; the spiky-looking letters meant nothing to him.

The hay was moldy, but soft and comfortable to sit on. Amos lay back, wishing he had something to eat. From now on he was going to store a little bit of food somewhere about him—a candy bar or something—and carry a small flask of something to drink, whenever he flew over enemy territory. A canteen of water and a sandwich or two would be no heavier than this damned pistol, he reflected, and much more useful. And a little packet of bandages, in case of crash injuries, and maybe some aspirins, and a pocket compass and a map. . . .

He whiled away quite a bit of time, lying there on his back on the spoiled hay, making up a list of things a pilot ought to carry on these missions. He knew he would never remember any of it, but it helped pass the rest of the day. Maybe, he thought, something to read ought to go on the list; getting shot down seemed to include a lot of waiting. They ought to issue something like a small combination Bible and German phrase book. Couple of grenades in case of hostile contact, prophylactic kit in case of friendly contact—

Amos became aware that somebody was moving about outside.

He lay perfectly still for a moment, analyzing the sounds. One person, moving a little clumsily but purposefully; none of the clink of pack buckles and rifle sling swivels and the like that usually characterized the movements of an infantryman, but the man outside was definitely wearing some sort of hard-soled boots. Amos moved toward the side door where he had come in. The man was coming toward the barn now, walking pretty fast. Amos flattened his back against the wall, next to the door, and took out his pistol.

The door creaked a little as it swung open. A man appeared in the rectangle of light, silhouetted against the graying sky, and stepped hesitantly into the barn. He was not very big, and he carried no weapon.

Amos's arm went around the man's neck from behind, yanking him back and pinning him in a choke-hold. Amos stuck the muzzle of his revolver into the man's ear and felt all struggles cease.

After giving his prisoner a moment to consider the situation, Amos let go and stepped back, keeping the heavy pistol trained on the man's head. He said, "Turn around," in English, and realized he didn't know how to say it in French or German.

The shadowy figure turned around. A familiar voice said, "Jesus *Christ*, Amos, don't scare me like that."

Amos said incredulously, "Bill? Is that you?"

Faulkner said, "No, it's Admiral von Tirpitz. What the hell?" He stepped into the light from the doorway and Amos saw that he wore only his gray uniform trousers and blouse and his black officer's boots. And, Amos noticed, quite a bit of mud and grime. One arm rested in a sling made from his white silk scarf.

Amos said, "What got you, the Albatroses or the ground fire?"

"Damned if I know. Seemed as if all of Kaiser Bill's subjects were shooting at Bill Faulkner at the same time. Engine just quit . . . think my arm's broken," Faulkner said cheerfully, "but the plane caught fire right after I got out, so I'm not complaining. You?"

"Pretty much the same. Ground fire damaged something, I didn't know it at first, then I spun her to get away from some Albatroses and I think the strain tore things loose. What about the others?'' Amos asked. ''Did you see anything before they got you?''

''Not really. Saw one Nieuport on fire, but no way to tell whose . . . no stripes, though, so it wasn't Lucas, unfortunately. Son of a bitch,'' Faulkner said bitterly. ''Stuck all our heads into the shit so he could impress High Command and give Cassidy fresh copy. I hope he at least got some shell fragments in his ass.''

He looked around. ''Nice place you've got here. Planning to stay long?''

''Just till it's good and dark. Then I thought I'd make for the front, try to find some way to get across to our lines.''

Amos hesitated. ''Bill—are you going to be able to travel with that arm like that? Shouldn't you just find some Germans and turn yourself in, let them get you to a doctor?''

''Oh, hell, no. It's not that bad. I'm not even sure it's broken, might just be dislocated, or a bad sprain or something. My legs are all right, and that's all I'm planning to use this evening. The only thing I'm letting the German Army examine,'' Faulkner said, ''is my ass, and that only through a dense cloud of dust.''

''You won't find much dust at the front,'' Amos said drily, ''if it's anything like I remember. Well, come on, you can lie down on this hay here, give it a rest anyway—''

''Sounds good. My feet are about to mutiny; they say they didn't join the infantry. At least I didn't wear those silly fur-lined things like you, though, how the hell do you stand it?'' Faulkner gestured with his good hand. ''And by the way, could you possibly put that howitzer away? Or at least quit pointing it at me?''

''Oh. Sorry.'' Amos stuck the revolver back in its holster, feeling his cheeks flush. ''Well, I thought after about an hour—''

He stopped, listening. Faulkner said, ''What,'' and then he heard it too.

Men were coming across the farmyard, a considerable number of men in military marching gear. Boots clumped and slings creaked and metal bits jingled and someone said distinctly, ''*Scheisse.*''

As footsteps approached the barn, Amos considered the possibilities. There was no way he and Faulkner could burrow into that moldering hay without being found, even if they didn't smother themselves; anyway, there was no time for that. A ladder led up to a small loft, but Faulkner couldn't climb it one-armed.

Seeing Amos's glance, Faulkner said quietly, "Go on, get up there and try to hide. I'll stay here, let them find me. Maybe they'll take me and you can get away."

Amos thought about it. "No. If we get captured we'll do it together—"

The big main door creaked and groaned and swung open. It was gray twilight outside, but the light that came into the barn seemed very bright. A couple of German soldiers stood in the doorway, looking inside, holding rifles. One said, "*Wer da?*"

Amos said, "Shit."

There was a shout and a burst of activity around the door. The barn seemed to fill up instantaneously with *feldgrau*-clad troops, most of them pointing rifles at Amos and Faulkner. There were repeated shouts of "*Hände hoch!*" even though Amos already had both hands raised as far as they would go and Faulkner had raised his good one and was nodding urgently at the sling and saying, "Broken, see? Bro-ken. Amos, what the hell's German for a busted arm?"

A small, angry-looking man, wearing the stripes of some sort of junior NCO, pushed forward and took Amos's revolver. "*Sprechen Sie Deutsch?*" He glared at them, mustache quivering, as if daring them to deny it. "*Sprechen Sie Deutsch?*" And to Faulkner, "*Hände hoch!*"

Amos searched his memory. "I speak a Little," he said lamely. "My Friend speaks not. See, he has his Arm injured. He can his Hand not raise. He must to a Doctor taken be."

The little man was still glaring in suspicious incomprehension. Amos said, "Speak You not English?"

There was a general stirring and muttering among the soldiers. The small man said, "*Engländer?*"

"No, no. We are—" Amos stuck, floundering. He had no notion how to convey "Confederate" or anything like it.

"Southern America" might suggest Brazil or Argentina, which would be interpreted as a lie—at the very least they might demand that he prove it by dancing the tango—and might in turn make these irascible *Herrenvolk* even more suspicious. Amos lowered a hand nervously, despite shouts and upward-jerked rifle muzzles, and pointed to his CSA belt buckle. "Know You not what this means—"

He was spared further effort, and the German language further mutilation, by a new arrival. Suddenly the soldiers fell silent and those near the door fell back to make a passage.

Amos saw a short, broad-shouldered man, about his own age, in the uniform of an Imperial infantry officer. Pale blue eyes peered out from under a visored cap; high black boots clumped slowly across the hard-packed earth floor of the barn. Both hands were stuck negligently into the pockets of an unbuttoned *feldgrau* jacket. An Iron Cross dangled from a slightly soiled red-and-white ribbon.

The small man jabbered excitedly. The officer silenced him with a careless wave. "Gentlemen. Pardon me if the peasants have been a bit discourteous." There was not the least trace of an accent, though the English was the British variety rather than American. "Good lads, but no breeding whatever. For God's sake lower your hands," he said. "Lieutenant Maximilian Ritter, at your service." He bowed; there was just the faintest click of heels. "And you are of the Confederate American forces, I believe?"

"William Faulkner," Faulkner said, after a moment. "Lieutenant, Confederate Flying Corps."

"Amos Ninekiller." Amos tilted his head in a token response to the German officer's bow. "Do you have a doctor with you?"

"I'm afraid not. We will, of course, see to it that this man receives medical attention as soon as possible." He looked curiously at Amos. "What an odd name, if I may say so. . . ."

The little man handed over Amos's revolver, mumbling something. Ritter examined it with raised eyebrows. "A certain brutal efficiency, if not as elegant as our Luger," he murmured. "Since our beautiful Luger also lacks reliability,

I thank you for your gift." He stuck the big .45 into his belt. "No sidearms?" he said to Faulkner. "Of course I never did understand why pilots wear the things. But then when I was in the cavalry, only last year, we rode about on horses and carried lances. To say nothing of those grotesque spiked helmets our troops used to have to wear. Excuse me, please."

He barked a series of orders. The men began dispersing to the rest of the barn, sitting or stretching out on the hay or the floor, stacking their weapons and getting out canteens and cigarettes.

"We are on our way to the front," the officer explained. "Been getting a little badly needed rest in the rear, but back to the real war now. I'm afraid I cannot offer you anything to eat. We will be receiving our own rations only after we arrive at our position and relieve the poor devils who are there now. However," he said, "if either of you would like a drink? We have water—"

They both nodded. "Water," Amos said, a little hoarsely, "yes, thanks."

Ritter snapped his fingers and spoke. The little man with the bristling mustache came forward, holding a canteen. Amos waited while Faulkner drank.

The little man said something in his high-pitched voice. Amos caught only the word "*Jude.*" Ritter laughed. "The *Gefreiter,*" he said to Amos, "wishes to know if you are Jewish."

Amos shook his head, taking the canteen from Faulkner. "American Indian," he said. "Cherokee." He tilted the canteen to his lips. The water was warm but clean-tasting. "Thanks," he said, handing the canteen back.

Ritter's eyebrows went up again. "So? Are you serious?" Amos nodded. "Remarkable," Ritter said. He turned to the little *Gefreiter.* "*Indianer,*" he explained.

There was an instant reaction among the soldiers: sharp intakes of breath, grunts of amazement, a few oaths. "These men," Ritter said to Amos, "are great admirers of you people, you know. Like all German boys, they grew up reading the stories of your American frontier. They will greatly impress their friends, back home and in other units, when they tell them they have met a real Indian. Although I think they are disappointed that you do not wear buckskin and feathers and paint your face.''

Amos said with a straight face, "Tell them that I am forbidden to do so by the regulations of the service. Naturally, at home, I wear these things, as well as the scalps of men I have killed.''

Ritter's eyebrows almost disappeared under his cap, but he translated, deadpan, and there was a chorus of excited sighs. "You have made them happy,'' he said to Amos. "Like children, all of them. Fascinated by the idea of the noble savage.''

Faulkner said, "But not as admiring when it comes to Jews, I gather.''

"Ah, well,'' Ritter sighed, and grinned. "The prejudices of the lower orders, you know. Of course, I have no more use for a Jew than does any other gentleman, but give me a Jew of breeding, a Rothschild say, before a vulgar little guttersnipe like this one.'' He indicated the *Gefreiter* with a tilt of his head. "A conscientious soldier, all the same, and utterly loyal; I should not mock him.''

He gestured. "Rest yourselves, gentlemen. As I shall.'' He spoke sharply and the men on the hay moved hastily away. Amos sat, holding out a hand to help Faulkner. Ritter eased himself down beside them. "Ridiculous, is it not?'' Ritter said. "Men such as ourselves, trying to kill each other, and for what? The squabbles of a lot of degenerate Slavs and inbred Austrians.'' He glanced briefly at the little *Gefreiter*, who was pacing restlessly near the door. "A despicable people, the Austrians. Almost as despicable as the Russians and their Serbian cousins. We should be fighting side by side against the Asiatic Slavs, you know.''

Amos said, "There are those on our side who would agree with you.'' He realized suddenly that Ritter reminded him of Lucas; there was something very similar in the pale blue eyes. "Are there other German officers who share your views?''

Ritter smiled cryptically. "You might be surprised. We Germans,'' he said, "of the better classes, that is—we have long admired the American Confederacy. We did not understand why you freed the niggers, but then we saw that it was a brilliant stroke—by making them technically free, yet carefully depriving them of any actual rights, you still have a useful labor force of inferior beings without the trouble of housing and caring for them. Perhaps one day we too—'' He broke off abruptly and got to his feet. "Enough. We have spent enough time here. Fascinating as this conversation has been, I have a war to fight."

He began giving orders in a high sharp voice. The men rose quickly and began gathering packs and rifles, putting out cigarettes, returning canteens to their belts. There was, Amos noticed, no grumbling or muttering, as would have been inevitable with a group of Confederate soldiers. It was nearly dark outside now; the men moved in deep shadow, but with the ease of men long accustomed to working in the dark.

"As for you two," Ritter said, "obviously I cannot take you along, much as I would enjoy your company. At the same time, I cannot spare a detail to take you back to the rear. In any event, I can hardly order an injured man to walk so far."

His eyes glinted faintly. "And, since you are officers and gentlemen—and since you are not French—I don't care to shoot you. Therefore—" He snapped his fingers. "The *Gefreiter*, here, will stay with you. When we reach the front, I will send a message to the Field Police to have someone come for you."

He spoke quickly in German. The *Gefreiter* said, "*Zum Befehl, Herr Leutnant,*" and saluted. Unslinging his rifle, he pointed it at Amos, then at Faulkner, and said something in German.

Ritter said, "Please don't do anything foolish, gentlemen. The *Gefreiter* here may look like a fool and sometimes act like one, but I assure you he is nothing of the sort. Among other things, he is an excellent shot and has outstanding reflexes. Incredible night vision, too; he usually serves as my runner when we're in action. Believe me, he'll kill you without hesitation if you try to escape."

He spread his hands. "And anyway, where would you go? You could never get through our trenches, and the wire, and across No Man's Land, without being detected and shot—and even if you did, the pickets on the other side would shoot you on sight. You must have noticed that your uniforms are quite similar to ours.''

He shouted an order. The soldiers began filing out the door.

''Good evening, gentlemen,'' Ritter said, clicking his heels again and saluting. ''Perhaps one day we will fight on the same side, eh?''

As he walked out the door, Faulkner said under his breath, ''Do you suppose there's some sort of contagion going around? A German Lucas, for God's sake.''

The *Gefreiter* jabbed the air with his rifle and spat out something in German. The words were unclear but the meaning was unmistakable. Faulkner shut up.

Outside, they heard the sounds of the soldiers moving off toward the road. Then there was silence, except for the artillery that still boomed and rumbled to the west. By now they had ceased even to be aware of that.

A long time went by: how long, Amos could not tell. He could see a bit of sky through the open barn door behind the *Gefreiter*, but it held only a single star, which he could not identify. It was not really important. He had other things on his mind.

They could, he knew, rush the little soldier who guarded them; with that clumsy bolt-action Mauser he would get off only one shot before they could reach him, and in the dimness he might miss even with that. And Amos thought that he might have tried it, if Faulkner hadn't been injured; but if the German shot Amos, then Faulkner might not be able to take him one-handed. The *Gefreiter* was small, but so was Faulkner.

And there was no question at all of waiting till the soldier let down his guard. Amos thought he had never seen a man take his job so seriously; the rifle muzzle never lowered, only swung slowly from side to side to cover the two pilots. The *Gefreiter*'s eyes fairly gleamed in the dark; it was obvious he would love to shoot them both.

Faulkner said suddenly, ''Water. I want water.''

The guard poked the air with his rifle and jabbered. Faulkner said more loudly, "Water, God damn it. What's the word in your stupid language? *Wasser*." He pantomimed the act of drinking, with noisy gurgling noises in his throat. "Let's have some *Wasser*, boy."

The *Gefreiter* shouted angrily for silence. Faulkner continued to make drinking gestures. In a pleading voice he said, "Please, *Wasser*, you don't understand English, do you, you syphilitic little asshole? Your mother must have done it with an unusually diseased pig," he went on, still in that abject whine, "to produce something as ugly and stupid as yourself." He pointed at the canteen on the little man's belt. "He doesn't understand a word, Amos," he said, still gazing beseechingly into the *Gefreiter*'s eyes. "Get ready."

The German took a step forward. He was still too far away for a grab. He pointed the Mauser at Faulkner. There was a dry metallic *flink* as he thumbed the safety off.

All at once Faulkner fell to the ground, writhing and clutching his stomach with his good hand, moaning and making choking sounds. His feet kicked spasmodically and drummed on the earth·floor.

Amos jumped to his feet. The rifle muzzle swung to cover him but he raised his hands and gestured angrily. "This Man is sick," he shouted indignantly in his best Freshman German. "Will You not this Officer help? Please, You must make quick—"

"Oooooo," Faulkner moaned. "OoooooooOOOOOO-aaaugh." He began to retch violently. Amos bent over him. "Bloooooch," Faulkner added. "Yocknapatawpha. Guhhh."

The *Gefreiter* took two steps forward, moving with surprising speed and precision, and looked down at Faulkner. "*Schweinhund*," he said contemptuously, and drew back his foot and kicked Faulkner hard in the ribs.

Faulkner said with great sincerity, "*Oof!*" and rolled over. The German took another step, the Mauser coming up in his hands, reversed, the iron-shod butt poised to come down on Faulkner's kidneys.

Amos turned, palming the razor from the top of his boot,

flicking open the hollow-ground blade as Tyrone had shown him, the back of the blade resting against his knuckles, the edge outward, braced by the thumbpiece. The fine-honed edge took the little *Gefreiter* just under the corner of the jaw, slicing back under the ear, through the big blood vessels of the neck. A spurt of warm blood drenched Amos's hand.

The *Gefreiter* made a choking noise and started to turn, bringing his rifle down toward Amos. Faulkner kicked him on the kneecap. Amos dropped the razor and grabbed the rifle and wrenched. There was not much resistance; the man was dying on his feet. Amos hit him alongside the head with the Mauser butt on general principles and watched as he fell across the oblong of dim light from the doorway.

Faulkner got up, none too steadily. "Christ," he said, "the little bastard kicked like a mule. Nice work there, Amos."

Amos bent over the body. Faulkner said, "What are you doing?"

"Boots," Amos said, pulling one off. "His feet look a little smaller than mine, but I think I can get into his boots. I'm tired of trying to walk in these things, and we may have to run . . . give me a hand, if you would? Oh, that's right, you can't, sorry."

Faulkner knelt beside the body and went through the pockets. "Suppose I better get his papers," he said, "might be something the Intelligence people can use."

"If you're recaptured with that stuff on you," Amos pointed out, "they'll shoot you, you know."

"So? If we're recaptured they'll shoot us anyway, now. Sooner or later they'll find the body, and Ritter knows our names and faces." Faulkner straightened up, shoving the German's papers into his breast pocket. "It's home or Hell tonight, Amos. How are the boots?"

"Too tight, but I can stand it. I don't think it's far enough for me to get blisters, anyway." He picked up the *Gefreiter*'s cloth cap and set it on his head. "As Ritter said, our uniforms do look a lot like theirs, don't they? Butternut gray and *feldgrau*, wonder how many men get shot by mistake on both sides." He strapped on the wide leather belt with the ammunition pouches and the canteen and the sheathed bayonet.

Picking up the rifle, he said, "Don't happen to know *Lili Marlene*, do you? I mean, these people sing a lot, everybody knows that. Great natural sense of rhythm."

"Shut up," Faulkner said crossly as they walked across the farmyard toward the road. "You get to be the hero again, I just get kicked. Now I think I've got a broken rib too. . . ."

The road was a busy place now, filled with columns of marching men and horse-drawn wagons and guns, most of it headed toward the sound of the artillery, here and there a single ambulance or a file of walking wounded struggling against the flow, trying to get to the rear. The moon was up and shining through an open patch among the gathering clouds; Amos felt obvious and exposed as he walked along head down, rifle on his shoulder, cap pulled low. And Faulkner, bareheaded and weaponless, arm in a sling—he had at least smeared some earth over the gleaming white silk—was downright spectacular, at least to Amos's eye. Yet nobody seemed to notice them; everybody was busy, intent on whatever business they were about, and as they neared the front the press of men and vehicles was too thick for individuals to be noticed. There were Field Police stationed along the road, checking papers and orders, but they seemed to care only about men moving the other way; anyone moving toward the fighting was evidently assumed to be all right.

Many of the soldiers, Amos noticed, wore a new type of helmet, a steel pot with a kind of flange that came down over the wearer's ears and protected the nape of the neck. Seeing one hanging on the side of an artillery caisson, he paused to pilfer it for Faulkner. The effect was excellent, and even better after the addition of a long-handled shovel which Amos stole from a passing wagon. Discarding the sling, Faulkner shoved his bad arm into the front of his blouse and rested the shovel on his good shoulder: just another soldier on his weary way to, or from, another work detail.

The shellfire was now loud and quite close ahead. On either side of the road, off in the dark, the big German guns blasted the night, returning fire, an occasional long-range shell bursting among them. Now and then a shell hit close to the road;

twice, Amos and Faulkner dived to the ground along with everyone else when a round whizzed down and struck nearby. Shell craters began to appear in the roadway, surrounded by groups of men struggling frantically to make repairs. A demolished wagon lay amid the bloating corpses of its horses.

They were getting right up into the lines, now. Trails led off the road toward the reserve trenches; up ahead, the road obviously became impassable. Amos and Faulkner followed a file of soldiers down a narrow pathway and then down a flight of board steps into the darkness of a big deep trench, where they stumbled along almost blind, guided by the narrow strip of night sky overhead. No one challenged them; no one seemed to notice them at all.

Amos shook his head in wonder as they turned up a communication trench that zigzagged toward the front line. Even in the darkness, it was obvious that the German trenches were infinitely better than the crude muddy wallows on the Allied side; solid board and stone walkways covered the bottom of the trench, and the walls were cut with mathematical precision and lined with timber. Moving down the next trench, they paused as a man emerged from a dugout ahead; through the entrance, before the curtain fell back, they caught a glimpse of a spacious, well-lit room with board-paneled walls. A smell of cooking sausage and cabbage drifted to their noses.

The German earthworks stretched on and on, trench after trench, the notorious defense-in-depth principle that made mockery of the simple-minded Allied assaults. Amos tried to remember how the German lines had looked from the air, how many lines of trenches there were, but his tired mind refused to supply pictures. He kept moving, following the communication trenches; the pattern was predictable enough after the first few turns, and he thanked the Germans in his heart for being such methodical, unimaginative bastards. It would have taken him all night to get half this far in the Confederate trenches he had seen, and then he would probably have gotten lost.

The quality of the trenches deteriorated rapidly as they neared the front; there was mud underfoot now, squelching under the *Gefreiter*'s boots, and Faulkner had begun using his shovel as a cane. The sky overhead had clouded over; down in the trenches it was pitch dark. Amos rammed into someone who said explosively, "*Zum Teufel*!" and pushed past, going the other way, muttering oaths.

There was no mistaking the forward trench, when they finally reached it. Amos felt firing steps cut into the forward wall; here and there men stood watching over the lip of the trench, heads and shoulders silhouetted against the dim sky. There was a tension in the air, like the forward edge of an approaching thunderstorm. Somewhere not far away a machine gun fired a short burst.

Faulkner whispered in his ear, "What the hell now?"

Amos grunted meaninglessly; he was wondering about that himself. Dark as it was, they still couldn't just climb over the top of the trench and walk, or even crawl, toward the other side; someone would definitely notice such odd behavior, and probably shoot without stopping to ask any questions. A narrow trench nearby led off toward No Man's Land, probably ending in a listening post or a sniper's position, and he considered following it, but even then they would have the fantastic German barbed-wire belts ahead of them. There had to be openings in the wire for patrols and raids to pass through, but finding them in the dark would be impossible.

Yet they couldn't hang about the trench much longer; dark or not, somebody was certain to notice two strangers, or speak to them, or give them an order they wouldn't understand. After which . . . whatever happened, it was safe to assume they wouldn't enjoy it at all.

There was a sound of men coming down the trench. Amos and Faulkner stepped back, pressing against the sandbagged wall behind them, as half a dozen Germans pushed past, slogging doggedly along in the mud, talking softly among themselves. A flare burst over the lines, off to the north; in the brief flickering light Amos saw that the men were carrying tools and strange-looking loads.

Without stopping to think it over, he tugged Faulkner's jacket and they fell in behind the work party, trying to match the soldiers' pace and spacing as they passed the sentries and the mouths of dugouts. Someone up ahead stumbled and a voice said tiredly, *"Der Herr Jesus."* Amos checked himself just in time to keep from running into the man ahead of him.

The work party stopped; Amos heard the sounds of the leaders climbing a ladder. Following slowly, groping in the darkness, he saw the lip of the trench black against the slightly lesser black of the sky, and the forms of men disappearing over the top.

The ladder was solid and steady, but its wooden steps were slick with mud. Amos climbed carefully, wondering if Faulkner could make it one-handed. The sounds behind him indicated the Mississippian was managing, with some difficulty.

Another flare went off, farther away, casting a dim light where it reflected off the clouds. Amos could just make out the work party up ahead, moving slowly and carefully out toward No Man's Land, and he hurried to catch up. The sound of shellfire and the occasional machine-gun burst masked any sound he might be making as he slogged through the mud; if the last man turned around he was dead, but that seemed unlikely. The work party was obviously following some sort of established path, requiring full attention.

A light rain had begun to fall.

Amos was aware of barbed wire, now, on either side, the top strands higher than his head, faintly visible against the sky. The pathway was narrow, barely wide enough to clear a man's shoulders, and it zigzagged sharply at regular intervals so as not to offer an avenue of attack. The wire went on and on; Amos estimated they must have passed through fifty or sixty feet of entanglements, yet there seemed no end to it. He had a sudden awful mental picture of men trying to get through this in broad daylight, with machine guns and rifles cutting them down, and he shivered slightly. Patton was right, he thought, they could go on for years and never break through. The white people had begun to outdo the Aztecs at human sacrifice. . . .

He realized suddenly that the work party had stopped. They seemed to be getting ready to go to work; he heard the faint sounds of metal tools, somewhere beside the path.

Amos stood, feeling Faulkner bump softly into him from

behind, waiting for light. When the next star shell went off, this one down to the south, he saw that they were almost to the forward edge of the wire. Beyond, the bare scorched desert of No Man's Land stretched off into the darkness. The German work party was bunched up a few paces to the left of the trail, setting up stakes and stretching wire. None of them looked around.

Amos and Faulkner stood absolutely still until the light had died. Then, moving with glacial slowness and surgical care, they eased down the narrow path through the wire, past the work party, toward the open space beyond.

There was a sudden movement to the left. Someone said, "*Wer da?*"

Amos held the *Gefreiter's* rifle at the ready, his thumb pushing the clumsy safety off. Then, after a moment, he put the safety back on, lowered the Mauser, and began walking on toward No Man's Land, not looking back. Behind him he heard Faulkner slipping and sticking in the mud, coming after him.

There was a low rustling sound behind then, voices whispering and muttering urgently, and the sharp click of a couple of safeties being thumbed off. Then there was a low but clear "*Nein, nein*," and another burst of muffled speech, followed by silence.

Amos moved on, using the rifle now as a cane to probe ahead for shell holes and boggy spots, freezing every time an illumination round went off nearby. As he had guessed, the wire party had realized they didn't really want to open fire on whoever was passing in the night; even one shot would have brought down an instant withering fire from the other side, rifle and machine-gun bullets at least, and possibly even mortars and light artillery. Anything could trigger catastrophic reactions, here in the nerve-jangling night; for a few men out in front of their own trenches, without cover and trapped by their own wire, it wasn't worth it. On the way back they would undoubtedly agree that they had seen nothing and heard nothing.

It was not far across No Man's Land, here, perhaps a little less than two hundred yards; any fit man could have run the distance, in daylight and on dry ground, without getting badly out of breath. In the dark, in the mud, in the rain, it took several hours longer than forever.

Approaching the other side, Faulkner suddenly grabbed Amos by the arm and then knocked lightly with his knuckles against Amos's rifle and his own steel helmet. Hastily they got rid of the German equipment, dumping it in the mud along with the rest of the litter of war, Amos remembering at the last minute to take off the *Gefreiter*'s cloth cap. He thought for a moment about sticking it in his pocket and sending it to Chief Watie as a kind of souvenir or trophy, but the idea seemed silly and he threw the cap into the darkness.

Standing there, then, he heard the patrol leaving the trenches ahead. He put his hand on Faulkner's shoulder, pressing downward, signaling the Mississippian to get down and stay there; then, willing his aching feet to move silently in the too-small German boots, he moved off into the darkness.

The Australian Corporal in charge of the patrol was standing there in the rain, trying to get his bearings, wondering what the bloody hell he was bloody supposed to be bloody doing in this bloody muck. His heart almost stopped when Amos Ninekiller suddenly rose up in front of him and said, "Good evening. Please don't shoot me, I'm on your side. I think."

13

BLANKENSHIP SAID, "Jack Yancey's dead. He went in and took an Albatros off Cobb's tail and two more jumped him. I saw the whole thing. His plane burned but I think he was already dead by then."

He paused to light a cigarette. Amos saw that his hands had a constant, barely visible tremor; the match flame fluttered and almost went out before he could get his cigarette lit.

"Christ," Blankenship said, "I never saw so many Kraut planes in my life. I didn't know the bastards even *had* that many . . . nobody had a chance, Amos. They just by God slaughtered us up there."

Amos said, "I thought I saw some damage to your plane. Big hole in the wing, wasn't it?"

"Best God-damned piece of luck I ever had," Blankenship said with feeling. "When I pulled up from the balloon, I already knew I was hit, so I didn't go rushing up to get in on the action, just got clear as quick as I could and headed for home. Hole that big, even Lucas couldn't say anything. Even then, I picked up a lot of bullet holes before I got away."

Blankenship closed his eyes and dragged on his cigarette. The skin was very tight over his cheekbones.

"They got Lynch, too," he said, "and Barnett and Hill. Bodine went down, but he managed to land near some Kraut troops and they were seen carrying him away, so maybe he's alive. That's what they tell me, anyway, I didn't see any of it." He blew smoke through his nostrils and opened his eyes and looked at Amos. "And Shoemaker got back in a shot-up plane and cracked up on landing and they hauled him off with burns all over. He'll probably live, but he won't be very pretty any more."

"God," Amos said. "Anybody else?"

"That's what I'm getting to," Blankenship said.

It was three days after the balloon attack. Amos had spent a day and a half in the trenches with some Australian infantry, fighting off a German counterattack—he had a memory of firing a rifle, but almost nothing else; by then he must have been little more than an armed sleepwalker—before it was possible to get anyone out. Then there had been an exhausting and confusing series of rides in various military vehicles, wrong turns and botched communications, and a night in a nameless village with some Canadian bicycle troops, before he could finally make contact with Confederate command and get a ride back to his squadron.

Lucas was gone, leading a patrol. Hardly anyone was around, but Amos found Blankenship sitting in the mess, drinking. It was not yet noon.

"By the way," Blankenship said, "how's Bill?"

"They took him away in an ambulance, after the front-line aid people put a crude cast on his arm and taped up his ribs. I haven't seen him since," Amos said. "They told me the hospital where he'll be. Some of us can go and see him, first chance we get, if he's there long."

Blankenship snorted. "Won't be too damn many of us going anywhere. There's not a hell of a lot of the old bunch left. Right now this squadron's more than half replacements, and still understrength. Only reason I'm here right now," he said, "my engine wouldn't start this morning. I'm gonna buy that mechanic a bottle of bourbon. Two if he can't get it fixed by tomorrow."

He crushed out his cigarette and looked out the window. The field lay quiet and empty in the late-September sunshine.

"What happened next," he said quietly, "I can't tell you all the details firsthand. Some of it I know, some of it I can piece together, some of it's just guesswork and suspicion . . . Lucas was all pissed off, of course, because we didn't get the balloon. Handed out a bunch of shit all around—that didn't go down too well," Blankenship said, "considering how many people we'd lost, and the fact that the attack was his plan to begin with, but he was pretty wild that afternoon. I guess he knew he was going to catch a certain amount of shit himself, from his own bosses, for not getting the balloon."

"And for losing so many planes and pilots," Amos suggested.

"Hell," Blankenship said, "you think they mind that? That part probably impresses the hell out of them—aggressive tactics, hard-charging leadership, all that crap. I've seen it all before." He made a face. "That God-damned reporter, Cassidy, was up here the next morning, asking a lot of questions, talking about how we're all gonna be heroes. You watch, they'll hand out medals for that business and Lucas'll get the biggest one."

Blankenship paused and took a deep breath. "Now comes the good part," he said grimly. "Next day—day before yesterday, wasn't it?—Lucas sent out another attack against that same God-damned balloon."

"For God's sake," Amos said. "He tried the same thing again?"

"Oh, no. Obviously that didn't work, had to try something else." Blankenship's mouth twisted. "This time the plan was to send in just a small attack force, with no top cover. Three planes, coming in low like before but from another direction, taking the Krauts by surprise. Instead of climbing out, they were supposed to stay down low to make their getaway, so any fighters would have a hard time getting after them."

"That's crazy," Amos said, baffled. "He actually sent three men out after that thing, with nobody covering? Who did he pick?"

Blankenship stretched his mouth in a ghastly smile. "Oh, our Major didn't *pick*—they all volunteered. At least that's what he says. You understand, this wasn't announced in a regular briefing; he set the whole thing up in his office, without telling anybody else. First thing most of us knew was when we saw them take off." He held up three fingers and folded them down as he called the names. "Eubanks. Weaver. Cobb."

Amos felt as if he had been kicked in the face. He said, "Oh, Christ. Oh, Jesus Christ."

"Yeah," Blankenship said bitterly. "*He* might could have saved those three poor bastards. Nobody else could."

He got out another cigarette and lit it. This time he did not try to conceal the trembling of his hands.

"Nobody knows for sure how it went," Blankenship said. "The only eyewitness report was by the pilot and observer of a British photo-recon plane that happened to be in the area, and they didn't see it close up—you don't go flying close to balloon sites in a Sopwith Strutter—or have any way of knowing who was flying which plane. You understand, nobody was even supposed to know that much, but I bribed Sergeant Hawkins with a bottle of whisky and he let me read the Sopwith crew's report."

He held up a fist to represent the balloon, flew toward it with three outspread fingers. "They came in like this, all spread out, all at once, way to hell too high—Cobb and Weaver didn't know what they were doing, of course, and Eubanks never had any sense—and the Kraut gunners just shot them out of the air like so many low-flying pigeons. There were some Albatroses in the area, but they never had a chance to get a piece. The Sopwith observer said he didn't think any of the Nieuports even got off a shot at the balloon."

Amos put his head in his hands, cursing. Blankenship said,

"Yeah, I think you pretty much got the picture. They need to add three more to Lucas's official score, because he sure as hell killed those three, just as good as if he'd shot them down himself."

"I don't know, sir," Sergeant Hawkins said dubiously. "I could get my ass in a lot of trouble, letting people see things they're not supposed to see. Major Lucas already gave me personal orders. All that stuff is restricted information— nobody's supposed to see it without personal authorization from the Squadron Commander. Said he'd bust me and send me up to the line in an infantry outfit."

Amos sighed. "Which means the price has gone up?" He held out a handful of bills. "Take whatever you require."

Hawkins scratched his head. "Well, I tell you, sir—"

"Or," Amos said, "I could just tell Major Lucas that you let Blankenship see that report."

Hawkins reached out and took the money, not looking at it. He said, "I'll be right back, sir."

Amos took the typed sheets into the officers' latrine and sat studying the dry stiffly-worded paragraphs: the file copies of Lucas's reports on the two balloon attacks, and the British report Blankenship had seen. It did not take long to read; it took even less time to determine that he had brought them to the most appropriate spot possible, and that it was too bad he couldn't leave them there.

Last was a single sheet, an official message form from Headquarters:

You are commended for aggressive action. Casualties regrettable but presumed unavoidable. Continue offensive operations against this and other targets.

Lucas said, "By God, Ninekiller, if you aren't the hardest man to please. Nearly as hard to please as you are to kill." He sighed. "What a hell of a story Gabe Cassidy could make of that escape—but of course Headquarters would never allow it, because if you ever got shot down and captured again they'd have a big showy trial and shoot you. They'll probably do it anyway, but that's the official policy on such things."

Amos said, "You sent those three out alone against that God-damned balloon. The whole squadron got butchered trying to get it, so you sent in a reckless showoff and the two worst pilots in the squadron."

Lucas grinned broadly. "I'm surprised at you, Ninekiller," he said mockingly. "As I understand it, you and Eubanks weren't exactly bosom buddies, were you? The way I heard it, you had a fist fight the first time you met. And he certainly made no secret of his contempt for your people . . . I'd think you'd be glad he's gone."

"If I'd wanted Eubanks killed," Amos said, "I'd have killed him myself."

"Hm. I think you would, Ninekiller. I really think you would." Lucas tapped the desk top with his fingers, studying Amos. "It's not Eubanks, though, is it? It's your little friend Cobb. Such devotion is remarkable. Is it possible there's something that I've overlooked here? I don't know how your people look on such relationships, but of course many great warrior nations—the Spartans, the Romans, the Arabs—" He stopped, holding up his hands, seeing the look on Amos's face. "All right, maybe not, I didn't really believe it. All the same, you're certainly reacting badly to the loss of a young fool you hardly knew. To say nothing of an enemy, and that lard-assed nitwit Weaver."

Amos opened his mouth, but words would not come. His throat felt very tight.

"Well," Lucas said, "I'm sorry if you felt any personal attachments to any of the late departed. Don't ask me to mourn for them, though. I'd trade a hundred like them to get Jack Yancey back, or Bodine. Those three were a God-damned liability to this squadron and a menace to everyone else who flew with them."

Amos said with difficulty, "If they were so bad, why did you pick them for a mission like that?"

"Why, Lieutenant Ninekiller." Lucas wiggled an eyebrow, still grinning. "How you talk. Those lads volunteered, didn't you know? Willingly gave their all in their country's service. It says so right here." He held up a sheet of paper. "In the report I just wrote recommending them for posthumous decoration. After all, I'm not without decent feelings, you know."

Amos said harshly, "Horse shit."

Lucas frowned slightly. "Lieutenant, I know there's been a certain informality between us, but I still have to insist—"

"Horse shit," Amos said again. "You can sell that to Headquarters, Cassidy can sell it to the people back home, but nobody in this squadron is going to buy it. Eubanks was a damned fool and a bigger glory hound than you. He'd have volunteered for anything, however crazy, because he didn't have any sense and he didn't really think he could be killed. Cobb and Weaver didn't know enough to understand what they were getting into. Anyway," Amos added, "I've checked around, and nobody else was ever given the opportunity."

"So?" Lucas was unruffled. "Even if you could prove it, who's going to do anything about it? Headquarters doesn't want to know things like that, and the people at home don't want to know anything at all. Start questioning whether a soldier knows what he's volunteering for, you'll threaten the whole fabric of modern society."

He leaned forward, his face serious now. "If you won't accept natural selection of the fittest," he said, "try command necessity. Eubanks was one of the three senior pilots left after the previous day's battle; I couldn't avoid making him a Flight Leader except by turning in an unfavorable report and getting him kicked out of the squadron, and he had important family connections that would have made trouble for me if I'd done that. Would you have had me assign four men to fly with Eubanks as their leader?"

"You did it to get rid of Eubanks?" Amos said incredulously.

"Headquarters wanted somebody to go after the balloon again." Lucas shrugged. "In the circumstances, Eubanks seemed more than expendable, so I expended him. The others were merely useless clowns, but I couldn't very well send

Eubanks out alone; it would have been a bit too obvious . . . and they were certainly expendable too. And if one of them *had* gotten lucky and flamed the balloon, everybody would have been happy.''

He looked soberly at Amos. ''Better get rid of that Sunday School morality, Lieutenant. Better get on the team.''

From outside came the sounds of engines revving up. The afternoon patrol was getting ready to take off: four planes, one of them sounding rough.

Lucas said, ''If you want to sit around and cry, though, save the tears for the next people to go after that balloon. Or the men flying understrength patrols with green wingmen because we're using up our strength on these balloon-busting raids. Because it's not over, you know. Headquarters has got a wild hair up its collective brass-bound ass over this balloon business.''

He tapped the bronze oak leaf on his collar. ''I don't plan to stay a Major the rest of my life, Lieutenant. Besides, if I don't keep after the damned gasbag, they'll just sack me and get someone who will.''

Amos said, ''You want that balloon?''

''I take it the question is rhetorical.''

''Bad enough to go after it yourself?''

Lucas frowned. ''Where's all this leading, Ninekiller?''

''With me.'' Amos stared into the pale blue eyes. ''Do you want that balloon bad enough to go across the lines, just you and me, and get it?''

''Son of a bitch.'' Lucas stood up. ''I think you're serious.''

''Believe it. You want the God-damned thing, let's go get it ourselves.''

''Well, I'm damned.'' Lucas rubbed his chin. ''You're actually proposing that you and I get up in the morning—''

''No,'' Amos said. ''Late afternoon, after the second patrol's returned. We've never done that before. They won't be ready for it. Their fighter cover will have gone home and the gunners will be relaxing, figuring we've packed it in for the day.''

''Hm. I like that,'' Lucas admitted. ''Damned good idea,

whoever does it . . . but two one-gun fighters, Ninekiller, could they do the job? So far we've riddled the bastard and can't seem to get a fire built.''

"Load with nothing but incendiary and explosive rounds," Amos said. "We've never had enough to load more than one in four—seventy-five percent of the bullets we fire are regular solid ball that don't do anything but make little holes. But even with the shortage of Brock and Pomeroy bullets, we can load a drum apiece for two guns. Alternating explosives and incendiaries ought to blow holes in the envelope and ignite the gas as it escapes, even if half the damned things don't go off.''

Lucas was nodding. "All right, makes sense, makes sense. Good plan of attack, Ninekiller. Only," he said with a slight grin, "why you and me? Why shouldn't I send someone else out to try your clever ideas?''

"Because you and I are the two best pilots left in this squadron," Amos said bluntly. "If anybody can do it, we can. You damned well know it.''

And, as Lucas considered this, Amos added, "And because you'll get the credit for destroying the balloon. No matter which of us actually flames the thing, on the record it'll be Major Lucas who took out the target nobody else could destroy. Unwilling to send more of his men to their deaths,'' Amos said, "heroic commander flies a daring private mission. Christ, I've been around Cassidy so much, it's getting so I can do it too.''

Lucas was looking at him strangely. "You'd do that? Give up your share of the credit, no matter which of us gets the balloon?''

"My word, if that means anything to you. As far as I'm concerned you don't even have to mention that I was there," Amos said, "except I suppose you'll want a witness.''

Lucas said, "Why? I know you don't care much for scores and credit for kills and the like, but why is this mission so important to you?''

"Because—you just said it—you're going to keep sending men after that balloon, and more of them are going to get killed. I've lost too many friends already. That's something else you ought to understand," Amos said. "I've got a score to even. You're the only one here good enough to help me even it."

"Revenge?" Lucas looked faintly amused. "I wouldn't have thought you'd go in for that sort of thing."

Amos folded his arms. "Don't make assumptions about me, Major. Don't be misled by the university degree and the short hair and the other civilized trappings. Underneath this itchy gray monkey suit, I'm still a Cherokee warrior. When the enemy kills my friends and wipes out my war party, I have to do something about it."

"Huh." Lucas looked genuinely astonished. "Well, kick my ass. Just when you think you've seen everything. . . ."

He turned and looked out the window, watching the afternoon patrol take off. For a moment the racket of the passing engines was too loud to allow conversation in the little office.

When the last Nieuport had disappeared over the trees Amos said quietly, "Of course, if you're afraid to go with me—"

"God damn it, Lieutenant, don't you try to bait me." Lucas's face went very pale. "Don't you *ever* try that crap on me. I don't have to prove a God-damned thing to you."

He stopped, turned his back for a moment, his hands making fists behind his back. After a few seconds he said in a calmer voice, "When did you have in mind to do it?"

"Today," Amos said. "I figure we've got just about enough time to work out the course and be ready to take off when the last patrol returns."

"What about those specially-loaded drums you suggested? It'll take time," Lucas pointed out, "to have them made up."

"No, they'll be ready. Ought to be ready by now, in fact," Amos said. "I put the armorers to work on them before you came back from morning patrol."

Lucas turned, laughing. "By God, Ninekiller, you've got enough balls for a whole tribe of Indians. All right," he said, "we'll do it. Come over here to the map."

The sun was dropping toward the western horizon, but the light was still good and the sky clear, as Lucas and Amos crossed the lines, angling to come at the target from the southwest, where the flare of afternoon sunlight would mask their approach. The usual spatter of ground fire came up at them, but they were flying low and moving fast, already beginning to drop toward attack height, and nothing came close.

There were several German balloons visible up and down the line, some right up above the trenches, others farther back, hanging at various heights from a thousand feet or so to nearly twice that. There was no mistaking the one they were after, though; it was no more than a little black dot at this distance, but by now they could have found it in the dark.

Lucas flew smoothly, surely, with an almost lazy grace; hanging off to the right and a little to the rear, Amos watched as the gray Nieuport banked slightly and increased the angle of its descent. The stripes that marked a Squadron Commander's aircraft flashed as they caught the sunlight.

Amos glanced up at his own machine gun. The upper wing hid all but the breech and a bit of the ammunition drum with its load of Brock and Pomeroy cartridges. He wished he had had a chance to test the airplane and the gun; he was using Blankenship's Nieuport and he would have liked to know exactly where the Travis gun was sighted. But it would do, for this flight.

Amos sighed, put his hand to his chest and felt the warm presence of the little medicine bag against his skin, and reached for the throttle.

As his Nieuport fell back and then took up station behind the other aircraft, he saw Lucas sit up and look around. The distance was so short he could see Lucas's mouth open in an expression of surprise and annoyance. A gloved hand came up, waving him back into position.

Amos steadied the Nieuport and fired.

The Travis gun rapped quickly, a short burst, no more than a dozen rounds. There was nothing wrong with Blankenship's sights.

The bullets punched through the thin taut fabric of the Nieuport's fuselage and slammed Lucas forward in the cockpit. For an instant he stared back at Amos, his mouth still open, his hand still raised. Then the hand fell limply against the side of the fuselage and, a moment later, Lucas slumped in his seat and slid downward until only the top of his head was showing.

For a few seconds the Nieuport continued to fly straight, still in its shallow dive, headed toward the distant balloon site. Then Lucas's body, settling, must have pushed at the controls. The stubby nose went down and the white-striped Nieuport streaked earthward in a power dive, its engine note rising to a banshee shriek. As Amos watched, the upper wing peeled slowly away and folded back, while the Nieuport went into a wild spin.

He laid the stick over and kicked right rudder, circling, as he looked back to see the impact. There was not much to see, just an already wrecked airplane shattering itself against the ground and, an instant later, a quick bright fire.

Amos looked the other way as his own plane came around, seeing the balloon still hanging in the near distance.

He thought about it briefly and said, "The hell with it," and let the Nieuport continue again around the circle, turning its nose toward the sun and toward home.

But then suddenly he said, "Shit," and wrenched the stick over and then forward, wheeling and going down to the ground, leveling off at bird's-nest height, seeing the trees and fields blur beneath his wings and the balloon growing huge against the sky, lifting the Nieuport's nose and feeling the momentary downward pressure on his body as the shells started to explode around him and machine-gun bullets popped through the fabric of his wings and the balloon filled his sights and then his whole view.

He opened fire as soon as he was within range and he held the trigger down, hosing the gray-streaked bulk of the gasbag, emptying the drum into the hydrogen-filled envelope. As the Travis gun snapped empty he climbed for the sky, the balloon passing so close under his wheels he could have hit it with a rock, the anti-aircraft guns falling silent as the balloon shielded the little Nieuport, then opening up again as he clawed away.

There was a great soundless rush of yellow light. Suddenly the balloon vanished in a ball of strange-looking flame. Beneath the blaze, two observers floated earthward, hanging from their parachutes.

Amos looked back long enough to take in the scene. His face showed no particular reaction at all, any more than when he glanced briefly, on his way westward, at the thin column of smoke rising above the distant trees.

14

GABRIEL CASSIDY snapped his leather-covered notebook shut and said, "Well, well. Quite a story, Lieutenant Ninekiller, quite a remarkable story. And told very well, by the way. I had heard that you people were gifted narrators." He flashed his teeth in his patented meaningless smile. "If you ever decide to write your memoirs of the war—after it's over, of course—you might get in touch. I'd be happy to offer any advice, put you in touch with the right people in the publishing industry."

He gave Amos a sidelong glance. "Or you might like to try your hand at fiction, like your friend Mr. Faulkner. Somehow I have a feeling you would be good at it—making up exciting and plausible tales, I mean."

Amos said expressionlessly, "If you say so."

Cassidy laughed. "God," he said, with as much sincerity as Amos had ever heard in his voice, "what I'd give to know what really happened that afternoon. And why." He shrugged. "Not that there's a chance in hell I could ever write it down for publication, of course. I'd just like to know for myself."

"The truth," Amos said, "is what Gabriel Cassidy says it is. Or so I've been told."

"Touché. Or, at the moment, the truth is what Amos Nine-killer tells Gabriel Cassidy. Major James Lucas went out on a personal mission to destroy the balloon that had claimed so many of his men. He took with him only Lieutenant Nine-killer, a volunteer. Attacking the balloon, the Major was hit by ground fire and killed. A gallant airman gives his life for the South. Et cetera, et cetera."

"You've got it," Amos said flatly.

"Hm. And you're absolutely sure, now, that it was Major Lucas who destroyed the balloon, not yourself? I mean," Cassidy said, "that's going to be the permanent story? No changing your mind later on—or now, for that matter?"

"If it helps," Amos said, "I give you my word as a Confederate officer and a gentleman."

"Oh? Of course, as you yourself once pointed out, you aren't technically a Confederate officer. And as to the other part, not being a gentleman myself—as I have so often been told, no one in my profession can truly be considered a gentleman—I'm not in a position to judge."

Cassidy tapped the tip of his fancy pen against his front teeth for a moment. "Now if I were a suspicious man," he said, "the sort of person who looks for hidden meanings and deep secrets behind innocent events, like some of my colleagues in the cheaper papers—if I were such a person, I might just possibly attach some significance to an obscure bit of information that happened to come my way just last night."

He looked away, his face wholly innocent. "Seems a Confederate patrol captured a prisoner," he said. "Seems the fellow, in the course of the interrogation, told some bizarre tale about having seen one Allied aircraft shoot another down. What an imagination, eh?"

"Amazing," Amos agreed. His own face was blank as a plaster wall.

"And what makes the story doubly ridiculous," Cassidy went on blandly, "is that the approximate time and general area of this hallucinatory event would have coincided closely with the attack on the balloon by Major Lucas and yourself. So if any such thing had happened, you would surely have seen it. But you didn't, did you?''

Amos looked Cassidy in the eye. "There weren't any other planes in the area," he said. "I told you that already."

"So you did, so you did. See, it just proves you can't trust these lying Huns. As I so often remind my readers."

Cassidy paused, slapping the palm of his hand lightly with the leather-covered notebook. "Lieutenant," he said softly, "I wouldn't worry too much about anything coming of . . . whatever happened up there. There are people in positions of influence who, shall we say, will not be altogether sorry that Major Lucas is no longer with the Confederate forces."

Amos said carefully, "I had the impression that he was connected with some pretty powerful people. People with what you might call big plans."

"True, true. You probably know more than you should, actually; Jim always did have a tendency to run off at the mouth, especially after a few drinks. Which is just one of the reasons his, um, mentors and associates will not miss him as much as you might expect."

Cassidy sighed. "Oh, he was an ambitious man, Lieutenant Ninekiller. As you put it, he had big plans, visionary schemes, dreams of power and destiny. Unfortunately," Cassidy said, "these things did not always endear him to others, even others who shared his vision. Some of them, you see, had more years and more rank than our late friend, and at times he struck them as a little too big for his breeches. The Confederacy isn't some Levantine or Latin American country, you know. Junior officers do not stage coups and seize control."

"And more senior ones do?"

"Not so far," Cassidy chuckled, "and no, you aren't going to bait me into an indiscretion; I was making a living at that game before you were born. Just remember what I said." He touched Amos on the forearm. "Even if they suspect, they will leave you alone—as long as you are, um, circumspect."

Amos said, "It should have been you."

Cassidy looked startled. "What?"

"It should have been you up there," Amos said. "Or you should have been with him. I thought about that, on the way home. I got the wrong one."

Cassidy was shaking his head vigorously. "I know you don't like me, Lieutenant, but—"

"Stay away from me," Amos said almost in a whisper. "Stay away from me or I swear it *will* be you, next time. I'll find a way and I'll do it."

Cassidy opened his mouth and Amos said, "Or if you say anything else, anything at all, I'll do it right here and now. I just don't give a damn any more."

Cassidy moved rapidly backward, like a man backpedaling a bicycle, bumping into a table and knocking over a glass. His face was very white. At the door of the mess he turned to go, but he looked back over his shoulder all the way out the door, watching Amos. The whites of his eyes were like those of a frightened horse.

Amos said, "Steward? Bring me another of those."

Mary Wildcat said, "Put your arms around me, Amos."

He held her close, feeling her body pressing against his, smelling her thick black hair. They stood in the doorway of the Paris building, holding each other, not speaking. It was a cool day, not really cold yet but smelling of colder weather on the way. The wind fluttered the hem of her skirt. A few leaves spun past and crashed into the street.

She said, "I missed you, Amos. I didn't know I was going to miss you so much."

She looked up at him. "And I'm going to miss you. This town's going to be like an old hollow barrel without you."

He said, "Well, I'll be coming to see you now and then—"

"No you won't." She pulled away and turned toward the door. "You might as well come on inside and find out about it."

Sam Harjo was sitting in the parlor, surrounded by books and maps and papers. He looked flushed and excited. "Amos," he cried. "You've come just at the right time. I was about to get in touch with the Confederate Embassy."

He waved a handful of papers. "Lots of red tape to get through, but we'll manage. I don't suppose you've got your citizenship papers with you?"

Amos said, "Would you mind telling me what the hell's going on around here?"

"For you the war is over," Harjo said happily. "This war, anyway. You're to be separated from the Confederate service as soon as the necessary tiresome formalities are completed. Chief Watie has already sent the requisite message to Richmond. You're going home, Amos my boy. Back to the Nations."

He stood up, tossing papers into the air. "Only, by God, it's not the Nations any more. Word just came from home. The secret convention finally thrashed out the details and the Five Nations are agreed. From now on," Harjo said, "there'll be a new nation on the map of North America, a single, united Indian nation—and maybe it's not much, compared to what we used to have, but it'll be ours."

He came forward and put his hands on Amos's shoulders. "And they need you there, son. Chief Watie's got some special plans for you. God, I wish I could go with you. This is an old, old dream of mine."

Amos said, "What are they going to call it? The new country, I mean?"

"Interesting, that," Harjo said. "There was some talk of naming it after Sequoyah, the great Cherokee. Then there were some other proposals—United Indian Republic, that sort of thing. But," he chuckled, "trust the Choctaws to come up with a commonsense idea. Call the place what it is, they said; call it Red People's Land. And since it was the Choctaws' idea, the convention decided to use the words in their language. *Oklah Homah*," Harjo said, rolling the words impressively off his tongue. "I think it's going to be spelled as one word, but they haven't settled that yet."

Amos felt dazed. Everything was happening too fast again.

"But for now," Sam Harjo said, "you're still an officer of the Cherokee Flying Corps, on the all-important paper record. So we've got to get things fixed up—"

Amos said, "Go ahead and work on it. I'll be back later."

Sam Harjo and Mary Wildcat stared at him. "Where are you going?" she asked.

"Yes," Harjo said, "hell, you can't go anywhere right now, son. All kinds of things have to be done—"

"It won't be long," Amos said. "I just have to go see somebody."

The hospital was a large sunny place in a Paris suburb, a former estate with broad lawns and clean-swept walks where men in robes walked on crutches and nurses pushed wheelchairs. Amos looked and wondered; he had seen the ghastly abattoirs that passed for surgery stations at the front.

He found Faulkner walking about the grounds, his arm in a plaster cast. "A little worse than I thought," Faulkner said when Amos made the obvious inquiry. "And it seems that you, and *Leutnant* Ritter, were right; all that stumbling around in the rain and mud wasn't good for it. But they assure me it's going to be all right, and soon I'll be able to play the violin, which I never could do before. . . ."

He held up his notebook. "Getting a lot of writing done, these days. Some interesting stories in here. I'm working on a novel about a Confederate soldier from an old Mississippi family who gets involved with a French nurse. I think she dies at the end," Faulkner said. "I'm thinking of calling it *Farewell To The Sound And The Fury*."

Amos said, "Will you be flying again?"

"Oh, sure. The doctors are under the strange impression that I'm chafing at the bit to get back to the war. There's a nurse here with the most magnificent bottom. I may have to fall downstairs and break a few more bones just to get to stay awhile longer."

He leaned against a tree. "Meanwhile, you get to go back to the Nation—pardon me, to Oklah Homah. Nice sound," he said. "Tell me about the squadron. I haven't heard much in here."

Amos told him. The narration seemed to consist mostly of names of men who had died; the realization depressed Amos, and he hurried through his account. "Christ," Faulkner said at the end. "So much for the old crowd. Who's running the squadron now?"

"Ashby, temporarily. They're bringing in somebody next week, I don't know his name. Hell, I don't know the names of half the men in the mess, now."

"Damn. And Mad Jim went after a balloon and got himself killed. Can't say that I'm prostrated with grief, but it's hard to imagine."

Faulkner sat down on a nearby bench and stroked his mustache pensively. "Lahaie was here," he said unexpectedly. "They saved enough of his foot that he'll be able to walk, eventually, but not very well. I thought it was a hell of a thing, but if he hadn't been hit that day he might have been killed later on. I've come to the conclusion that the stupidest words in the language are 'What if?' "

Amos stood there a little while, wondering if Faulkner meant to go on, but the Mississippian seemed to be off in some private world. Finally Amos said, "Well. I've got to get back—Sam's having fits. I'll try to come see you again before I leave, of course—"

"You killed him," Faulkner said suddenly. "I just figured it out. You killed Lucas. Didn't you?"

Amos said, "Yes."

"Why?" Faulkner cocked his head, watching Amos's face. "For revenge? To keep him from killing more people? Why, Amos?"

Amos shrugged. "Both those things, I guess. At the time I didn't really think it out in any detail. I just did it."

He looked away across the lawn. A couple of nurses were leading a man whose entire face seemed to be covered by bandages.

"I told him," Amos said, "when the enemy kills your people, you have to do something about it. I didn't tell him I'd just realized who the enemy was."

"The enemy being Lucas?"

"Along with others. Ritter, and Cassidy—oh, Christ, yes, Cassidy—and I suppose you could make out a pretty long list, all the way up to the crowned heads and brass hats. You said something once about wishing you had them in your sights," Amos said. "But you have to take what you can. I took Lucas."

Faulkner was chuckling softly, a little sadly. "Oh, Amos, what am I going to do with you? I talk about things like that when I've had a few. So do a lot of people. Only you go out and do it."

He thumped Amos lightly on the arm with his good hand. "Haven't I told you enough times? You can't change things by killing individuals. Killing Lucas," Faulkner said, "as satisfying as it may have been—and I'm not saying I'm sorry you did it—won't make any difference at all in the long run. Any more than you changed the German war effort by killing that poor crazy little *Gefreiter*."

"Probably not," Amos admitted. "At least, though, I did it to Lucas for personal reasons. The German—hell, I didn't even know his name. Never will."

"Actually," Faulkner said, "as it happens, I do know his name. I got his wallet and his paybook, remember? And he wasn't a German, technically, but an Austrian; it was on his identification. Now what was that name?" Faulkner mused. "Hibbler? Hitler, that's it," he said, snapping his fingers. "*Gefreiter* Adolf Hitler."

The liner *City of Chattanooga* (Dixie Lines, in Confederate service for the duration of hostilities) pulled slowly out of Bordeaux harbor on the morning of October 30, 1916. Flanked by the slim gray shapes of her escort, the destroyers *Raphael Semmes* and *Jean Lafitte*, she steamed toward deep water, zigzagging to make a harder target for U-boats.

Standing at the stern rail, Amos Ninekiller pulled his long gray trench coat tighter against the cold wind and watched the dark outline of Europe sink beneath the eastern horizon. He shoved his hands into his pockets and thought about various things. The occasion seemed to call for some sort of memorable sentiment or significant insight, but nothing much came to mind.

Another uniformed figure appeared at the rail beside him: a stocky, fair-haired young man in the dress grays of a Lieutenant in the Confederate Marines. One sleeve, Amos noticed, was empty and pinned shut. A black patch covered one eye.

The stranger was holding out a box of matches. "Could you give me a light?" He indicated the cigarette hanging from his mouth. "I still haven't got the hang of striking these things one-handed. At least I can't seem to do it in this wind."

Amos struck a match and held it, shielding the flame from the wind with his hands, while the Marine puffed gratefully. "Thanks. What I get for forgetting to duck, huh?"

Amos said, "Trenches?"

"Oh, no, no. Never even saw the front lines, the whole time I was over here. Raid on some Kraut coastal installations," the Marine explained, sounding almost apologetic. "Up on the North Sea, you know. Didn't quite go according to plan." He coughed. "Ought to quit smoking these things, I guess they're bad for me . . . raid went all right," he went on, "we blew up what we were supposed to blow up, these British torpedo boats took us off, but then on the way out of the harbor this Kraut destroyer showed up. Wonder we made it back home at all."

He looked at Amos's uniform. "Aviator?"

"Yes."

"Damn, I never met a flyer before. What'd you fly, scouts?"

"Yes. They call them fighters, now."

The Marine nodded slowly. "Sure, that makes sense. Shoot down any Krauts?"

"A few."

"Boy, you wouldn't get me up in one of those things." The Marine was watching the vanishing mass of land in the distance. "Well, anyway, we both made it through alive, didn't we? Getting to go home."

Amos took his right hand out of his pocket, holding a bit of shiny metal at the end of a length of ribbon. The Marine said, "Croix de Guerre, huh? I got one too. You get kissed?"

Amos glanced down at the medal. "Yes."

"Me too. Man, I about shit when that old Frog got me on both cheeks."

The coastline was almost invisible now, only a smudge along the line of the horizon.

The Marine said, "So tell me something. Did you ever figure out what the hell it was all about?" He gestured in the direction of France. "What was it all for?"

"Not a God-damned thing," Amos said flatly, not looking at him. "It was all for nothing."

He snapped his wrist in a fast vicious motion, flicking the Croix de Guerre out over the rail in a flat spinning trajectory toward the sea. The medal hit the water and vanished in the ship's wake, its tiny splash lost amid the turmoil of the waves.